Binding Energy

Binding Energy

stories

Daniel Marcus

LASTIC
PRESS

Printed and Bound by Biddles, King's Lynn, Norfolk

Cover design by Richard Marchand (www.richardmarchand.com)
Cover layout by Dean Harkness
Typeset by Andrew Hook

Published by:
Elastic Press
85 Gertrude Road
Norwich
UK

elasticpress@elasticpress.com
www.elasticpress.com

For Chris and David

"In their range, and the articulation of styles, and in their balancing between self-aware referentiality and fist-clenched passion, Daniel Marcus's brilliant assemblage of stories in BINDING ENERGY could be seen as a kind of map for the future of literary SF."

– Jonathan Lethem, National Book Critics Circle Award-winning author of Motherless Brooklyn

"You never know, entering a Dan Marcus story, where he is going to take you. His work is eclectic, beautifully told, imaginative, and always, always intriguing."

– Marta Randall, author of Journey, and Dangerous Games

Edgy, dark, and fascinating, these vivid tales showcase Daniel Marcus' amazing range, original voice, and deep understanding of the human heart.

– Pat Murphy, Nebula Award winning author of The Falling Woman

Marcus has put together an outstanding collection – emotionally taut, tough-minded, and beautifully rendered, these stories are models of compression and power.

– Karen Joy Fowler, World Fantasy Award winning author of Black Glass and Sarah Canary

Thanks to the writers who have workshopped these stories, to the editors who have bounced or bought them, and to readers past and future. Special thanks to Gardner Dozois, Andrew Hook, and Clarion West 1992.

Table of contents

Same Ear

Introduction

A struggle between science fiction and the so-called mainstream of American literature has gone on for a lifetime. It truly began in the 1950s, when hardcover publication of science fiction by mainstream publishers began, when critics like Knight and Blish began insisting on higher standards, when writers like Bradbury and Vonnegut first achieved crossover success. It continued through the 60s, when 'speculative fiction' was a short-lived synonym for stylistically advanced sf. It reached a tipping point, I'd say, in the mid-70s, between the publication of *Gravity's Rainbow* and the release of *Star Wars*.

Science fiction readers and writers of a certain age and temperament instantly recognized and embraced Pynchon's novel as kin; it was nominated for a Nebula. Many saw in Lucas's technological fairy tale (in the accomplishment of its effects, not in its narrative content) a level of innovation that challenged and would transform traditional print sf; it won a Nebula.

These two works are emblems to me, from my period, my coming of age. They are the far outliers of the territory that could then plausibly be called science fiction, maybe the widest territory ever so claimed. Since then the category has fragmented; most of the audience and the money has gone to mass entertainments – films and tv and other media. The writing of sf for and as print has become a minority and embattled occupation, with even master practitioners of long standing increasingly published in small press. The large firms that still publish independent sf writing (as opposed to media tie-ins) have mostly retrenched to what we might call 'core' sf – not necessarily 'hard' sf (which has always been a misnomer), but sf that has a thorough understanding of the field's history, tropes, and idiom, and identifies strongly with its major themes and common practices. Outliers on the Pynchon side are more likely to be published, if at all, as mainstream. But in certain quarters the memory and the imprint of that once-wide territory remains. Writers who matured during or after that watershed have a particular way of seeing sf and the mainstream as sharing a lot of ground that has since been subdivided. 'Slipstream' doesn't half cover the territory.

So I see Dan Marcus as a post-Pynchon, post-Lucas writer as far as sf goes, but there's more to him. The stories in *Binding Energy* are, beyond question, core sf; they also cover, with unlabored mastery, that maximum territory from space opera to contemporary alternity, and they do it with a bit of Pynchon's bemusement at the complexity of the world, with something like James Joyce's scrupulous attention to meanness, and with a fair measure of Lucas's attention to an audience. If a few of the stories wander outside the stricter precincts of the sf genre, it's not because Marcus is a dabbling litterateur who doesn't understand the rigors of science fiction; he is deeply read in the field; its tropes and idioms hum in the fine bones of his cochlea; he has a PhD in Engineering and has worked as an applied mathematician at the Lawrence Livermore Lab and Princeton's Institute for Advanced Study. He's also a musician, so when he goes for the higher registers of what some call 'literature' (I wish I had a less conflicted term that I wouldn't have to define from the ground up), that same ear responds; he doesn't falter in his command of pitch and tone (as some core sf writers have been known to do). He expects a savvier audience than Lucas, but he doesn't have much patience for longueurs or postmodern vaudeville. He wants to get on with the story.

And so he does, as directly as Elmore Leonard, by simply and firmly taking it as given that scientific and literary values are not at odds, nor should they be that we listen to all narratives with the same ear (same mind is a discussion for another day). He grasps that nettle, and it works because he has the same ear for science, for futurity, for alternity, that he has for the present, the everyday, the street. He sees that the spirit of core sf has taken up permanent residence in our daily lives. That vast territory has collapsed to a singularity.

These stories are so accomplished, so easy in their tone, that you can miss their import on a first reading. Go back and read them again. You'll be surprised and rewarded. That's pretty much my highest praise.

Carter Scholz, 2007

Those Are Pearls That Were His Eyes

The only window in Suki's bedroom opened onto an airshaft that ran through the center of the building like the path of a bullet. She would lie in bed in the hot summer nights with the salt smell of the drying seabed coming in through the open window, a sheen of sweat filming her forehead and plastering the sheets to her body like tissue, listening to her downstairs neighbors. When they made love, their cries echoing up through the airshaft made her loins ache, and she brought release to herself silently, visualizing men with slender, oiled limbs and faces hidden in shadow.

Sometimes the neighbors sang, odd, sinuous music redolent with quarter tones. The melodies wove counterpoint like a tapestry of smoke and for some reason Suki thought of mountains. Jagged, fractal peaks thrusting out of an evergreen carpet. Summits brushed with snow. Tongues of cloud laying across the low passes.

Sometimes they argued, and the first time she heard the man's deep voice raised in anger she was sure he was a Beast, possibly an Ursa. She was less certain of the woman, but there was a sibilant, lilting quality to her voice that suggested something of the feline. They'd moved in three weeks before but their sleep cycles seemed out of sync with hers and she still hadn't met them.

Suki tried to imagine herself going downstairs to borrow something: sugar, yarn, a databead. His broad muzzle would poke out from behind the half-closed door; his liquid brown eyes would be half-closed in suspicion. They would chat for a bit, though, and perhaps he would

1

invite her in. They would teach her their songs and their voices would rise together into the thick, warm air.

Some nights there was no singing, no arguing, no love, and Suki listened to the city, a white-noise mélange of machinery and people in constant flux, like the sound of the ocean captured in a shell held to the ear. Beneath that, emanating from the spaceport on the edge of the city, a low, intermittent hum, nearly subsonic, so faint it seemed to come from somewhere inside her own body.

On those nights, she had trouble sleeping, and she would climb the rickety stairs to the roof. She couldn't see the Web, of course, but she imagined she could feel it arching overhead, lines of force criss-crossing the sky. Ships rode the Web up to where they could safely ignite their fusion drives for in-system voyages, or clung to the invisible threads all the way to their convergence at the Wyrm.

Newmoon hung in the sky, its progress just below the threshold of conscious perception, like the minute hands of a clock. She had visited there as a child, a crèche trip, and she remembered the feel of the factories humming under her feet, the metal skin pocked with micrometeorite impacts stretching to the too-close horizon, the tingling caress of her environment field.

Heat enveloped the city like a glove around a closed fist. It kept people indoors, and business in her little shop was slow. Suki fed and watered her animals, trimmed the heartplants, and carefully tended the incubator, where she was nurturing a quintet of silkpups. Not much more than embryos now, but they would bring a good price when they birthed. Tuned to imprint themselves upon the bio-field of whoever first touched them, they were quite the rage among the Ken, who viewed their intense loyalty and affection with something like amusement. Of course, with the Ken, you never knew what that really meant.

When Suki returned home that evening, the message light was blinking over the console in the kitchen alcove. She brushed her hand across it and the burnished surface faded, replaced by a ghostly rendering of Tam's head and shoulders.

Suki jumped when she saw him.

" – been such a long time, and I just wanted to see how you were doing," Tam was saying. "The Hyaloplasm is *cold*, they never said it would be like this. And you never call me any more." He paused. "Sometimes it feels like no one remembers me."

His image faded to black. Suki stared at the screen for a long time afterwards. They had called each other a lot after the aircar crash, but it made her feel strange. It wasn't quite Tam anymore – something of his essence had been lost in the upload – and there was a feeling of unhealthy enmeshment about staying in relationship with a Ghost. She hadn't taken a new lover yet, but she was ready.

She didn't want to call him back and a tendril of guilt nagged at her as she prepared her dinner. It soon gave way to resentment.

Damnit, she thought. Let the dead stay dead.

He'd turned a corner and she couldn't follow – wouldn't even if she could. Why couldn't *he* let her move on? Why couldn't he move on?

Leaving her plate of stew half-eaten, she went to the console and activated the recorder. The steady, yellow light above the blank screen stared at her and she took a deep breath, trying to visualize Tam's face in place of her own shadowy reflection.

"I don't want you to call me any more, Tam. I have to get on with my life. I'm sorry – " Her voice caught and almost broke, but she recovered. "Goodbye."

With a few shaky keystrokes she set the console to play back the message in response to Tam's signet.

She returned to her meal, but she was restless. After pushing bits of vegetable and tofu from one side of the bowl to the other for the third time, she got up from the table, went to the console, and downloaded *Versala Dreams*, a lavish historical romance she'd been meaning to scan, rich in costumes, intrigue, and sex. She put the databead in the reader and leaned back on the couch. The induction field wrapped around her optic nerve like an invisible, coiled worm.

On the eleventh day of the heatwave, she awoke with the feeling that things were about to change. It was still oppressively hot, but there was a smell of clean moisture in the air, of something besides death and age wafting in from the salt sea.

She ate a spare breakfast of cracked wheat and blood oranges, and left early for work, treading quietly as she passed the Ursa's apartment on the floor below. She could picture them in there, all the shutters

3

drawn, he and his cat-woman curled together on a padded mat, deep in the shadow of sleep.

The streets were almost deserted – it was the hush before the morning flurry of activity – and she enjoyed the feeling that the city was hers alone. She had to walk nearly half a click before she found a bicycle, and the one she found had its front wheel bent slightly out of alignment so that she wobbled from side to side as she rode down the Avenue of Palms toward what used to be the waterfront.

As she rode, the city seemed to awaken around her. The tree-lined street filled with men and women on bicycles, with Beasts pulling wheeled carts. Low residential buildings of pink desert stone gave way to a chaotic clutter of commerce. Mechs wove through the traffic on silent cushions of air, full of purpose.

When she got to the Boardwalk, she stopped and leaned the bicycle against a lamppost. Almost immediately, a pleasant-looking young man took it with an apologetic smile.

"Careful," she said. "The wheel is bent." He shrugged, smiled again, and wobbled down the Boardwalk before she could say anything more.

Suki sighed.

In the distance, wavering in heat haze, the sea hugged the flat horizon like a layer of mercury, almost too bright to look at. Long wharves stretched out into the salt flats. A strong, coppery smell hung in the air.

There was a faint pop from the direction of the spaceport, like the sound a small boy might make expelling a puff of air through his lips. The ionization trail from an ascending ship cut the sky in half, faded, and was gone.

The silkpups were almost ready. Their vitals scrolled past on the incubator display, slender threads beginning to bear the full weight of life. The pups themselves still didn't look like much – hairless rats, primitive and inert.

She heard a noise and looked up. Standing at the counter was an elderly female Ken and her Speaker. She hadn't heard them come in.

"Hello," she said, a little too abruptly.

The Speaker's eyes rolled up in his head. "Good morning," he said.

"We didn't mean to startle you. Please forgive." His voice was metallic and brittle.

"It's all – "

"You have silkpups for sale?"

Conversations with the Ken were always like this – off-balance and skewed, full of sharp corners.

Suki forced herself to look in the Ken's bird-like eyes as she replied. "Yes. Well, no – not yet. But this brood will birth tomorrow."

The Speaker's eyes returned to focus on Suki. She turned to him and he nodded brusquely. Together, he and the Ken turned and walked out of the shop. A musty odor, like old, damp cloth, hung behind them in the still air, noticeable even over the familiar smells of animals and hydroponics.

Suki didn't know if she'd offended her or not, but she resolved to put it out of her mind. She was dealing with Ken, after all.

Business after that was slow, but a wealthy, young couple bought a rare icebird from Nortith, complete with an environment-field generator to maintain its habitat. The sale more than adequately fleshed out Suki's profit margin for the day.

Feeling pleased with herself, she closed up shop early and walked down to the waterfront. The Boardwalk was crowded – Beasts, Ken and their Speakers, human tourists from all over.

An old jetty stretched out into the salt toward the distant, retreating sea like an accusing finger. It was much less crowded than the Boardwalk, and Suki found herself drawn to it. As she walked down its length, hearing the wood – *wood!* – creak beneath her feet, she wondered what it had been like when the sea was right here. She tried to imagine it, soft blue-green, gentle on the eyes, sails and hovercraft drifting lazily to and fro.

She sat down on a low bench at the end of the jetty and closed her eyes. Images of Tam's face kept intruding into her consciousness, and she pushed them away. She tried to empty her mind, to reduce herself to a simple, animal presence basking in sunlight. After a short while, though, she heard footsteps tapping hollowly along the jetty, coming closer. She opened her eyes.

A tall, young man was approaching. There was something strange about the way he carried herself, and it wasn't until he came closer that she could see the crystals embedded in his temples. He was blind. When he came closer still, she saw the fine, radial scars around his eyes. A Void Dancer.

A shudder passed through her. *A Void Dancer.* She'd never met one, but everyone knew what they did. Take a one-person jumpship and dive into the Wyrm at a velocity and angle of incidence nobody had ever tried before. Mapping the Universe by throwing darts, blindfolded, in an empty room.

"May I join you?" he asked.

"Of course," she stammered.

He sat down next to her and sighed. She looked over at him. Handsome, except for the scars, and not as young as she had first thought.

"Sometimes," he said, "the crowds..." He faced the salt flats. "The empty space is soothing."

She tried to imagine the crystals in his temples sending out a silent screech of ultrasound, receiving echoes, constructing a pattern to send to his brain, bypassing his withered optic nerve.

"What do you see?" she asked, surprised at her boldness.

He smiled. His eyes were mottled pools of grey jelly, but Suki still had the sense of being held in that lifeless gaze. "It's like an old photographic negative. Do you know what that is?"

She nodded.

"But that's just the interpretation my brain makes of the data from the tweeters." He tapped his temple. "What it actually looks like..." He shrugged. "What does that really mean?"

They were silent for awhile.

"What do you see when you're out *there*?" Suki asked.

He smiled again. "It's ... different. I don't know if I can explain it. The ship is my whole body; my awareness of things around me comes through as a kind of kinesthesia. Or that's what the medicals say, anyway." The curdled jelly in his eye-sockets seemed to quiver gently. "I sense a nearby mass as a sort of plucking at my skin. The electromagnetic spectrum gets filtered through to me as olfactory sensation – a deep, hot smell for the infrared, a sharp whiff of ozone up in the u.v. – "

He paused. "But I'm prattling on. Tell me about yourself. You have a name?"

"Suki."

"Roan," he said, and held out his hand. It was dry as paper and completely smooth.

"Do you work here in the city?"

"Yes, I have a little shop on Front Street, not far from the spaceport, actually. Organic complements. Mostly grown in-house, but I get a few naturals from time to time."

He nodded. "I know Front Street. Do you know that I grew up not far from there? That was a long time ago, of course." Had he eyes, they would have rolled heavenwards as he calculated the dilation. "Eleven hundred and seven years, to be exact. The sea was still lapping at this pier!"

"A long time ago," she agreed.

Again, they were silent. Strangely, the silence did not feel awkward to Suki, but rather like they were occupying the same space together.

"Perhaps you'd like to come by the shop sometime," Suki said, again a little surprised at her boldness. "Something for your ship – a bonsai tree, a heartplant..."

His smile was a bit forced this time and she winced at her stupidity. "I would hardly be able to enjoy it," he said.

"Of course – "

"But I would come by to see *you*."

Suki felt her face flush and she wondered if his tweeters could detect the warm blood rushing to her cheeks.

She took the long way home, through the administrative district on the other side of the Lhoss Gardens. A new building was going up – a crew of Oxen on the ground pushed wheeled pallets piled high with building materials, while Cats climbed the scaffolding that surrounded the blocky, unfinished pyramid.

Suki stopped her bicycle and balanced on one foot, watching, listening. The Oxen called to each other in low, bleating tones that mingled with the sibilant cries from above. It was recognizable as her own tongue, but there were words she couldn't understand. Always a few more, it seemed, each time she heard them speak. Each time she stopped to listen. The Beasts were changing, drifting off onto their own trajectory. She envied them their transit of undiscovered territory.

*

The neighbors sang again that night. Lying in bed, her gaze angling up through the window, she imagined the close, hollow harmonies lifting her like a cushion of air toward the box of starry sky at the mouth of the airshaft.

She thought of Roan. He'd said he would come by the shop tomorrow. She wondered if he would.

She thought of Tam. Her system had logged two calls from him, so she knew her message had been received. She pushed aside the feelings of guilt that began to take shape and tried to construct a picture of Roan's face in her mind, but it was elusive. All she could evoke clearly were the eyes – moist flecks of cloudy jelly set in hollows of leathery, scarred skin.

If the eyes are truly windows to the soul, she thought, what do they reveal of his?

Her hand stole between her legs and she imagined his hands moving across her body, his sweet breath warm on her neck. The peak of her pleasure braided with the music echoing up through the airshaft and segued seamlessly into a dream. They were sitting on the bench at the end of the pier. The water, blue as his eyes, made gentle sounds lapping up against the pilings. A dense, organic smell hung in the air like a fog hugging the surface of the sea. Birds wheeled across the sky. The sun was a shrunken, glaring wound.

The silkpups birthed overnight, and when Suki came into the shop they were squirming in their padded nest, crawling across one another, taking shaky, hesitant steps and collapsing in a tangle of limbs.

Their psychic energy, too, was almost palpable. The air around the incubator seemed charged. Each of them was a *tabula rasa*, engineered to bond with the first person that touched them.

There were no customers all morning and Suki busied herself with small jobs – cleaning cages, maintaining nutrient baths. The heartplants hung heavy with fruit, the tiny, fist-like buds pulsing faintly. She snapped one off, leaving a moist scar on the smooth branch. Red sap dribbled down her hand. She popped the fruit in her mouth and bit down, wincing at the explosion of salty sweetness.

Just before she was about to close up shop for lunch, Roan walked through the door. Suki was surprised and a little frightened at the surge of joy she felt.

"Hello," she stammered.

He took her hands. "Hello, yourself." The gray jelly in the hollows of his eyes seemed expressive, but of what she wasn't sure. "I don't have much time. I'm leaving tomorrow and I have a great deal to prepare."

He paused. Suki felt something inside her wither and begin to fold in upon itself.

"Could you meet me tonight?" he asked. "Midnight, the pier where we met yesterday?"

She nodded. "Midnight."

"Good." He smiled, squeezed her hand, and was gone. A bubble of silence filled the shop; gradually, the familiar rustle-whirr-whisper of animals and machinery reasserted itself.

She took her lunch down to Lhoss Gardens and sat in the shadow of the Sundial, dangling her feet in one of the fountains that marked the hours.

Roan. She realized that her excitement was made keener by anticipation of loss, but she didn't care. *Maybe he would take her with him.* Even as the thought formed in her mind, though, she rejected it. Ridiculous. She was no Void Dancer.

A crèche-group passed on the far side of the Dial, moving almost as a single organism. Whispers and giggles floated across the plaza. Suki tried to study their faces, but from this distance they shared a bland sameness.

The group passed behind the black, glassy wedge at the Dial's center. They must have stopped there to rest, because they didn't emerge. It seemed to Suki that they had just walked off the face of the world.

She was bent over the silkpups' nest, lost in their restless, wriggling motion, when her nostrils filled again with that damp musk.

She looked up. The Ken and her Speaker were standing in front of her. Once again, she hadn't heard them come in.

"Hello," she said.

The Ken's bead-like eyes stared impassively back at her. She had to look away. The Speaker smiled kindly at her, and for the first time she noticed laugh lines around his eyes. She wondered what he had to laugh about, a Speaker for the Ken. Then his smile vanished and his eyes rolled back in their sockets.

"You have silkpups today?"

Suki nodded, stepping back from the nest. Before she could say anything, the Ken reached into the enclosure and picked up a tiny, squirming pup. She held it up to her shriveled face and stared at it. Gradually, the pup stopped squirming and began to emit a low, contented hum.

The Ken looked at Suki. "Fascinating," said the Speaker. She replaced the pup in its nest, turned on her heel, and walked out the door.

Suki couldn't believe what she was seeing. Dimly, she was aware of the Speaker entering something on her credit pad. He touched her arm.

"I'm sorry," he said. It was the first time she had heard him speak with his own voice. It was low and musical. He hurried out the door after the Ken.

The silkpup lay in a corner of the nest, shivering. Suki leaned close and she could hear a high, keening whimper. Already, its littermates were shunning it – they clustered in a writhing mass of tiny arms and legs on the other side of the nest, as far away as they could get.

The imprint disrupted, the connection broken, the silkpup would soon die. There was nothing she could do.

Almost nothing.

She picked up the animal and held it, trembling, in her hand. With her other hand, she took it by the neck, closed her eyes, and gave it a quick twist.

She put the body in the disposal, and for the rest of the afternoon the shop smelled of burnt hair and ozone.

Suki parked her bike in the alley next to her building, hoping nobody would ride off with it. She felt a small stab of guilt at her selfishness, but she didn't want to wander half across the city looking for a bike and be late for Roan.

Two more attempts from Tam on her console log. When would he give up? She thought of him, bereft of flesh, suspended in purgatory, reaching back to life and light. She could no longer make the connection between that Ghost and the ghost of her own memories. He was finally gone to her.

To her relief, the bike was still waiting where she had left it. The night air was cool, the Avenue of Palms empty at this late hour. She arrived at the old waterfront fifteen minutes early and walked her bike out to the end of the pier. She sat down on a wooden bench to wait.

Midnight came and went. By twelve-fifteen, Suki was beginning to think that Roan would not come. The salt flats spread out before her, luminous in the blue Newmoon light. Behind her, the city asleep and not asleep, hollow as an open mouth.

By twelve-thirty, she was sure. As she mounted her bike, the ionization trail from an ascending ship lanced across the sky, followed by a faint popping sound. She blinked back the afterimage, a straight, bright scar across her vision, and wondered if it was Roan.

She rode home slowly, through quiet side streets. She felt nothing.

As she passed by the Ursa's apartment on her way up to her own, she paused to listen. They were singing – his low voice a modal drone, hers above sinuous and agile, weaving in and out of the tonal center.

She walked up to the door, pressed her cheek against the cold, smooth surface. The music seemed to enter her body through that contact, sending delicate tendrils down her neck, spreading through her chest and out her arms and legs, filling her with warmth.

Random Acts of Kindness

The fog brought me a gift this morning. When I woke in the pre-dawn stillness to relieve myself it lay over everything like cotton ticking. I stepped out onto the porch and held my hand in front of my face. I could barely see it, a splayed dark outline, the space between the fingers like webbing in the half-dark.

I went back to sleep and when I awoke again the fog was thinner. Not completely gone, but the sky had that bright gray look like there was blue up there somewhere. On the porch railing, next to a small potted cactus, was the head of a mountain lion. There was a dark, irregular stain on the wood underneath it and the fur around what was left of its neck was torn and bloody. Its eyes were open and its mouth was fixed in a snarl. As I watched, an ant crawled up the matted fur of its cheek, explored for a moment, and disappeared into a nostril.

Even in death, there was something magnificent about the creature and I thought of Egyptian gods in hieroglyphic profile. I looked beyond it to the sloping, rock-studded hill disappearing into the fog still hugging the ground.

I had been looking for that cat. In the last month I'd lost two sheep, and the day before, I'd come home to find my goat, Mama Cass, lying in a pool of blood, eviscerated and partly eaten. There was no sign, nothing to track – the killer left about as much spoor as the fog.

I walked to the head of the rickety wooden stairs and looked around, hoping to catch a glimpse of whoever or whatever had graced me with this offering, knowing I wouldn't. I had an urge to shout, just to hear my voice damped, absorbed into that mist like rain into dry dust. I didn't see anything I didn't expect – just the fog, the gentle contours of the hillside, and off to the left, just visible through the whiteness, my old, blue Chevy rustbucket sitting under a listing, tin-roofed lean-to.

Beyond the truck were the woods. They went on for miles, almost all the way to the ocean, uninterrupted except for patches of clearcut. I remember, years ago, flying low over the coastal range in a small private plane, seeing miles of deep, mysterious green scarred and broken by wide swaths of nothing. Dead zones. It made me want to cry. Not too much of that this far out in the boonies, but the lumber companies and the Feds managed to make a sorry mess of things before they stopped. Before everything stopped.

I was hungry, and debated with myself whether to make something before heading down the mountain, or wait until I got to Stores. I never liked to pass up an opportunity to sit down to some of Evy's hash, but I was going to be bartering for gasoline to keep my generator going and needed a clear head, so I went back to the kitchen and grabbed an oatcake to give my blood sugar a kick. On my way out, I stopped at the hall closet and got the box of .22 longs that I planned to use for trade. There was only about a case and a half left and I felt a sharp stab of worry as I wondered what I was going to use for currency when that was gone. I didn't want to think about it. Under a tarp in the back of the truck there was also a small buck I'd bagged the day before. That and the ammo should get me five gallons at least, maybe a box of nails.

As I walked out through the porch again, breaking off crumbs of cake and putting them in my mouth, I took another look at the cathead. It had lost most of its magic for me and just looked dead, the eyes glazed over, the fur taking on the dull gloss of old carpet. I felt a chill run down my spine though as I wondered again how it got there. The hairs on the back of my neck were standing on end.

The truck was hard starting. There was always fog up here and I think the dampness got into the electrical system somehow. It turned over and over but wouldn't quite catch. Just when the starter was about to call it quits, cranking slower and slower and groaning with the effort, the engine kicked in. I saw a cloud of blue smoke rise in the rear view mirror and mix with the fog. I opened the glove compartment and took out my Walther, took the safety off, and jacked a shell in the chamber.

I laid it gently on the seat next to me. I thought of Annie and pushed the thought away. Two years since she died, and I was still hurting. Everything in the house and the rough land around it shouted her name at me.

The road wound down the mountain, hugging the contours, switchbacking a couple of times. I could drive it in my sleep. By the time the hardpack dirt gave way to asphalt, I was out from under the fog and I could see plumes of woodsmoke rising from behind the curve of the next hill. As I rounded its side, the twin windmills that provided power for the little community came into view – tall, spidery things perched at the mouth of the valley like birds of prey. Only one of them was spinning – the other was down again, waiting for a trader to make the long trip up from Tehachapi with spare parts.

I pulled up in front of the trading post, a low, ramshackle building with a sprawling collection of additions. There were a couple of trailers off to the side, and a long aluminum storage shed. A neatly lettered sign reading *Stores* hung over the main entrance. Behind the main building, scattered throughout the woods and down the road, were about thirty houses, most of them new – makeshift dwellings that sprouted up around Stores like mushrooms on nightsoil after they got the windmills going. It was still pretty early and the dirt lot in front of the shed was empty. I stuck the Walther in my belt and walked in.

Evy was behind the counter. She was wearing a rough homespun shirt and her long gray-streaked hair was pulled back into a thick braid. Behind her, pots and saucepans perched on Coleman burners, filling the room with the smells of chili, chicory, and kerosene. Through a door next to the stove I saw a jumbled confusion of merchandise – bolts of cloth, tools, barrels of dry goods. There was a single customer, someone I'd never seen before. He wore a scarf over his head that didn't quite cover an ugly burn scar and he sat hunched over his joe like he thought someone was going to take it away from him. Evy smiled when she saw me.

"Blair," she said. "How goes it?" There was a gold star inlaid into one of her front teeth and it flashed at me as she spoke.

"Some strange shit, Ev'." I told her about the offering I'd received. When I was finished, she rolled her eyes and whistled softly through her teeth. "Thing is, though," I went on, "I don't know whether to feel threatened or graced. I mean, I *wanted* that cat, but this is pretty damn strange."

As I talked, the stranger became more and more agitated, mumbling to himself and slopping his chicory on the counter in front of him. Finally he turned to me. The burn scar sprawled across his face like an open hand. His eyes peering out from behind it held a sick, flickering light.

"It's happening, man," he said. "They're coming back. Cowboy Neal at the wheel, man. Four dimensional beings in three dimensional bodies looking out two dimensional windshields. Ashes to ashes, man. They're coming *back*."

I looked at Evy with a questioning frown. She shrugged and pointed down, meaning, I guess, that she figured he had come up from the South, from the ruins around Sacto or San Francisco. People didn't travel much anymore, but we still got a steady trickle – techno-junk traders, musicians, storytellers, and the occasional crazy.

"I seen it, man. It's happened to me. I was up to Shasta, up near the summit, and I got caught in a storm." Something happened to his eyes then – the fevered light dimmed and he seemed almost sane. "Man, I had half a biscuit in my pocket and the shirt on my back and the temperature dropped from sixty to zero in about twenty minutes. I thought, 'This is it, man. Thank you, Great Spirit for giving me this life, see you in the next one,' you know?" I nodded. I knew about those storms – he wasn't exaggerating. Evy had stopped wiping down the counter and was staring at him.

"Before long it was total whiteout," he continued. "Nowhere to go, so I just sat down right where I was, closed my eyes, and waited. Pretty soon my feet and hands got all numb and I just went to sleep." He giggled. "I just went to sleep, man." He shook his head and stared down into his mug. He was silent for so long I didn't know if he was going to continue speaking. "I just went to sleep," he said again, so softly it was almost inaudible. He looked up at me and grinned. "You think I'm gonna tell you I dreamed this long tunnel with a bright light at the end, right?"

I shrugged and he shook his head. "Nothin,' man. No dreams at all, but I woke up in the old abandoned base camp cabin at the foot of the northwest approach. A good ten miles away. There was a fire in the stove and a big fat squirrel on the table next to it, gutted and cleaned and ready to cook. And standing there looking down at me was God's own angel. She was an angel, man..." Evy looked at me and rolled her eyes. He didn't seem to notice. "She gave me this slow, sad smile, like she knew me, and then she turned and walked out the door. I remember the smells in the room, man – blood and woodsmoke."

He looked at Evy, then back at me, with a defiant expression, like he was daring us to call him crazy.

He beckoned me closer. "You know who I think it was?" he asked. I shook my head. He continued without pausing for an answer. "There were spirits who lived here before we came and fucked it all up. The Indians knew them and they had sort of a peaceful thing going. Then we came and started tearing down the forests and pissing in the streams and they went into hiding. I think they were always there, but they kept a low profile. Then the shit hit the fan and we almost blew ourselves off the planet. They're coming back, man..."

"Wait a minute," Evy said. "If that's true, don't you think they'd be a little, well, pissed off? Why would they help us?" I'd been thinking the same thing.

He shook his head. "You don't get it, man. They're not like us. They don't hold grudges. It's a clean slate – we can all start over. A clean slate..."

Then something in his face sagged and he looked back down into his mug. Evy and I looked at each other and shrugged.

"We've got some business to transact, Evy," I said after a long moment.

"What you got?" she asked.

We went through the motions of dickering and barter but neither of our hearts were in it. I got my five gallons, she got the .22 longs, and she agreed to salt all the meat and give me half. Somewhere during the course of the negotiations, our friend had disappeared.

"Hey," I said. "Where's Cowboy Neal?"

"Beats me," she said with a shrug. "Probably stepped out to score some 'shrooms."

"No shit," I said. "The band's playing but the amps aren't plugged in."

She chuckled softly. "Rock and roll will never die. You think there's anything to his story?"

Binding Energy

"Fuck if I know," I said. "I did wake up with a cathead on my porch, but I think our friend's been smoking a little too much Humboldt Polio Weed." I was trying to make light of it, but there was something nagging at a corner of my mind and it wouldn't let go. I had heard similar stories, especially since the war. Impossible rescues, strange gifts left in the dead of night.

I spent the afternoon in the 'machine shop' at Stores – little more than a garage with an old lathe, a hoist, and a meager collection of hand tools – helping Jacob Ross tear down and rebuild a generator. Jacob was Stores' resident doctor, Evy's Significant Something-or-Other, and he was pretty good with his hands. He had patched me up more than once, and had done all he could to save my wife Annie when she took two rounds in the chest from a .357 Magnum. A biker gang, up from what was left of Oakland. He wasn't a miracle worker, though – the life leaked out of her slowly but steadily, and she was gone before the night was through.

It was good working with him. We knew each other well and there was an economy of words and motion that made the work seem almost like a dance. I told him about the macabre gift I'd received and about Cowboy Neal and he just grunted and nodded. It was pretty much what I needed to hear from him. By the time I got back up the mountain to my place, the shadows were starting to lengthen and the high clouds in the western sky were streaked with gold fire.

The cathead was still on my porch and the ants had been having a field day. A line of them stretched up the side of the porch to the railing and the head itself was teeming with them. There was a cloud of flies circling and buzzing and a whiff of decay hung in the air. I wrapped a kerchief around my hand, grabbed the head by an ear, and tossed it as hard and far as I could. It bounced a couple of times and rolled into the woods. Like ringing the dinner bell for the 'coons and skunks, but I just wanted it out of my sight. I got some water from the reclamation tank and washed down the railing.

I'd been thinking about Annie again on the drive back and missing her more than a little. I decided to pay her a visit. First, though, I wanted to leave something in case my visitor showed up again. I looked around the living room and settled on the God's-eye hanging over the mantle –

black and yellow yarn wound around the arms of a rude, wooden cross to form a textured pattern of concentric diamonds. The arms of the cross were tipped with hawk feathers. Annie made it the summer before she died. I didn't know why, but it seemed right. I brought it out to the porch and laid it on the railing where the cathead had been.

Annie wasn't far, just about a half-mile further up the mountain, but it was deep woods and I maintained the trail as lightly as possible – just enough to let me find my way. She would have wanted it like that.

It was one of those clearings that just opens up out of the woods like God lifting the lid from a teakettle. About half an acre of green so deep it hurt the eyes, peppered with wildflowers in the spring, studded with an array of smooth boulders perfect for sitting. It had been a favorite place of ours, even before the war. Her grave was near the uphill end of the clearing, marked by a sort of mandala of small stones, a simple spiral set into the rich earth.

Some people talk to their departed loved ones. I couldn't do it. It was too much like wishing for something that could never happen. I liked to be near her sometimes, though, when I needed to be alone with my thoughts. I sat on a boulder near her grave, stretched my legs out, and remembered...

...being out on San Francisco Bay in a sailboat under a perfect blue sky, the wind ripping through my hair, fingers completely numb. I remembered ice cream, the cold sweetness, the way the really good stuff sort of coated your tongue and the back of your mouth. I remembered what it felt like to play an old Martin, the rosewood fretboard silky beneath my callused fingers, the rich harmonics ringing out underneath the chords, vibrating the body of the guitar.

In all of those images, Annie was there, somewhere just outside my field of vision. I began to get that tight feeling across my forehead like I was about to cry, and before long my shoulders were shaking with dry sobs. After a while, the tightness went away and my breathing returned to normal. I took a last look at Annie's grave and walked back down the meadow to where the trail disappeared into the woods.

As I made my way along the overgrown path, I had a distinct feeling that I was being watched. I stopped and looked around. It was almost dark and the woods were deep in purple shadow. The mosquitoes were out and they hovered around me in a cloud. Off to the left I heard the deep drone of a wild beehive. The air smelled of pine and leaf mold. Nothing. I thought wistfully for a moment of my Walther, lying in the glove compartment in my truck.

By the time I got home it was pitch dark and my neck was sore from looking over my shoulder. The God's eye lay on the railing where I left it. I made myself some dinner and, afterwards, brewed myself a pot of coffee from my dwindling hoard. I brought it out onto the porch and settled into the big wicker chair to wait. I had a long night ahead of me. As an afterthought, I went down to the truck and got the Walther out of the glove compartment. I didn't think I'd need it, but I was still spooked from my walk, and I had learned to trust my intuition.

I leaned back and looked up at the sky. There was a pretty good aurora. We'd been getting a lot of those since the war – gauzy, iridescent curtains hanging cold fire from the heavens. There were a lot of shooting stars, too, and at one point I saw a dim light make a slow, steady crawl across the sky. Probably Space Station Kyoto. I didn't think there was anybody up there any more, but I wasn't sure. I felt a sharp sadness at the thought.

I must have dozed off, because when I woke the sky was beginning to take on that colorless pre-dawn shade, just before the light starts pushing itself up from the East. There was someone on the porch with me. I couldn't make out her features very well (I knew somehow it was a 'her'), but I had a sense of fine cheekbones, of grace and slenderness. And I knew that she was not human. I reached behind me and rested my hand on the cold hardness of the gun.

She stepped forward, out of the shadows. Huge, liquid eyes, catching the dim light like a cat. Body covered in a fine layer of glistening fur. I wanted to reach out and touch it. She wore no clothing, but a belt slung low on her hips held a long knife, an axe, and a small pouch. She smelled faintly of ginger.

She picked up the God's-eye and held it up in front of her face. She rotated it around a quarter-turn, then back, then she returned it gently to the railing. She looked at me then. Cowboy Neal's words echoed in my mind. *It's a clean slate, man.* With a falling sensation, I lifted my hand from the gun and met her gaze. Behind her, on the mountain, the fog was coming in.

Angel From Budapest

Claude Wilczek guides the old Caddy past the empty storefronts and abandoned warehouses of downtown New Haven. The buildings rise up in front of him like the undersea temples of a decrepit, post-industrial Atlantis. Moonlight glints off jagged tips of glass in the brooding windows. He takes a left on Division Street, heading towards the bus station. Towards the women.

There are three of them, equally spaced down the length of the block. They lean against lampposts and parked cars, in postures of casual allure. He slows down as he approaches the first. Her skin is dark as bittersweet chocolate, smooth and shiny in the light from the streetlamp. She is wearing a red vinyl jacket open almost to her navel, fishnet stockings, short, black skirt. Small gold hoops pierce her left nostril and eyebrow.

A look is exchanged, a nod. He stops the car and reaches over to open the passenger door.

"You want to party?" she asks.

Claude nods nervously.

"Twenty I suck your cock."

He nods again and she gets in the car.

"The money."

Claude reaches into his shirt and hands her a crumpled bill.

They drive back down Division Street, away from the bus station, and park behind an abandoned factory. She reaches over, unzips his pants, and goes down on him. He feels the warmth spreading out from his groin and his hips begin to move.

"Yeah, baby," she says unconvincingly, pausing for a moment at the top of a stroke. She looks up at Claude. The rings through her nose and eyebrow glitter in the dark. She runs her tongue lightly down the length of his cock and engulfs him again.

Claude closes his eyes and the images wheel through him. His second wife, her face flushed with desire, half in moonshadow. His lover going down on him, her blonde hair falling over her face. His father, rough-cheek perfume of tobacco and vodka. Budapest, rain-slicked cobbled street, smell of sausages grilling on a sidewalk cart, Soviet tanks rumbling past the Government Palace.

"Oh, yeah, give it to me, baby," she says between strokes, managing to sound breathy and listless at the same time.

He opens his eyes. There is a woman standing under a streetlamp twenty feet away, facing him. She is wearing a long overcoat and her blonde hair falls limply on her shoulders. Her face is hidden in shadow, but her stance, the shape of her, resonates someplace deep inside him. Full recognition skips back just out of reach, though, flickering behind the pleasure coursing up from the center of him.

He ducks down in the seat, hoping she will not see him. His orgasm surges through him and he cries out in Hungarian, clutching the steering wheel.

When he opens his eyes again, the woman is gone.

As he is driving home, WCLA is playing Kodaly, the cello sonata. The music moves from sharp, staccato passages, the notes bitten off like broken sticks, to deep, seductive long tones, and it seems to draw the Caddy out of the crumbling downtown sprawl.

Claude feels the shame begin in a quiet place within him and work its way outwards. It is almost pre-verbal, a dark, formless shape in his mind. He knows the feeling well, and knows how to wall it off so that he can sip its exquisite bitterness in small doses.

He turns onto a tree-lined street and pulls into his driveway. As he walks up the path to his front door, he hears his daughter's footsteps pounding down the stairs.

He opens the door and she throws herself at his legs, giggling.

"Daddy, Daddy!"

He reaches down and strokes her thin, straight hair. She looks up, a dull, happy light in her too-close eyes. One of them veers wildly off to the left and the other looks straight at him. She is smiling, and it seems to push her features even closer together, accentuating the Down Syndrome signature.

"Daddy!" she says again, with a slight, muffled slur.

He leans down and kisses the top of her head.

"Hello, Zoe. Hello, baby."

He feels a wave of fierce love wash over him and he buries his face in her hair. She is so pure, he thinks. The only pure thing in my life.

His lover, Mary, is standing in the hallway, her hand on her hip, a sardonic half-smile on her face that could go either way.

He gently untangles his daughter's arms from his legs and he walks over to her.

"And you," he says. "Hello to you."

He leans over to kiss her and she turns her head so that his lips just brush against her cheek.

"We were going to try to catch the Yale Symphony's dress rehearsal tonight. Did you forget?" She steps back. "I really wanted to hear what they did to the Brahms. Callie came over from next door to babysit but I sent her home."

Claude smacks himself on the forehead. "Shit! Shit! I'm very sorry." He really had forgotten. "I was preparing Fourier analysis lecture. Classes – "

" – start tomorrow," she finishes for him. "Yes, yes, I know. I've hardly seen you at all for the last two weeks."

"I am sorry, baby. I am space cadet."

This time, she leans towards him and kisses him on the mouth. "This is what I get for living with a mathematician. Wait until opera season opens, though. Between my rehearsals and your lectures we'll hardly recognize each other come Christmas."

He awakens in the middle of the night. Mary's sleeping form is curled beside him in a fetal apostrophe. He puts on a robe and pads softly downstairs, careful so as not to awaken his daughter. He sits down at the table next to the hall phone and dials his sister's number from memory. The phone at the other end rings six, seven, eight times. Finally, a sleepy voice answers.

"Hello?"

Like Claude, Alya's accent is still very thick. Frozen, he thinks. We are frozen in time like bugs in amber. The familiar voice seems to echo in his ears over the oceanic hiss of the long distance connection. Ghost conversations weave in and out of the susurrus, faint and fragmentary.

"Hello?" she says again. "Who is this?"

Claude holds the receiver to his chest. The moonlight coming in through the living room window throws a geometric pattern of light and shadow across the hall carpet. He has not spoken with his sister for over ten years.

"Hello?"

There is a muffled curse and a sharp click.

Passing through the gates of the Yale campus is like entering a medieval keep – crumbling tenements outside, academic stone and ivy inside. Claude has a headache, and a vague feeling of incipient depression. He remembers dreaming vividly the previous night, but no details. As he pulls into his parking space behind Courant Hall, the encounter with the prostitute comes flooding back to him. Her flat, dull monotone as she snatches a breath of air. *Yeah, baby. Give it to me, baby.* Her head bobbing up and down in his lap, the rough, even texture of the corn rows in her hair. He is getting an erection, and a hot flush creeps up his cheeks. He looks at himself in the rear view mirror, feels a rush of loathing at the delicate features – pale skin stretched tight across slight, feminine curves of bone, fine tracery of blue veins just visible beneath the surface.

Claude has never lacked for attention from women, though. Forty-four years old and he has been married three times. The first two were dancers, the third an opera singer. All three marriages blossomed and collapsed in the same pattern – two or three years of numb bliss, a sudden pulling away, a volley of joyless infidelities. And always the prostitutes.

His daughter, Zoe, is the product of his second marriage. Her mother moved to L.A. four years ago and sank like a stone. No letters, no postcards, nothing. She blamed him for Zoe's condition, but he knew there was no blaming. It was dumb luck – like winning the lottery or choking to death on a bit of gristle. He has been told that he is fortunate, though; that Zoe is 'high-functioning.'

It's different with Mary, he thinks. They met while he was still married to Nedda, the opera singer. He used to come to rehearsals at the big, old hall in Bridgeport and sit in the back. Mary was a cellist in the orchestra and sat with him one afternoon when the director was putting the chorus through its paces for a production of *Boris Gudonov*. Together they ate the ham sandwiches Nedda had made for his lunch and sipped hot tea from his thermos. The first thing he noticed was her hands. They were large and strong, with long, supple fingers. The hands of a cellist.

Claude takes a last look in the mirror and mentally strokes his shame again, like a small animal cupped trembling in his hand. He puts his glasses on. The frames are small and round and gold, the lenses clear, unground glass. As he walks through the vaulted entrance to Courant Hall, the familiar smells fill him – ivy and stone, wet from the morning rain.

He walks up the stairs to the third floor and steps into the Mathematics Department office to check his mail. He almost collides with Tom Magdar. Magdar is a burly Englishman who specializes in differential geometry. He towers over Claude, and has the coarse, scrubbed look of someone who revels in outdoor activities. Claude was on his tenure committee last year and held out with the only dissenting vote until finally succumbing to pressure from the other committee members.

"Claude, how are you?" Magdar claps him on the shoulder.

Claude forces a smile. "Fine, fine. Getting ready for another semester." He looks past Magdar at the doorway into the hall. Magdar stands there like a tree, an expression of stupid good cheer on his face.

"What are you teaching this semester?" he asks.

"Modern analysis. Light load." He puts his hand on Magdar's shoulder and gently pushes him aside. "Excuse me. Lecture to prepare."

"Right-o. Good man." He claps Claude on the shoulder again as he passes.

As Claude nears his office he realizes his fists are clenched into tight balls. *Two-faced swine.* He has heard, in confidence of course, that Magdar knows about his efforts to block tenure. Since then, Magdar has played 'hail fellow, well met' to the hilt, but Claude senses a mocking tone beneath the effusion. He emerges from their interactions with the feeling that he has failed at some subtle jockeying for power.

In his office, the message light is on and he plays back the calls. His student Lee Ming, in a mild panic about a particularly sticky bit of analysis. Harvey, the department chairman, about the faculty parking committee. Then several clicks, a long, whispering hiss. Music, very faint. A woman's voice, speaking in Hungarian.

"Hello? Claude? Hello?" The crackle and static is cut off abruptly. There are several clicks, then a dial tone.

Claude feels a cold knot in his stomach, as if he had just swallowed a glass of ice water. At first he thinks it is his sister, but no. He knows that voice, though. Suddenly, his office feels impossibly close to him. The faint, dusty musk of the mathematics books lining the shelves hangs in the air like a fetid mist. He staggers over to the window, opens it, breathes deeply.

He is standing in front of the classroom. Before him are rows of faces, some eager and open, some jaded and full of the arrogance of the gifted young. There are about thirty students, a lot for a first year graduate seminar. His reputation has preceded him – Claude is a good teacher. He slides into his lecture persona easily, like a loose fitting suit. There are the inevitable questions about what will be expected for the exams, how much homework 'counts,' how he curves his grades.

"Grading policy is simple," he says. "If you argue with me, you get 'A'. If you don't, you get 'B.'"

A polite chuckle ripples through the classroom. Claude lifts an admonishing finger.

"I am quite serious. That you have come this far shows you have rudimentary mathematical ability. But this is real thing." He lifts up the Korber text. Actually, he isn't very fond of the Korber – too chatty and informal. Good mathematics shouldn't read like a cheap detective novel. But Harvey had been adamant. Claude suspected he was getting kickbacks from the publisher. "Part of your training as mathematicians now is to learn to ask questions, to develop critical habits of thinking." He looks around the room. "Any questions?"

Another chorus of chuckles.

"I didn't think so. Let us begin. We review your entire undergraduate analysis course in the next three lectures. We do it right this time. Purpose is to establish lexicon for functional analysis."

He launches into a discussion of elementary point set topology. Sets, open and closed; neighborhoods; vector spaces. He sketches out a proof of the Bolzano-Weierstrass theorem at the blackboard, turns around to face the class, and sees a woman sitting alone in the back row. He didn't hear her come in. She is wearing a long coat of cheap wool, the narrow lapels looking old-fashioned and out of place. She has straight, blonde hair parted at the side and it hangs limply down to her shoulders. She has a strange detached expression on her face, as though she is unaware of her surroundings.

Budapest. The summer heat lying heavily over the city, radiating back in ripples over the cobbled streets. Her face framed by an open window, sun catching gold highlights in her hair. *Mother.* It was the last time he saw her, that August in 1956 when the Soviet tanks rolled through. But it is a young woman sitting there in front of him. *Impossible.* And last night, the woman standing there half in shadow, the prostitute's head bobbing up and down in his lap, his back arching, hips thrusting.

Her.

Claude drops the chalk and staggers back against the blackboard. A swell of whispers rises up from the class. "Excuse me – " he mutters, and lurches towards the door.

In the hallway outside the classroom, he leans against the wall, breathing in short gasps. *Mother. It isn't possible.* Gradually, his breathing slows. He takes a handkerchief from his pocket and wipes the sweat from his forehead. He takes a deep breath, lets it out, and walks back into the classroom. The white-noise murmur of conversation stops abruptly. The back row is empty.

Claude sits in the cool darkness and oiled mahogany smell of the Faculty Club. He has a glass of Chablis in front of him, barely touched although he has been there for an hour. He is looking through a many-paneled window with a curved Gothic frame at a quadrangle of grass bordered by shady cedars.

For someone who is having a mental breakdown, he thinks, I am doing pretty well. He takes another sip of Chablis. His mouth puckers with the sourness of the wine and he thinks of his father. Dedicated alcoholic. Professor of economics at University. He rarely thinks of him. Tries very hard not to think of him.

He cannot summon up a picture of his parents together – he remembers them as voices raised in anger from another room, remembers the fear he felt huddling with his sister under a scratchy blanket as his father beat his mother, remembers the sound of her crying as if the sobs were being torn out of her. When his father used a belt, the blows were sharp, loud cracks; when he used his hands, the impacts were low and meaty. Claude thought that she was taking the blows for him and Alya, that nothing stood between them and their father's rage but their mother's wispy presence.

She disappeared during the Soviet invasion in 1956. There was no note, no call from the authorities to come identify a body in a basement morgue. She just stepped out to market one day and never returned. The sense of betrayal Claude felt was absolute. How could she leave them? How could she?

After Claude's mother disappeared, after the tanks rolled through Budapest, it was as if something in *himself* had been flattened by their relentless progress. The focus of his world narrowed down until it encompassed nothing but the daily business of survival under the new regime – the lines, the black market, avoiding the watchful eyes of the police who were suddenly everywhere.

His father, too, changed. He still beat Claude and Alya, but intermittently and without relish. Mostly he sat in the kitchen with his vodka bottle, clattering away on the old typewriter, chain-smoking foul-smelling cigarettes smuggled in from Turkey. He had connections in the right-wing intelligentsia, and managed to arrange an escape to the West for all of them. It was not an uncommon thing in those days. But he could not secure an academic position in the States and drank himself to death. Claude and Alya dropped out of touch shortly thereafter – it was as if each reminded the other that they shared a secret too raw to acknowledge.

Claude tries to imagine a Budapest without the secret police, a Budapest without the heavy pall of deprivation and hopelessness hanging over the city, thicker than the smoke from state iron works. He cannot. He just cannot get his mind around it. It is as if the stories of hope and new opportunity he reads in the paper are of some other place, some Avalon he has never seen.

*

By the time he leaves campus, it is dark. Before going home, Claude drives into the crumbling ruins clustered around the bus station. He drives past the women, goes around the block, and drives past them again. His prostitute is there. She looks at him each time as he passes by, but shows no recognition. The rings in her nose and eyebrow flash gold in the light from the street lamp.

Mary is at a rehearsal and Callie is babysitting for Zoe. Callie is the daughter of a literature professor at Yale, fifteen-years old and very pretty in spite of a fluorescent pink Mohawk and a constellation of acne on her cheeks and forehead. She wears a wicked-looking cluster of cuffs and hoops all up the curve of her right ear, and Claude has never seen her in anything except black jeans and t-shirt. She is very good with Zoe.

"How is she?" he asks, taking off his jacket and setting his briefcase down next to the hall table.

"Quiet, man. Really quiet. She's been hanging with the toad." She nods her head in the direction of the living room. Her earrings jangle faintly.

Claude looks past her. Zoe is sprawled asleep on the couch, her arms wrapped around a stuffed toad the size of a large cat that he gave her for Christmas the year before. The toad is wearing a short vest and an expression of comic seriousness. Its arms are opened wide, as if asking for a hug.

Claude picks her up and carries her to her room. He tucks her into bed and nestles the toad in the crook of her elbow. He bends down, kisses her gently on the forehead, and steps back, looking down at her. He stands there for a long time. Cars pass on the street outside and shadows from their headlights crawl across the room at irregular intervals. It scares him how much he loves her. His high-functioning daughter. Finally he sighs, turns around, and walks out of the room, leaving the door open a crack behind him.

There are no apparitions that evening. Mary calls to tell him that rehearsal has been extended, that she will be home late and he shouldn't wait up. Again. Claude feels something like sorrow surge through him and recede, like a wave coursing through a rocky channel.

*

Claude is dreaming of his father's incest with his sister. He hears her cries in the bed next to his, hears his father's heavy breathing and muffled curses, senses the weight of that huge presence in the dark like something undersea. Then, suddenly, he is in the shower, warm water beating against his back. His father is with him, rubbing the rough scratchy soap down his arms, up his legs, between his thighs. On his knees, leaning over him, brushing his lips against his face, his neck. Rough-cheek perfume of tobacco and vodka, scratchy abrasion trailing down his chest, down his stomach. He wants to run away, but he cannot. He feels torn open, flayed, a pulling at the very center of him, pulling something out of him in long, ropy streamers.

He awakens in the middle of the night. Mary is next to him, sleeping. Her breathing sounds very loud in the still darkness. He slides carefully out of bed. She snorts, groans quietly, and rolls over. He has a blinding headache. He knows he has been dreaming, but does not remember the details. A crystal doorknob. Running water. Steam.

He walks down the steps to the hall phone, dials the number.

"Hello?"

He opens his mouth to speak, but no words come.

"Hello?"

An hour before class, he realizes he has forgotten his lecture notes. If he runs a red light or two he can just make the round trip in time.

As soon as he walks in the door, he knows that something is wrong. He *knows*. Zoe runs up to greet him, dragging the toad behind her by one of its webbed feet. He picks her up in his arms and walks into the hall. The feeling of dread intensifies.

"Mary?" he calls. He hears faint sounds coming from the upstairs bedroom. He puts Zoe down. "Go into living room, baby. I will be right there."

He walks up the stairs and the sounds resolve into the rhythmic squeaking of bedsprings and low, throaty moans that he recognizes too well. He pushes the door open, knowing what he will see.

Mary is crouched on the bed in the darkened room, her naked back to him, her hips rocking up and down. All he can see of the other man is legs and hands, and his cock pumping rhythmically into her. Claude walks into the room. Mary's eyes are closed and a deep flush is on her cheeks. He closes the door behind him.

Mary's eyes open and widen in horror. She rolls off and kneels on the bed looking at him, resting her weight on her hands, her breasts swaying heavily. The man rolls off the other side of the bed and grabs frantically at the pile of clothing on the floor. He is very young, nineteen or twenty.

"Get out of my house," Claude says. The man nods and scurries out of the room, clutching a bundle of clothes to his chest.

Mary is still crouched on the bed, looking at him.

"You too," he says. "Get out."

They look at each other for a long time. Several times, she opens her mouth as if to speak, then stops.

"Get out," he says again. He walks over to the window, pulls open the drapes and looks out at the backyard. He hears her moving about the room behind him, getting dressed. The dresser opens and shuts several times and he hears the zipper of an overnight bag closing. Then silence. He can sense her presence there behind him, looking at him.

"I know you don't want to talk now – " she says. He doesn't turn around. Finally, he hears her footsteps leaving the room and padding down the stairs.

He sits on the bed and puts his head in his hands. The ecstasy on her face burns into his brain, segues to the cold, dead eyes of the prostitute. *Give it to me, baby.* He thinks of the gun in the locked strongbox on the top shelf of the closet. He cleans it regularly and keeps it loaded. *Give it to me.*

The door creaks open and Claude looks up. Zoe is standing there. Her mouth is open and a small rivulet of drool trails down her chin.

"Zoe – " His voice catches in his throat. "Come here, baby."

He puts his arms around her, buries his face in her hair. He strokes her shoulders, her back, reaching down over the small, innocent curves of her buttocks. His erection is straining at his pants; he feels it coming up from somewhere deep in the center of him. Part of him watches on in horror, but he can no more stop himself now than he could have stopped the Soviet tanks that long-ago summer.

Suddenly, he senses another presence in the room and looks up. She is standing in the doorway, her form shot through with coruscating streaks of light, coalescing into substance. *Mother.*

"Little honey bear," she says in Hungarian. She walks towards him and sits next to him on the bed. He is still holding his daughter, but the desire he felt roaring inside him is gone like smoke in a sudden breeze. His mother puts her arms around both of them. It is strange – she is a small woman, but her arms easily encircle them. She begins to sing in a quiet voice. He recognizes the melody immediately, rich in Eastern European half-tone grace notes. It is a song she used to sing to him and Alya when they were little.

> "She builds her city
>> the white goddess
> builds it
> not on the sky or earth
>> but on a cloud branch
> builds
> three gates to enter it
>> one gate she builds
> in gold
> the second pearls
>> the third in scarlet
> where the gate is dry gold
> there the goddess' son
>> is wedded
> where the gate
> is pearl
>> the goddess' daughter
> is the bride
> and where the gate is scarlet
>> solitary
> sits the goddess."

"Mother – ", he croaks, the Hungarian phonemes thick and awkward on his tongue.

She nods, a sad smile on her face. He can see himself there in the delicate curve of cheekbone, and in her eyes, his daughter.

"I've been trying to get through to you," she says. "It is very difficult, but the greater your need, the clearer the path is for me."

"The visions, the phone call – "

She nods.

A sudden rush of horror sweeps through him. "Zoe – "

Again, she nods.

Tears fill his eyes. "Why – ?"

She cradles his face in her small hands and he is there in the sticky August heat. Budapest, 1956. A tank with a bright red star on its side forces the jostling crowd down one of the narrow streets that fan out from Government Square. The treads alternately rumble and whine as the tank pushes away a burning car the crowd has placed in its path.

Bird-like panic. *She* is not a student, *she* is not an activist. She has been caught in the madness and swept along like a cork in a river. Someone hurls a Molotov cocktail at the tank. It bursts, sending a sheet of liquid fire across the armored hood. It dissipates quickly, flickers feebly, and is gone. The hatch of the tank opens and a head emerges. It is a very young man, his eyes wide with fear. A machine gun is cradled in his arms. Her eyes lock with his for an instant, then he pulls the bolt back and fires into the crowd. She feels a bursting in her chest, white light, impossible pain...

She lifts her hands from his face. He looks in her eyes, searches in those clear, blue depths for something, some piece of himself.

"I thought you'd just left us, that you ran away." His voice stumbles, cracks.

She shakes her head. "Forgive me, Claude. I was never really there for you and Alya, never strong enough to protect you from your father. I wanted to. I would lie awake with the pain from his beatings, praying to God for the strength to take you away. But God had other plans for us." She pauses and looks away, bites her lip in a gesture that reminds him achingly of his daughter. She looks at him again, deep into his eyes. "Love is all there is, Claude. It is all you have. Stronger than fear, stronger than shame. It is all there is." She caresses his cheek. "You can begin to heal. This I can give to you."

She begins to fade, the pressure of her hand on his cheek like a wing, like a feather, gone.

"Daddy – " Zoe looks up at him.

"Yes, baby. I'm here." He puts his arms around her again.

They stay like that for a long time, father and daughter breathing together. Soon, she is asleep. He picks her up and carries her down the hall to her room. He tucks her into bed, pulling the sheets up under her chin. He rescues the toad from the corner and lays it next to her, folding her arm across its green, velvet stomach.

He walks down the stairs to the hall phone and dials the number. It rings twice and a voice answers.

"Hello?" Her accent fills him. He takes a deep breath.

"Hello," he says in Hungarian. "Hello, Alya."

Note: The author gratefully acknowledges TECHNICIANS OF THE SACRED, Jerome Rothenberg, Ed., University of California Press 1985, for the Eastern European folk song excerpted herein.

Prairie Godmother

Sometimes it got so bad the only thing Will could do was put a 12-pack of Budweiser in the old 4X4, some Hank Williams on the tape machine, and burn up the two-lane straight as a carpenter's rule out into the empty heart of the prairie.

He wasn't a drinking man, not really. But it kind of built up in him slowly, that hollow feeling, like he was one of those dried Indian gourds and there was nothing inside him but a handful of tiny, rattling seeds, hard as stones.

It was more than just missing Rose, although of course he did miss her, every day, even after five years. Will still slept alone under the bedspread she'd made for them with her own small hands, and her needlepoint Lord's Prayer still hung on the living room wall, right over the television.

No, it was more like when she died it left a space in him that never filled, and these trips were like the wind rushing in to claim it.

He was well out of Salina now, coming up onto the intersection with County 7. Will reached over to the carton on the seat next to him, pried out a beer, and pulled the top up one-handed as he turned onto the little blacktop road. It stretched ahead of him, winking in and out of sight with the gentle contours of the land, and Will felt it pulling him forward like a wire to some place beyond the low, distant hills.

Hank was singing *I'm So Lonesome I Could Cry*, and Will crooned along with him, belting out the words loud in the cab of the pickup. He caught a glimpse of himself in the rear-view, his leathery face scrunched up like he'd caught his foot in a door. He laughed, and he felt the borders of that darkness in him push back a little farther.

You just keep doin' it for me, Hank. Just don't stop talkin' to me.

Will loved the prairie, everything about it. When you looked at it from a distance it looked smooth and featureless, just miles and miles of tall, waving grass, but when you got up close you could see the wrinkles and scars. There was a rolling motion to the land that was gentle on the eye but sucked the strength out of you on foot, and the contours hid a cross-hatched pattern of stream-beds and hidden arroyos. A person could get lost out here and never get found.

Will had a favorite spot and that's where he was headed. He turned onto a rutted dirt road that snaked around a low hill, and when the road widened just a bit, he pulled over and stopped. He put the beers in a rucksack along with a couple of ham sandwiches neatly wrapped in wax paper, and walked straight out into the waist high grass, following the faint path.

The land gradually fell, and as it did the grass got higher and higher, until it was over his head and Will felt like he was walking on the bottom of an ocean of rustling tan.

Suddenly, the high grass opened up in front of him and he stood on the edge of a dry stream bed. Rocks of all sizes were scattered in the shallow bed, ranging from stones no bigger than a baby's fist to huge, rough boulders the size of a Buick. There was a cluster of big ones downstream a bit, just above a fork in the bed. One of them had a flat, sloping surface perfect for sitting and Will picked his way towards it, stepping from one stone to another along the rough stream bed as if water still flowed between them.

He dropped the rucksack and sat down next to it, wincing with the familiar protest in his knees and back.

Won't be able to do this for much longer, he thought, and shook his head.

He reached into the rucksack and pulled out another beer and a sandwich. He unwrapped the sandwich, carefully re-folded the wax paper into a tight, neat square, and returned it to the pack. He took a big bite and followed it with a long pull of beer. It was so good – the sharp, salty taste of the ham, the cool bitterness of the brew – it almost brought tears to his eyes.

He sat there, drinking and eating, not really thinking about anything. Will liked the way the forks of the stream bed ran off in front of him, gradually diverging, separated by a widening 'V' of tall, waving grass. It was getting on to his favorite time of day – late afternoon, the heat coming up out of the ground in waves and the slanted, golden light of the sun just beginning to lose its harsh, mid-day edge. He wished there was someone around to share it with, and he felt a small surge of sadness wash through him.

Rose. They'd tried to have kids but it just didn't happen. After a few years of disappointment and a cold, growing fear, they took her in for some tests.

"Her equipment's in tip-top condition," the doctor said. Rose was still in the examination room, getting dressed. Will didn't like his false heartiness or the cold, limp handshake he'd proffered. "If I were you," he continued, "I'd see about getting a sperm count for yourself."

Will was quick to anger in those days, and he almost took a poke at the clean, smug face hovering above the stethoscope-collared jacket like a pale balloon. Instead, he nodded sharply and muttered something, and when his wife emerged from the room he took her arm and hustled her out of there like they were late for something important.

They drove home in silence. About halfway there, when they were sitting at a stop light, Will turned to her.

"They don't know what's wrong," he heard himself saying. "They don't know what the problem is. We could get some more tests, but I don't know how much good it'd do."

Her eyes filled up with tears, but she took his hand.

"We'll just have to keep trying, Will. Something's gotta happen sooner or later."

He turned away and put both hands on the steering wheel, waiting for the light to change.

On his own, without telling Rose, he went to another doctor and had his own tests done. Sure enough, all those years he'd been shooting blanks. He'd worked the machine shop at Rocky Flats for a few years back in the sixties, and that must've done it. They'd handed out some safety pamphlets – comic books, really. Will remembered the stylized logo stamped across the front of the gaudy covers – the looping, crossed ellipses of the electron orbits framing a round, smiling face where the nucleus was supposed to be. Andy the Atom. The pamphlets made radiation sound safe as shuffleboard. Just take a few simple precautions and you'll be fine.

Will never told her. He waited for years for the cancer to take him like it took so many of his friends from the plant, but it got her instead. He never told her and now she was gone and it was too late to take back the lie. His stupid pride. Too late.

He upended the beer, draining out the last few drops, and put the empty in the rucksack, smiling to himself a little as he heard it rattle against the growing collection of empties.

We're gettin' there, he thought. *Feelin' no pain.*

As he was reaching around in the rucksack for another full one, he heard a low whistling sound coming from out of the western sky, getting louder. He looked up and his mouth fell open. The beer slipped out of his hands and rolled down off the rock, bursting open with an explosive hiss when it hit the stream bed.

It came in low, about a hundred feet above the prairie. It was long and thin, a featureless ellipsoid about the size of a jetliner. A dull, metallic black, it seemed to suck the waning afternoon light into itself like a sponge. And it was burning.

It passed over Will's head with a roar that nearly burst his eardrums, trailing a wake of oily looking smoke, and went down somewhere beyond a low, grassy hill about a quarter-mile away.

Will tensed, waiting for an explosion, but none came.

What the hell was that thing? he wondered.

Maybe something new out of the SAC base up at Omaha. He'd heard plenty of stories, and the pictures he'd seen of the new B-1 bomber looked like something out of a science fiction movie. Even if the damn thing couldn't fly. A part of him knew, though, that this thing was just too strange, even for SAC. It didn't have any wings, for one thing. And the way it held the light – kind of rippling, almost disappearing, when you looked right at it...

Will laughed out loud and shook his head.

A goddamn spaceship. Little green men. Boy howdy, Will, have another beer.

Still, he couldn't tell how hard the thing went down – there might be someone hurt. He slung the rucksack over his shoulder and headed down the left fork of the stream bed. A wisp of smoke curled up beyond the hill, marking the spot.

He was a little drunk, and he stumbled a couple of times on the uneven ground. He wasn't scared, not exactly, but he felt mixed up. A part of him was putting one foot in front of the other, pushing him forward, wanting nothing but to be there to help if someone was in need. Another part of him though, way down deep, wanted to turn tail and run like hell.

As he neared the spot, the breeze brought him a sharp, metallic, burnt wiring sort of smell, and underneath it, the familiar odor of burning grass. They'd had some rain recently, so hopefully it wouldn't catch. Will had seen a prairie fire once, and that was enough.

As he got closer, the feeling of unease intensified. Still, he kept walking, one step at a time, one foot in front of the other. *Like Hue*, Will thought. *Scared shitless but showin' up.*

He climbed up out of the stream bed and started pushing through the waist-high grass. A smoky haze hung in the air. Suddenly, he came to a wide swath of flattened grass and torn earth. Patches of fire licked feebly here and there, but they were well separated and looked like they wouldn't last long.

He looked down the length of the swath and could make out a shape a couple hundred yards away, partially hidden by the hazy smoke.

This isn't no Air Force stealth gizmo on a training run, he thought.

He wished suddenly for the Remington sitting in his gun rack back in the pickup. The smoke was starting to get to him – his eyes stung and there was a raw, rasping pain in his throat. Still, he had to keep going. Ignoring the clenching fear in his stomach and the protesting ache in his bones, he began to run down the corridor of ruined earth toward the thing, picking his way between the fires.

It materialized out of the haze, almost as if drawing substance from the smoke itself, a huge, black shape. It lay in a patch of scorched earth, crumpled and broken. A wide scar ran down one side, splitting it open, and Will caught glimpses of flickering lights through the smoke.

He stopped, trying to catch his breath. He drew in a great lungful of air and smoke, and he doubled over in a spasm of coughing.

He felt something then, a kind of tugging at the edge of his mind. *Here*, it seemed to say. *I am here*. But it wasn't really words – that was just the best way Will's mind could get hold of it. It was more like a kind of *knowing*. And it was also in that knowing that Will realized suddenly he had nothing to fear.

He approached the crippled ship. Near the tear in its side, half-hidden by the curved, crumpled fuselage, lay a human form. Will ran closer and saw with a shock that he was almost right. It had a rounded body covered in folds of metallic-looking cloth, and the right number of arms and legs, but the face was like nothing Will had ever seen before.

Green, scaly skin stretched tight across a triangular jaw. A lipless mouth revealed thin, needle-like teeth and there was a single vertical slit where the nose was supposed to be. Narrow, bony ridges protruded above wide, golden eyes that held Will's own in an intense stare. A thin line of dark blood ran out of the corner of its mouth.

Red, Will thought. *Red blood.*

He felt strangely calm. He knelt down next to the creature, reached out a hand, then pulled it back. He didn't know what to do.

The creature opened its mouth and made a sound from deep in its throat, like the last gulp of water emptying from a jug. It sounded like 'gog.'

Will spread his hands. "I don't – "

"Gog," it said again, more forcefully this time. It pulled aside a fold of its silvery garment to reveal a scaly pocket of skin along its midriff, rippling and bunching like there was something moving around down there.

Suddenly, a head popped up through the leathery flap. The same triangular face, the same big, golden eyes.

"Goddamn," Will said.

He felt it again, that *contact*, a feather-touch on the surface of his mind. Will didn't hear it in words, but he knew that this creature was dying, that it wanted him to save its child. He also knew somehow that they could live here, that their bodies weren't really all that different. And he knew, without that voice telling him so, that they weren't all that different as souls either, that they moved to the dictates of something that was larger than themselves, something like love. It was enough for Will.

"Come on, little feller." Will reached down and the thing crawled out of its pocket and swarmed up his arms.

Go.

He felt that touch in his mind again, but it was *pushing* this time. *Go. Leave. Go.* The voice was still powerful, even though Will could see the life beginning to flicker and fade in the thing's eyes. He took a last look, nodded sharply, and began to run back along the corridor of burned, flattened grass, the child-thing clinging tightly to his arms.

When they were back at the stream bed, about a half-mile away, the ground lit up like a flashbulb had gone off and Will felt a wash of radiant heat on the back of his neck. He could feel the presence of that voice in his mind wink out like a light being turned off. The creature in his arms made a whimpering sound and burrowed more tightly into his chest.

He turned around. A small mushroom cloud rose up into the darkening sky.

Destroying the evidence, Will thought. *Smart goddamn lizard.*

He looked down. The thing was curled up against his chest and all he could see was the top of its head. A pattern of fine scales caught highlights in the waning light.

"So what the hell am I gonna do with you?" he asked. "And what am I supposed to call you?"

He shook his head, then laughed out loud.

Sure. Yeah, why not?

He thought maybe he'd name it Hank.

Blue Period

Charcoal was good. Pablo liked the simplicity of it, the challenge of coaxing subtlety from the purest of elements. You begin with nothing. White paper. Black lump of coal. And like God shaping the Earth from light and void, you create a world.

Sometimes.

He had been working since early afternoon. A woman in the market giving an apple to her half-wit son. Something about the two of them, the set of her shoulders toward the boy, the way the light touched his hair, suggesting that some measure of divinity lay in him and that she was the one saddled with infirmity. But Pablo wasn't getting it. The thing emerging from the rough paper was a cartoon, a grotesque joke.

The shadows in the studio lengthened until the sun fell behind the buildings across the Rue Gabrielle. Pablo took no notice, working until it was almost too dark to see. Finally, when the charcoal smudges began to flow of their own accord into the unmarked whiteness of the paper, he stepped back and stretched his cramped shoulders.

He lit a lamp and the studio filled with warm yellow light. The large room looked like it had been visited by a whirlwind with an artistic fetish. Canvases in various stages of completion were scattered about; rough sketches littered the floor. To the left of the wide, bay windows, to catch the light of afternoon, a raised platform for the models. Heavy-breasted cows, most of them, but what could you do? Pablo loved Paris, but the women were pigs.

On a table near the door, a loaf of bread, three days old and hard as stone, a bottle of rough burgundy, a bowl of apples. And leaning against the south wall of the studio, about twenty finished canvases, Pablo's portfolio. They were set apart from the clutter as if a protective wall had been erected around them. His ticket to greatness. Nineteen years old and already he was breaking new ground, surpassing the work of the established masters. After all, he had been chosen to represent his native Spain at the Paris Exhibition! The canvases he saw in the Montmartre galleries would be better suited to wrap liver. Monet should have been smothered as a child. Smothered in flowers. Who cared a dog's teat about flowers? Even the best of the new ones, Denis, say, or Vuillard, couldn't paint their way out of a burlap sack. Dragonflies! Lilies! Swirling hair! It was crap, all of it.

The Spanish upstart, they were calling him. Dismissing him as if he were an insect. Deft but morbid, one review said. Uneven, said another. He would show those Symbolist faggots what a real artist could do. He turned back to the sketch of the woman and the idiot boy.

But not tonight, he thought. This is shit.

Pablo tore the page from the easel and ripped it in half, then in half again. He let the pieces fall to the floor and walked across the room to the table. He uncorked the burgundy and raised it to his lips, taking a long draught. It was rough but good, leaving a warm glow in his gullet. The French peasants were all right for something. He raised the bottle to his lips again when suddenly, a bright green flash lit the sky outside his window. It was gone in an instant, but it was so intense that the afterimage of the silhouetted buildings across the street stayed pulsing in his vision.

What the hell was that? He ran to the window and looked out. A few souls on the street, looking up. He scanned the horizon. There, beyond the basilica of the Sacre Coeur, a greenish glow pushing into the twilight, just beginning to recede.

Even as his eyes began to adjust, another green flash lit the sky. This time, Pablo could see its trail, like a shooting star but brighter, lancing downward to the west. It was accompanied by a roaring sound, something like thunder but with an edge to it, as if the sky were made of cloth and somebody was ripping it in two. There was a moment of preternatural quiet, the world itself holding its breath, then a flickering orange glow began to lick at the bottom of the sky. The Bois du

Boulogne? It was hard to tell. Pablo was still new to Paris and didn't quite have his bearings yet. In fact, he hardly ever left Montmartre.

His countryman, Casagemas, had said he'd be at Le Ciel on the Boulevard de Clichy, fondling women, no doubt, and getting drunk. Pablo felt a sudden need for his companionship. He grabbed his jacket and cap and began to head out the door.

Then, as if he'd forgotten something but wasn't quite sure what, he stopped, turned, and looked around the room. His eyes lingered on the stack of canvases leaning against the wall. His mind filled with an unfocused dread, almost crushing him under its sudden weight. With an effort of will, he pushed it aside. Everything was all right. Shooting stars. Big deal. God taking potshots at the lame and unrepentant. Pablo knew that God had other plans for him.

The streets were buzzing with energy. People clustered in front of shops, talking, gesturing up at the sky. As Pablo passed one such group in front of a patisserie on the Rue Saint-Vincent, he overheard someone say, "Men from Mars, I'm telling you! They've landed!"

Pablo approached the group. "Excuse me, my French still isn't very good. Did you say 'men from Mars'?"

"Yes!" The speaker grabbed Pablo by the lapels. He was drunk; his breath would have knocked over a horse. "A cylinder landed at Royaumont this morning and vile *things* crawled out. Gargoyles! The monastery is in ruins!"

Pablo pried the man loose and backed away. One of his companions laughed. "The monastery is seven hundred years old. It's already in ruins."

"Laugh all you want," the drunk said. "We aren't the only creatures in the cosmos God has graced with intelligence. They're here to test us and we'd better be ready!"

Another of the man's companions winked at Pablo and pantomimed drinking from a bottle. Pablo walked away. Their voices faded behind him, drifting up into the warm night air.

Men from Mars! Pablo had read in *Le Figaro* about the recent volcanic activity on Mars, jets of gas shooting out from the planet's surface, visible from Earth with even a modest telescope. Forty million miles away. Pablo shook his head. What did numbers like that mean?

And now men. No, *monsters*! Gargoyles sent by the God of War! He laughed. Casagemas was really going to get a kick out of this. He quickened his pace.

He cut through the Montmartre Cemetery on his way to the Boulevard de Clichy and quiet surrounded him like a velvet glove. Gnarled oak trees cast a protective canopy, muffling the street sounds. Neat rows of headstones, pale in the moonlight, followed the gentle, hilly contours like cultivated crops. The sky above the trees to the south was bleeding orange at the bottom.

Inside Le Ciel, the smoky air was charged with reassuring chaos. An acrobat tumbled across the stage, flanked on one side by a dwarf in formal evening attire and on the other by a grinning pinhead in a flowered nightshirt. A mustached pianist played a lively accompaniment. Near the bar, two men shouted at each other at the top of their lungs. It was business as usual at Le Ciel, Martians or not.

He scanned the tables for Casagemas. There, near the front, his friend's broad back and shaggy black hair. He was leaning over to whisper something into his companion's ear. She threw back her head and laughed. Pablo stared. This one was beautiful. Not painted like a whore, but flush with the bloom and innocence of youth. Casagemas was moving up in the world!

Pablo pushed through the maze of tables and wedged a chair between the two of them.

"Ho, Carles!" he said. "What have you been keeping from me?" Up close, the woman was even lovelier than he'd thought. Curly, brown tresses framed a heart-shaped face. Cool blue-green eyes, like the ocean under a tropical sun. "Casagemas and I are the best of friends," he said to her. "We share everything, you know."

She blushed and smiled, but Pablo saw first a flicker of anger pass across her face. Passion, too! Good!

"Hey, Pablo, behave yourself," Casagemas said. He turned to his companion. "He doesn't know how to act around a real woman. Just the whores. Germaine, this is Pablo Ruiz Picasso, the greatest painter in Paris, only nobody knows it but him. Nineteen years old and already he is a legend in his own mind."

"Yes, well, one day Carles will shock us all and sell one of his own paintings," Pablo said. He took Germaine's hand and brought it to his lips. "I am not only charmed," he said, in Spanish, "but stricken with envy that this pig will be taking you home tonight and not I."

Her eyes flashed again with anger, and she blushed a deeper red. She started to say something, glared at Casagemas, pushed back her chair, and stalked away.

Casagemas glared at Pablo. "Her father is Spanish, you fool. She speaks it like a native. You've really done it this time."

He got up and hurried after Germaine. Pablo grinned and watched him weave through the crowd, narrowly missing a collision with a waiter carrying a tray laden with bottles and glasses.

He picked up his friend's glass, still half full of ruby burgundy, took a healthy sip, and turned his attention to the stage. The dwarf was balanced on the acrobat's shoulders, juggling a wicked looking knife, an empty wine bottle, and a flaming torch. The pinhead looked on, his mouth hanging open. In the light from the stage-lamps, his lips were shiny with drool.

After a few moments, Casagemas and Germaine returned to the table.

"Germaine has consented to stay if you will apologize to her, Pablo," Casagemas said.

She was glaring down at Pablo so hard that he had to look away to keep from smiling.

"I'm sorry," he said. *That you're with Casagemas*, he added to himself. "We've gotten off on the wrong foot. Please stay."

She smiled, a little stiffly, though, to be sure, and sat. Casagemas did likewise. Pablo motioned a waiter over and ordered a bottle of wine and a plate of bread and hard cheese.

"So," he said when they were settled. "What do you think about the men from Mars?"

Casagemas laughed. "It's the Germans. Von Bulow's ambition has finally gotten the better of his common sense. We'll crush them like insects."

"The Germans!" Germaine said. "We're at war, then?"

"No, I'm kidding." Casagemas held up a hand. "But it seems more likely an explanation than men from outer space."

"Well, something is going on," Pablo said. "There were two explosions – at least two – and I think the Bois du Boulogne is burning."

Binding Energy

"Burning!" Germaine said. "Maybe we should try to find out what's happening."

"Maybe we should have some more wine," Casagemas said.

Pablo thought for a moment, then he grabbed the bottle and stood up. "Maybe we should do both. It's better to know what's going on than to be left in the dark."

He wrapped the bread and cheese in a napkin and stuffed it in his jacket pocket. Germaine and Casagemas looked up at him from the table.

"Well, what are you waiting for?" Pablo asked. "Let's go!"

They looked at each other. Casagemas shrugged and reluctantly pushed back his chair. He offered his hand to Germaine.

"I have a bad feeling about this, Pablo. If there was something wrong, the authorities would notify us. This is another one of your crazy expeditions."

Back in Barcelona, Pablo had persuaded Casagemas to come with him to the recent scene of an anarchist bombing. An outdoor cafe, reduced to rubble in the middle of the afternoon. Two hours later, it was still a charnel house, debris everywhere, a row of bodies in the street covered with bloody tablecloths. Due to their scruffy looks, Pablo and Casagemas were arrested at the scene and detained for several hours. Eventually, they were released, but not before some very rough questioning. It was all fuel for Pablo's artistic drive; he filled a whole notebook with sketches. Casagemas had nightmares for weeks. Disembodied hands, flesh cracked and burned, reached for him in the dark while faceless inquisitors hurled nonsense questions at him.

"Don't worry, Carles," Pablo said. "Germaine and I will protect you."

Germaine smiled uneasily.

Pablo took a last look across the room at the stage. The pinhead was looking directly at him. His eyes, which Pablo had first thought glazed with idiocy, burned, full of suffering and grace, into his own.   Pablo turned away.

Traffic was heavy on the Boulevard de Clichy; horses, carriages, the occasional motor car, wove through the thickening crowd of pedestrians. A tradesman, still in work clothes, had his wife and two

48

beribboned girls in tow. A trio of drunken soldiers passed a bottle back and forth, laughing. The overall mood was almost that of a holiday. It was as if they were saying, "This is Paris, after all, the center of the civilized world! What could possibly happen?"

Pablo thought back to Barcelona again, to Death himself laying waste upon the languid peace of an afternoon. *Anything* could happen. Anything. God is a cruel prankster and these Parisians are fools.

When he could get a glimpse of the sky to the west, Pablo saw that it was still tinged with flickering red at the bottom, but the crowd was moving in the opposite direction, towards the center of the city.

He stopped a young man in a blue watch-cap. "What's going on?"

"Something crashed in the Seine, near the Ile de la Cité! The river is boiling!"

Germaine and Casagemas clung tightly together to avoid being separated in the thickening crowd. She reached out her hand to Pablo and he took it. It was warm, soft, and strong.

Pablo heard several different stories, each of them more fantastic than the last. Notre Dame had been leveled. A great crater had been plowed into the Jardin des Luxembourg and grotesque things were crawling out. Another variation of the Royaumont story, only this time the Martians, after destroying the monastery, began striding across the land in great cowled vehicles hundreds of feet high, setting fire to everything in their path.

The crowd had a life of its own now, sweeping them down the Rue Rivoli. When they reached the Pont D'Arcole, Pablo shouted to his companions, "Let's stay on the bridge and let the crowd pass. We can see everything from here."

They pushed their way to the side of the bridge, buffeted by passing bodies. When they reached the railing they held on. Soon, the mob thinned.

Something *was* going on in the river. Just beyond the tip of the Ile de la Cité, a circular patch of water ten meters across pulsed a luminous green, the glow intensifying to eye-searing brightness and fading to cool chartreuse with a period of roughly thirty seconds. As it brightened, the water in the affected region bubbled furiously. Wraiths of steam floated above the river.

"This must be where one of the shooting stars landed," Pablo said.

A pair of barges bristling with grappling equipment floated on either side of the glowing area. Men clustered on the decks.

There was something wrong with the outline of the Notre Dame Cathedral. As his eyes adjusted, Pablo saw that one of the towers was gone, sheared off near the top leaving a jagged silhouette. The shooting star must have grazed the old cathedral in its descent.

A black tentacle broke the roiling surface of the water. Its motions were flexible, but it was clearly a mechanical contrivance, composed of a series of articulated segments. Tentative at first, it waved this way and that, as if sniffing the air, extending itself all the while above the river like a metallic beanstalk.

It stopped its weaving motion, leaned toward one of the barges, and struck with reptilian speed. The tentacle wrapped itself around the barge and, in an instant, dragged it down into the turbulent, glowing water.

Bits of debris floated to the surface. A few men struggled briefly, but they were being boiled alive like crabs in a pot. Soon their motions ceased.

Another tentacle, or perhaps it was the same one, broke through the water's surface. This time there was no hesitation; it went directly for the other barge, pulling it under in the blink of an eye.

All was quiet. The luminous patch faded to a dull, pulsing glow. A few scraps of wood bobbed in the water.

Pablo looked at Casagemas. His friend's face was pale. Germaine clung tightly to his arm.

"What *was* that?" she asked.

Casagemas shook his head. "I don't know."

"Germans, eh?" Pablo asked. He was badly shaken, but he didn't want his friend or Germaine to know just how badly. "Germans from outer space!"

He realized that he still held the wine bottle by its neck. He lifted it to his lips, took a long pull, and offered the bottle to Germaine.

She shook her head, and Casagemas shot him an annoyed look. "Don't be flip, Pablo. People are *dead*. What sort of horror *is* this?"

Pablo shrugged. "Maybe it's true. Men from Mars bearing the judgment of a cruel, stupid God." He took another pull of wine and winked at Germaine. "Or maybe they come to Paris for the women."

Germaine looked away.

Suddenly, the water began bubbling furiously again and a rounded shape broke through the roiling surface. It continued to rise; sheets of water cascaded off its surface. As it cleared the water Pablo saw that it was supported by three jointed legs. Curled tentacles dangled from its flat bottom. One such tentacle was wrapped around a box, affixed to one end of which was a shape like the funnel of a Victrola.

At its full height, the thing towered above the river, balanced on spidery tripod legs. The cowled head was level with the turrets of Notre Dame. It looked this way and that in a manner that was almost human.

Surely *this* thing is not one of the Martians, Pablo thought. It must be some sort of vehicle, with the creatures themselves inside.

Whatever it was, intelligence and malice guided its motions. It stepped out of the river onto the quay, raised the funneled box, and pointed it at the Notre Dame Cathedral.

A deep thrumming sound seemed to emanate from the device. Suddenly, a ghostly green beam, almost too faint to see, leapt from the box, and the face of the great cathedral exploded. Stone shattered, stained glass glowed and ran like wax. The remains of the south tower began to collapse, as if in slow motion.

It took Pablo a moment to realize that what he was seeing was the effect of great heat, but when the Martian swept the beams across the roofs of the surrounding buildings, there was no doubt. As soon as the beam touched them, they burst into flames as if ignited by a torch.

The crowd, so anxious a little while ago to get close to the spectacle, began flowing back across the Pont D'Arcole. It was a brainless mob; Pablo saw at least one person trampled under its relentless, panicked flight.

"Hold tightly to the railing!" he shouted to his companions.

As they were buffeted in the sea of bodies, trying to keep from being swept downstream, a ragged line of soldiers appeared on the quay from the nearby Prefecture de Police. They raised their rifles at the great machine towering above them.

Pablo could see muzzle flashes, like tiny fireflies in the night. Their effect upon the leviathan was little more than that. It swept the beam across the pitiful rank of soldiers and one by one as it touched them they burst into flame.

The machine then swung the beam across the river, leaving a violent wake of hissing steam, and as it touched buildings on the Rive Gauche, they exploded into fiery blossoms. The beam cut a swath across the mob on the Pont D'Arcole, not twenty feet away from Pablo and his companions. Pablo felt the heat on his face; it was like standing too close to a furnace.

Each person the heat-ray touched instantly became a wick encased in a billowing column of fire. One man was looking in Pablo's direction as the beam touched him. Time slowed to a halt; every detail imprinted itself on Pablo's vision. The dark hollows of his eyes in the flickering inferno, his skin peeling, blackening, cracking, his mouth open to scream, consumed by the fire before he could utter a sound.

Pablo ducked down, seeking the meager protection of the stone fence. Casagemas and Germaine stood clutching each other, frozen with fear.

"Get down, you idiots!" Pablo grabbed Germaine by the hem of her coat. She pulled Casagemas down with her to the stone walkway.

They huddled together, leaving as little exposed as possible to the panic of the mob and the return of the heat-ray. Countless feet kicked their hunched backs in passing flight. They huddled closer.

A deafening screech filled the air, exultant and alien.

"Aloo! Aloo!"

Pablo looked up. Almost directly in front of him, one of the tripod legs rose out of the water. Its strangely scaled surface held a dull sheen. Impossibly far above them, the cowled head swept back and forth. Suddenly, a jet of bright green steam hissed from one of the joints and the leg lifted out of the water. It passed over their heads, gone in an instant. The alien howl cut through the night again, fading as the thing strode west along the river toward the flickering glow in the sky.

Pablo was hyper-aware of his surroundings – the smell of Germaine's perfume, her rapid breathing. The scratchy feel of Casagemas' overcoat on his cheek, more real than the Bosch-like image of a three-legged monster towering above the river, laying swaths of destruction across the City of Light.

Soon, relative calm descended upon the bridge. The cries of those touched by the edge of the beam floated towards them. A greasy, burned smell hung in the air, singed hair mixed with meat left too long on a spit. Wisps of smoke rose from the pathetic charred hulks that had once been human beings. Scattered groups of survivors began looking dazedly around. A few began seeing to the injured.

"What are we going to do?" Casagemas asked. They had retreated to the safety of an alley on the Rive Gauche side of the Pont D'Arcole. In the distance, they could hear the hollow boom of artillery.

"My parents live in Versailles," Germaine said. "I have to get out there."

"I will accompany you, of course," Casagemas said. Germaine touched his arm gratefully. He looked at Pablo.

Pablo thought of the stack of canvases in his studio. His portfolio, the sum total of his work to date. It would be easy to dismount them and roll them up. He could no more abandon them than he could leave an arm or a leg behind.

Pablo nodded toward the orange glow in the western sky.

"That's probably Versailles," he said. "I don't know if there's anything left."

Germaine began to weep.

"Pablo, you are such an asshole sometimes," Casagemas said.

Pablo shrugged. "Do what you must. I have to go back to the studio and get my paintings. It would be a disaster if they were destroyed."

"A disaster!" Casagemas said. "What do you think is happening here? Your paintings mean nothing, Pablo. We have to survive, help if we can. Our chances are better if we stick together."

Pablo stiffened. "You are a woman, Carles. Go then. Run. Survival is nothing without art. Otherwise, we are no better than dogs pissing in the street."

Casagemas glared at Pablo and pulled Germaine closer. Without a word, he turned and walked out of the alley, his arm around her shoulders.

Pablo watched them turn the corner and disappear. His soul was filled with blackness. A part of him wanted to chase after them, to throw in his lot with them, flee the city and find a safe haven somewhere far away. But Casagemas was a fool. There was no safety anywhere. It was the Apocalypse. Grace had passed Man by and thrown open the Gates of Hell in her passage. The Beast was loose upon the world.

*

Pablo wandered the streets, trying to make his way back to the Rue Gabrielle. He quickly became lost. A detachment of mounted cavalry appeared out of nowhere and all but ran him down.

The sound of distant artillery shook the warm night air. Above it floated the sharp staccato of rifle fire. If he stopped to listen, he could sometimes hear the deep thrumming of the terrible ray. Several times, the uncanny cries of the Martian machines pierced the night.

Knots of people stood on street corners, talking and gesturing. Others huddled together in alleyways, passing bottles of wine and bits of food back and forth. The stories of destruction he heard were similar to what he'd witnessed from the Pont D'Arcole. Paris was being crushed under the weight of the Martians' onslaught.

The things weren't unstoppable, though. An artillery battery near the Bois de Boulogne had shot one of the tripod's legs out from under it and the thing toppled, sending a ball of flame hundreds of feet into the sky when the cowled head hit the ground. But for the most part, the resistance offered the Martians was sporadic and ineffective.

Somewhere near the Rue de Rivoli, Pablo came upon a small mob smashing windows and ransacking shops. A handful of soldiers appeared on the other end of the block and began firing into the crowd. Pablo ran.

The sky was beginning to segue through lightening shades of grey. He emerged from a labyrinthine tangle of streets onto the Quai D'Orsay. A bloody, swollen sun hung low in the sky over the Seine, peering through a haze of smoke.

Across the river, the spire of the Eiffel Tower scratched the bottom of the sky. Pablo loved Eiffel's creation. The juxtaposition of fluid curvature and implacable Cartesian logic epitomized for him Mankind's emergence into the new century.

A pair of tripods approached the tower from either side. They were dwarfed by the structure, their heads rising only to the second tier. They moved in and backed away, giving the appearance of nothing so much as a pair of dogs investigating a particularly troublesome artifact.

A bundle of tentacles descended from the belly of one of the machines and wrapped itself around the tower's leg. Its fellow likewise approached the adjacent leg. The machines pulled and strained at the structure, clearly trying to bring it down, but without success.

Then, the nearest machine stepped back and lifted one of the funneled boxes high in the air. Its companion stepped back and pointed its own device at the tower. In the daylight, Pablo couldn't see the heat rays, but their effect was immediately apparent. Currents tore at the air above the tower. Soon the entire structure was glowing cherry red. The Martians swept their beams up and down its length and the bottom arches began to sag. Suddenly, it folded over upon itself and collapsed onto the Champ de Mars.

Champ de Mars! Pablo began to laugh. Champ de Mars! He looked around for Casagemas to share the joke with, but there was nobody. Pablo shook his head, remembering. Casagemas was gone. Fatigue descended upon him like a dark, heavy cloak. Gone, his friend and countryman. Gone, his beloved tower. All gone.

The machines stood above it for a moment, like hunters gloating over a kill, then they strode off to the west, crossing the Seine and disappearing into morning haze made thick by the smoke of many fires.

Witnessing the tower's ruin tore at Pablo's heart, but it had a sobering effect as well. He resolved to get back to his studio. He wasn't sure, but he thought that Montmartre was vaguely north, so he walked with the rising sun at his right, trying to avoid the major thoroughfares.

The streets were strangely quiet. He could hear the distant sound of fighting, but it hadn't yet spread to this part of the city. He guessed that people had either left the city or were cowering in their apartments. He was grateful that he'd had the foresight to stuff some bread and cheese in his pocket back at Le Ciel, and he gnawed at them as he walked.

He turned a corner onto the Boulevard de Magenta and everything clicked into place. The dome of Sacre Coeur rose above the rooftops. Almost home.

His studio was just as he left it. Morning light cast stripes of light and shadow across the floor. His paintings leaned in a stack against the far wall, but his eyes were drawn to an unfinished canvas propped up in a corner, a commission from the Church of St. Genevieve.   It was a standard crucifixion scene. So far, he'd just sketched in the cross and the outline of a man upon it.

Pablo stared at it for what seemed like a long time. Then, moving as if he were in a trance, he dragged his easel into the light and placed the framed canvas on it.

He used oil, thick, viscous gobs of it. At first, he applied it with a knife, but before long he was using his hands, his fingers, the end of a smock, anything that would serve the image emerging onto the canvas.

Shadows crawled across the floor. The sound of artillery grew closer for a time, then began to recede. Smoke drifted in through the open window.

Pablo stepped back, wiping the sweat from his forehead with a stained sleeve. He was done.

There, the vacant idiot eyes and glistening lips. Slack-jawed, full of grace and pain. Behind Him, Judgment rose above the smooth, tawny hills of Calvary on spindly tripod legs.

Breeding Lilacs

"April is the cruelest month, breeding
Lilacs out of the dead land, mixing
Memory and desire, stirring
Dull roots with spring rain."

– T.S. Eliot –

The night before her father came back, Laura dreamt of his death. It was morning, and the light coming in through the living room window had the harsh, unforgiving quality of December in Manhattan. Shadows were thrown into sharp relief, and fat motes of dust drifted in lazy random motion through the wide, bright swaths of sunlight.

The phone rang. Her mother looked up, her face haggard and drawn. Where it was illuminated, her skin had an unhealthy, yellowish cast. She looked very frightened.

The phone rang again. No one moved. Laura looked over at her brother, John, and for an instant, she missed desperately the easy rapport they had shared as children. His eyes slid over hers like oil on glass. No one moved.

A third ring.

"Christ, I'll get it."

Katy, her mother's sister, pushed herself up off the couch and hurried into the kitchen. Laura and her brother followed. Her mother stayed behind in the living room, staring out the window at the jumbled, snaggle-toothed skyline.

Katy picked up the phone in the middle of the fourth ring and held it to her ear.

"Yes?"

She was silent, listening. She closed her eyes and, without speaking, replaced the phone on the hook.

"Tommy's gone," she said.

There was a noise from the living room – a sharp intake of breath, not quite a sob. Laura and her brother still couldn't look at each other. She felt a rushing sensation, as if she were moving at great speed, wind whipping past her face. Katy's hand rested on her cheek like a dry, paper wing.

Laura awoke feeling disoriented and upset, the dream-moment on her consciousness like a weight. She made her way through the tiny hallway into the kitchen, negotiating by memory the clutter of canvasses stretched on wooden frames. Some were blank, others were alive with shape and color. She had a gallery opening in three weeks, and she wasn't ready. Not at all.

It was an odd little apartment, even for New York. Three rooms connected to form a 'U', so that to get from the bedroom to the living room you had to go through the kitchen. The rooms were long and narrow, with elaborate deco embellishments on all the moldings and fixtures. If you leaned just right out the living room window, you could get a great view of Central Park. The pipes made horrible banging sounds at all hours of the day and night and there were mice, but no roaches. She loved it.

She got some coffee beans out of the refrigerator and was about to measure them into the grinder when she glanced into the living room and saw her father stretched out on the couch, one arm dangling, brushing the floor. She dropped the bag of beans, scattering them across the linoleum. She took a faltering step forward.

"But, you're..." She couldn't quite bring herself to say 'dead' – it sounded Gothic and absurd.

He looked much as he had in the weeks before his death, when the cancer had all but consumed him from within. The skin of his face was stretched across the bones of his skull like parchment; his eyes glittered from within sunken hollows like the pilot lights on some infernal machine. She was reminded of pictures she had seen of concentration camp inmates. Buchenwald, Treblinka, Dachau – the images of horror the names evoked seemed remote and distant compared to those last weeks of endless bedside vigil, waiting. The death watch, she had called it.

I can't deal with this, she thought. This isn't happening.

Survival instinct took over; her mind simply shut down. She swept up the beans and threw them away, dressed quickly, and left for work. She bought an orange drink and a cheese danish at the Nedicks in the Forty-Second Street station and stood there, eating, watching the crowds of people sweep past her. She would pick out a face and study it for a while as it bobbed up and down in the river of flesh and trenchcoats, until she lost it, and she would pick another. Sometimes the same face resurfaced, and she felt a small surge of joy. Her thoughts kept returning to the figure lying on her couch and skittering away.

This is denial, she thought.

When she got to the office, she threw herself into her work with a manic intensity. She had a pitch to upper management scheduled for the following week and, while the main ideas were sketched out, there was still a lot of detail work to do. It was completely absorbing and she wrapped it around herself like an oversized sweater.

'Working in advertising,' she had once told someone, 'is like being a whore, but you don't have quite as much self-respect.'

She actually enjoyed it more than she cared to admit. She considered her painting to be her real work, but she took an almost guilty pleasure in the honing of her craft as a marketable commodity. The money wasn't bad, either.

She worked straight through lunch and it wasn't until three o'clock that she took a break, realizing that she was hungry and a little dizzy. She left the office, and walked up Lexington Avenue, stopping to buy a hot dog and a Coke from a street vendor. The cool autumn breeze was a welcome relief from the stale, climate-controlled air of the office. The morning seemed very distant.

Aberration, she thought. Apparition. She repeated the words to herself like a mantra. Aberration. Apparition. She was certain that he would be gone when she returned. As she walked, eating her hot dog, she thought of the day he died.

*

A bleak pandemonium descended on the apartment after the news arrived. Arrangements with the hospital, the funeral home, endless phone calls, a steady procession of relatives bearing trays of food. She had a terrible argument with her brother.

"We shouldn't have let him die in that crummy hospital," she screamed at him. "He wanted to come home. We should have let him come home."

"Mt. Sinai is a good hospital," he said. "He had the best of care. He was sedated, he was comfortable. We just don't have the facilities here..." His voice trailed off.

She slapped him, hard. His glasses flew across the room and he stood there, shocked, an angry welt rising on his cheek.

"You're crazy," he said. "You're really crazy."

She raised her hand to strike him again, and Katy grabbed her wrist. She looked at John and tilted her head towards the door. He retrieved his glasses and stalked out of the room.

"Take it easy," Katy said, putting both hands on Laura's shoulders. Laura realized that her teeth were clenched so hard her jaw hurt. She exhaled slowly, willing herself to relax.

"I don't know," she said, shaking her head. "This has been going on for so long. I've wished that he would just get it over and die so we could all go on with our lives. Now that it's over ... I don't know. It's no relief, not really, but I expected to feel *something*." She laughed. "What I really want to do is get John back in here and hit him again."

Katy put her arms around her and they stood there holding each other, swaying gently back and forth. After what seemed like a long time, Katy stepped back.

"This is making us all a little crazy," she said. "The Van Gogh is still showing at the Met. Why don't we take off for a couple of hours? Your mother and John can hold down the fort."

It sounded like a good idea. Laura was overwhelmed by the prospect of spending the afternoon sharing the little apartment with her mother's grief, her brother's anger, and the cloying, Hallmark sentimentality of an extended family that flocked to death like fat, white seagulls to a discarded crust of bread.

"Great," she said. "Let's get out of here."

The morning sunshine had given way to clouds and by afternoon, a misty, bone-chilling drizzle was falling. The museum was nearly empty. They walked slowly past the paintings, saying little except to comment from time to time on this color, that texture. Laura particularly liked the pencil and reed pen sketches. They were so simple, just lines and curves, yet there was something about them that was absolutely transcendent. Her own work seemed leaden by comparison. She stopped in front of a seascape, admiring the technique – the broad pen-strokes for the rippled sea becoming tighter and finer as the sea approached the sky, the great, puffy cumulus clouds hovering above the horizon perfectly defined by a few well-placed arcs.

A memory came to her as she stood there. She was with her father. They were fishing off the coast of Block Island, the waves rocking the little boat in a gentle rhythm. She was very small, and a little frightened by the vast expanse of blue and the smallness of the houses still visible on the distant shore. It was good to be with him, though. Her mother and brother had stayed ashore. "Just the two of us," her father had said, and she felt very proud. She had snagged her thumb on a fish-hook, and it still stung with the salt of the ocean and her own sweat, but it was good to be there in the moment, it was perfect. The sun was huge and her father's face was huge, and the ocean was a flat, endless plain of silvered glass...

The cab ride downtown was spent in a sad, gentle silence. When they were nearly home, Katy turned towards her.

"Was he a good father?" she asked.

Laura thought about it for a few moments.

"Not really," she said, finally. "I don't think he ever really saw me, who I really was. The focus was always on John, his schooling, his career. I think he just figured I'd get married and start spawning..."

She was silent for a moment. Absently, she traced lines in the grime on the cab window. In six sure strokes she had sketched the unmistakable outline of a Madonna and child. She looked at her index finger, grimaced, and wiped it on the seat in front of her.

"You know what he said to me when I got the fellowship at Parson's?"

Katy shook her head.

"'That's good,' he says. 'So, you seeing anyone special?'"

Katy laughed. "That sounds like Tommy."

"Doesn't it, though?" She shook her head. "That house. It just revolved around his monster ego. Every year, Mom seemed to get smaller and smaller. You talk to her now and it's like there's nothing left. Don't kid yourself, either. Dad loved being sick. He *loved* it. No dissent. No back talk. Mom scuttling around like a cockroach on a griddle. I don't think I ever heard her use the word 'cancer,' though. It was always, 'Your father's health...'"

Katy put her hand on Laura's shoulder and pressed gently.

"You know," she said. "Maybe he didn't know how to love you. Maybe he didn't know how to love anybody. But I think he did the best he could, even if it wasn't much."

"I'd like to believe that," Laura said.

Someone jostled her and mumbled something. She looked up. She was at the corner of Forty-Second and Lexington, one foot on the curb, one in the street, and she realized that the light had changed four times as she stood there. She threw away the remains of her lunch and returned to work.

She put off going home for as long as she could. She knew that she was stalling, but it was easy to justify – the work was going well and there was a lot of it. She sent out for deli around seven, working straight through, and finally, close to nine, decided it was time. All the other designers had left, and there was no one in the outer office. In the darkened lobby, a lone, uniformed security guard sat reading the *New York Post*, surrounded by a console of closed-circuit television monitors.

"Good night, Charlie. Keep the crack dealers out of here."

"'Night, ma'am."

Her father lay where she had left him. He appeared to be asleep. His sunken chest rose and fell almost imperceptibly, and there was a dry, rattling sound coming from deep within his throat. She stood at the head of the couch, looking down at him, and felt a wave of despair wash over her.

His eyes opened.

"Hi, Dad," she said weakly.

The corners of his mouth moved slightly. It may have been a smile.

She sat down next to him in the big easy chair and turned on the television with the remote control. *Miami Vice* was just starting; she remembered that it had been one of his favorites. They sat there together in the flickering blue light, watching the images chase each other across the glowing screen.

When it was over, she carried him into her bedroom and laid him on her bed. He was very light. It was like carrying a sack of tinsel. She thought of movies she had seen as a child – beefy heroes carrying beautiful, helpless women to safety with casual ease – and she remembered her naive speculation that when the burden of consciousness left the body, the shell that remained must be nearly weightless. She returned to the living room and curled up on the couch. It was still warm from his body.

She awoke to muted traffic sounds and the light from a bright, metallic overcast coming in through the living room window. She performed her morning ablutions in a detached haze and, when she could put it off no longer, she looked in on her father. He lay there on her bed, his eyes wide open, staring at the ceiling.

"Do you...need food?" she asked. "Can you eat?"

He didn't respond.

She got a bowl of cereal from the kitchen and tried to coax a small spoonful into his mouth, but it just dribbled down the side of his cheek. She contented herself with moistening his cracked lips with a damp towel. She wondered if this was going to become a routine – shower, coffee, water her dead father, and off to work. She laughed out loud.

Am I going crazy? she thought. Is this what happens?

She looked down at him. A fly landed on his wrinkled, spotted forehead. She brushed it away, heaved a great sigh, and left for work.

The day rushed by her like scenery past the window of a speeding car. She felt possessed of a calm detachment though, and she watched herself as if from a great height – her steady, meticulous hand at the drafting table, the easy banter with her colleagues, the innocent, ongoing flirtation with one in particular who looked a little like David Byrne. The phrase 'business as usual' ran through her thoughts, as if spoken by another.

She worked very late again. On her way to the subway, she passed a man and a woman of indeterminate age sitting on the sidewalk with their backs propped up against a building, feet wrapped in rags, faces caked with grime. The woman held a tattered paper cup and shook it with a slow, steady rhythm. The sparse jingle of coins sounded hollow and sad. She looked at Laura as she hurried past, her gaze expressionless, unbeseeching.

Laura began to cry. It started slowly, with a tension in her forehead and a few tears grudgingly released, but soon her body was wracked with great, heaving sobs. She staggered into a lamppost and threw her arms around it for support. Gradually the spasms subsided, and she walked the rest of the way to the station with slow, measured steps.

She had the first car of the train to herself and she stood at the front window, looking out at the lights of the tunnel rushing past, letting herself be swayed back and forth by the rhythm of the train's motion. Her reflection stared back at her, an imperfection in the glass giving it a distorted ripple. She closed her eyes, and the tunnel lights made a stroboscopic flicker against her eyelids that seemed to penetrate deep into the center of her forehead. She could feel her body – the tightness in her calves as her weight shifted, seeking balance, her stomach contracting in anticipation of hunger, and in that moment, the rhythmic motion of the train could have been the rocking of a small boat, the intermittent shriek of metal on metal the call of sea birds, the flickering on closed lids sunlight scattered from the crests of a random sea.

When she got home, her father was lying where she had left him. She stood there for a long time, staring down at him. This time, he did not awaken. She bent down and brushed his forehead with her lips. Gently, she eased the pillow out from under his head and placed it over his face. She pressed down on it until she was leaning with all her weight. He did not struggle. After a short while, a small shudder ran through his withered frame, and she knew it was over.

She walked to the window and opened it, letting in the sound of the street, the cool night. She looked out at the city, and imagined herself turning around and finding him gone, the bedclothes wrinkled and bearing the impression of his body.

Love in the Time of Connectivity

The first time I met Kali her Proxy was wearing a bone through its nose, a necklace of rat skulls, mirrored sunglasses, and nothing else. We were at the Cabaret Sauvignon in the Paris Muse and she scorched me for an obscure violation of the Tannen Protocol – using a male pronoun in a designated Safe Zone. Big fucking deal.

She pinged me about a week later with a half-assed apology. Said she'd been a little hard on me but my politics were dim and somebody had to show me the light of day. I pinged her back saying yeah, she'd been a little hard-on, all right. We went back and forth like that a few times, each iteration producing more heat and less light, until she broke it off.

"And your Cockatoo looks like shit," she said. "You've got Moiré patterns up the yin-yang."

A cheap shot. The Cockatoo was one of my favorite Proxies, a seven-foot parrot with feathers so iridescent green they bled, leaving glowing, chartreuse trails even on a Mitsushita. The Moiré was a visualization artifact – I'd been using a cheap, Malaysian volume rendering algorithm. But I didn't think it was that bad.

Fuck the shareware fee, I thought.

After that, wherever I went on the Web, it seemed like she was always on the periphery of my radar. A Tapioca Buckshot concert. An interactive lecture series on Roger Corman, everybody wearing cheesy-looking rubber lizard Proxies. Ten Forward in the Trek Muse. We'd probably always hung at a lot of the same Sites, but I just started noticing her after we tangled.

I gave her a wide berth until one evening at the Sauvignon I saw her get stuck in an Event Loop with a pair of Libertarian automata. They were wearing Jehovah's Witness Proxies – cheap suits, horn-rimmed glasses, skinny black ties – and they had her cornered near the back of the club. You could say they were AI's, but you'd only be half right. Low-level Structs under a fairly convincing Proxy shell, if you engaged them at all they'd lock onto your port and spin the same five or six megs of retrograde, crypto-anarchist spew at you, over and over again. They were easy enough to subvert, but you had to know the interrupt sequence.

Kali had on a huge, white rabbit with a checkerboard vest. A pocket watch the size of a Frisbee dangled from a gold chain at her waist. Her shoulders were hunched in a defensive posture and her nose was twitching a mile a minute.

The Structs were really going at it.

" – if you agree that the only role government can possibly have is to ensure the primacy of the individual over – "

" – don't pay taxes. Schools, roads, hospitals all can be funded by private citizens if – "

The exchange was starting to draw a bit of a crowd. Victim identification. Almost everybody had been sucked in by one of those pestilent little automata at one time or another and they were enjoying Kali's discomfort.

I was too, but I was starting to feel a little sorry for her.

"– can you be so stupid as to think that government – "

"– if everybody owned a small tactical device, then – "

Enough. I coded up a Worm with the interrupt sequence and fired it off. The Structs disappeared in a soundless flash of white light.

There was a round of applause, then the crowd started breaking up. Kali just stood there looking stunned. I walked up to her.

"Thanks for the Control Cee," she said. Her myopic, button eyes were moist.

"No problem," I said. "Happens to everybody once in a while." I was wearing my Conan and I couldn't help but preen a bit.

She shook her head. "Yeah, but I ought to know better."

I shrugged. "Yeah, well ... see you around." I started to turn away.

"Wait – "

I turned back to face her. "Yes?"

If it's possible for a fuzzy, pink rabbit the size of a Barcalounger to look both contrite and provocative at the same time, she managed.

"What's your hurry?"

We started seeing a lot of each other. We roamed the Web together, exploring little, out-of-the-way Sites as well as the bustling, urban Nodes. There was one place in the Lunar Muse we particularly liked, a bar with a great view of the Sea of Tranquility. It didn't matter to us that NASA had been sold off piecemeal to the Chinese to re-boot the Social Security bankroll after Bushgate – this was better than the real thing.

After about a month of seeing each other nearly every day, we decided to go Vox.

I sat in the big chair in my study, clutching the plastic receiver to my chest. Everything around me had that odd, shimmering clarity things get when you've been online a lot. And I'd been online a lot. My catheter hurt like hell, probably a low-level infection. I rubbed a speck of crust out of the corner of my eye.

The phone hummed at me. I made sure the vid was off – I wasn't quite ready for *that* – and brought the receiver to my ear.

"Hello?"

"Conan?" Her voice sounded like spring water on green stone, like a warm wind caressing the strings of a golden harp.

I hung up.

She found me in the Sauvignon at a table near the back. She was wearing the Proxy she had on the first time I saw her. The skulls rattled against her chest as she stormed towards me.

"What the fuck was that all about?" she asked.

I shrugged. "I'm sorry. I just got, I don't know, nervous all of a sudden."

Her expression softened, but she wasn't going to let me off that easy.

"Look, I need to know that it's really me you're interested in, not this – " She spread her arm out in a vague, inclusive gesture. The skulls tinkled. " – this illusion."

"Of course it's you I'm interested in," I said. "How can I prove it to you?"

A pink nubbin of tongue peeked out from between her perfect teeth. She smiled.

"There's a cluster of Locked Rooms a little ways down the Pipe from here."

I smiled back. "What are we waiting for?"

Things really shifted into high gear after that. For the next few weeks, I don't think we were apart at all except to sleep, and even then we were on standby.

We tried Vox again and this time I didn't panic. It was kind of nice, actually. At first. But the novelty wore off quickly – it seemed like we had so many more avenues of expression available to us online. Kali insisted, though. She said it was for 'balance.'

It was during one of our Vox interactions that she suggested we go *f2f.*

I felt the blood drain from my cheeks. The background hiss on the phone line roared at me like frying bacon.

"Face to face?" I asked. "Why?"

I knew the answer, though.

" – need to know that it's really *me* you're interested in." I mouthed the words along with her. I was glad we were Vox-only.

So I caught the shuttle up the Corridor to Greater Boston and hopped a puddle-jumper to the Sturbridge Mall. They'd glassed over the whole town, but the Colonial feel was still intact. I walked over a covered bridge to the edge of the Commons and staked out an outside table at Ye Olde Cappuccino Mille.

I ordered a doppio alto low-fat decaf latté and a hazelnut-ginger-fennel biscotti from the tronbot. I was nervous. What if we didn't have anything to say to each other? What if she was ugly?

I didn't have long to wait.

Kali came sauntering up the cobbled street and heads turned to follow her. She was easily the most beautiful woman I'd ever laid eyes on. Long blond hair, green eyes, a perfect, heart-shaped face.

She walked right up to my table and stood there with her hands on her hips, smiling down at me. She was wearing spray-on jeans and a Parisian half-shirt that exposed her left nipple. There was a gold ring through it and I wanted to reach out and give it a gentle tug. Plenty of time for that later.

"Hello, Conan," she said.

"Hello, Kali," I replied.

Behind her, the sky rippled faintly in a shimmering Moiré.

Heart of Molten Stone

An early surveyor, tongue firmly in cheek, named it Styx – a river of molten lava running from near Altair V's north pole all the way down to its equator. It carved its way around jagged spires of obsidian, meandered across plains of rough, pitted basalt, sent glowing, fractal tributaries sprawling across half the planet. The first time I saw it, coming down fast out of the bottom cloud layer on approach to North Station, I felt like I was locking on to a landing beacon from Hell.

Which would not have been a bad name for Altair V itself. Its rocky surface tortured by volcanic activity, constantly bathed in an actinic, ultraviolet glare from its blue-white primary, cloaked in a wispy atmosphere of sulfur, ash, and carbon dioxide, it was one of the last places you would expect humans to try and carve out a foothold. But it had mineral riches beyond imagining – single crystals of emerald and sapphire the size of a jumpship, shimmering pools of molten gold, superconducting metglass splashed across the lava plains like spilled milk.

There were two mining stations on Altair V. The main station near the north pole served as the planet's spaceport, such as it was. The finicky mag-fields of the planet were weakest there and the location made for cleaner navcom. Follow Styx's spidery sprawl down to the equator and you'd hit Deep Station, clinging like a flea onto a landscape that made Earth's Dakota Badlands look like Avalon.

There was a skeleton crew of humans at both posts, a handful of andys, and a lot of expensive hardware. The mineral shipments from the planet had broken records at first, then dwindled down to a trickle in recent months. It was my job to find out why.

A yellow light was blinking on my nav-panel, indicating that I was receiving a carrier for a landing beacon but it was rejecting handshaking protocol for lock-in. I tongued my radio on.

"North Station, this is the jumpship *Conrad*. North Station, this is Martin, jumpship *Conrad*. I need a lock. Repeat, I need a lock."

Nothing except the hissing whisper of background static in my mastoid speakers and the rushing sound of my own blood in my ears.

"North Station, I need a lock. Goddamnit, wake up down there."

Crackle, hiss. "*Conrad*." Very weak signal. I boosted the gain. I could barely make out the words beneath the roar of static. It sounded like two voices. "...no... Schwartz... beacon."

"Please repeat, North Station. Please repeat."

Hiss, crackle. "... turn... Schwartz... No...!"

What the hell was going on down there?

"North Sta – "

There was a sharp click in my ears and the panel light went green.

"*Conrad*, you are locked. You are locked." Signal loud and clear.

About time, I thought. "Affirmative, North Station."

I tongued on the three-sixty display, saw a brief sparkle as the induction field wrapped around my optic nerve, then I was sitting on empty space, streaking down into a glowing hellscape.

I followed the river Styx upstream. It flowed quickly in the middle, glowing bright yellow and fading to orange and red near the banks. Patches of black crust seemed to grow out from the banks into the main flow and break off, careening downstream. Billowing clouds obscured parts of the river, glowing red and yellow as if with an inner light.

North Station was a sprawl of domes, blockhouses, and heavy equipment, scattered across a flat plain of black glass on the high side of the river. A crude landing field was marked off by an 'X' of blue lights. Beneath the faint shimmer of an environment-field, I saw a crew of black-skinned andys crawling like ants around a large, treaded vehicle.

I tongued back into realspace just as I landed with a slight bump. I powered down the drive, unstrapped myself, and removed my helmet. I felt cold all of a sudden, naked and exposed. I had been augmented for so long, it was like removing a limb.

I got my gear and strapped a portable environment-field generator to my belt. My ears popped as I walked out the port and the ship's e-field merged briefly with my own. The sky was red in the direction of the river, fading to deep purple on either side, framed by jagged cliffs and spires. Straight overhead, blue and green auroras rippled across the black sky, peeking out from behind an inconstant curtain of shredded cloud.

There were two men waiting for me at the bottom of the ramp. One of them was tall and lean, with long blonde hair pulled back in a braid and a slight Asian cast to his features. His companion was almost as big around as he was tall, and it looked like solid muscle. Definitely enhanced – hormones for sure, maybe surgery. The skin on his scalp was sculpted in an elaborate series of ridges. His lip was split and swollen, glistening in the light of the landing floods.

I raised my hand in the Company salute.

"Gentlemen." Raspy buzz of enhanced subvocalization.

"You're Martin," the blonde said. My jaw tingled faintly with the vibration of my mastoid speakers. "I'm Flint. This here's Drake." He nodded towards his companion.

I looked at Drake. "That lip looks nasty."

Drake returned my gaze with an expression of sullen defiance. "I fell," he said. A bubble of reddish spittle formed on his lower lip and dribbled down his chin.

I looked back at Flint. There was a faint, wry smile on his face. This clearly had something to do with the scuffle over the landing beacon, but whatever was going on here was between the two of them. I didn't want to get involved unless I had to.

"Fine," I said. "Well, you know why I'm here. Is there someplace we can talk?"

We walked across the black glass landing field towards a low cluster of prefab buildings. As we drew near, I saw that their carbon-fiberglass sides were streaked and pitted with oxidation scars. We entered a covered vestibule in front of the nearest one and walked through a doorway. My ears popped again as the e-fields adjusted.

We were in a large room, almost the size of an aircraft hangar, that clearly served as a live-work area. One end of the room was scattered with computer equipment, machine tools, and biomech gear. Spotlights mounted on ceiling tracks illuminated the area, leaving black shadows in the corners. The other end of the room was partitioned off by flimsy barriers into sleeping quarters and an eating area. A pair of andys stood motionless near a corner, gleaming, black synflesh dully reflecting the room's lights. There was something odd about them, but from this distance, I couldn't tell what.

Flint and Drake seated themselves around a large round table next to a porta-stove. Empty provisions crates served as chairs. Flint produced a bottle of clear, oily-looking fluid and three metal cups. He poured a round and handed out the cups. He looked at me expectantly.

I lifted my cup and took a sip. It was vile, some sort of compost Everclear. I hoped it wouldn't blind me.

"All right," I said, when I could talk again. "The Company sent me here to find out why production on this rock has dropped fifty percent in the last six terra-months. I'm supposed to review your procedures here, head down to Deep Station and talk to Schwartz, and take whatever action is necessary. I've been given full authority."

I looked back and forth between the two of them. The tension between them was almost a living thing. Drake was staring down into his cup, looking mean and sullen. His swollen lip gave the impression of a childish pout. Flint looked back at me with a blank expression that didn't quite mask a hint of supercilious amusement.

"Full authority," I repeated.

I kept staring at Flint. Finally, he shrugged his shoulders and looked away.

"I don't know what I can tell you," he said. "We can only ship out what we get from Deep Station – that's where most of the mining action is. Last few terra-months, though, we haven't been getting much out of Schwartz. A few days of big shipments of rock or metglass for processing, then nothing for weeks at a time – "

Drake broke in. "He's into some intense shit down there."

Flint shot him an annoyed glance and went on. "Only reason the Company's gotten anything at all the last month is we've been cleaning out our backstock."

He paused and took a sip, holding the cup up to his lips for a long moment, looking lost in thought. Finally, he nodded, as if coming to a decision, and looked up at me. "I sent Orbison down there in the flitter a few days ago and I haven't heard anything. We have a comsat in geosynchronous orbit but it went belly up just after Orbison left, totally dead. Can't bounce signals off the ionosphere with this planet's crazy fucking mag-field. Only jumpship on-planet is down with Schwartz, too."

He shook his head, and again I thought I saw a hint of wry amusement in his expression. "So we have been stuck here, mister Company man. High and dry. Incommunicado."

I took another sip and the raw whiskey burned my throat. I turned to Drake. "What kind of shit?"

He shook his head and stared down into his cup again.

Flint laughed abruptly, a short bark. "Let's just say that Schwartz has been working outposts a little too long. It didn't matter as long as he kept up his shipments..."

"*What* didn't matter?"

He waved his hand at me. "I'm getting to that." He paused and took another sip of whiskey. "He seems to be acting out some sort of... *fantasy*... with his andys. Some sort of God thing."

"What are you talking about?"

"Schwartz seems to believe that his andys ... worship him."

I looked closely at him. It was ludicrous. Andys were ... andys. They had a functional bipedal form, but they were just high-melanin synflesh stretched over a fullerene endoskeleton. There was a vat-grown knot of ganglia between their ears that gave them a rudimentary vocabulary and the ability to carry out manual tasks. They were outstanding tools, but they had about as much capacity for spirituality as a toaster.

"That's crazy," I said.

Flint shrugged. "Well, yeah, but you have to understand. It's different with andys out here."

I felt a sharp jolt in the ground underneath me. The lights in the shed flickered briefly. There was another, gentler jolt.

"Quake," Flint said. "We get them all the time."

"Great," I said. I'd lived in South California for a few years when I was a kid, just before the Big One. The holos of the Los Angeles Sea still gave me the willies. I didn't want to think about what a serious quake here might do to the e-field generators. I put both hands flat on the table, trying not to show my nervousness. "What do you mean, different?" I asked.

He shook his head. "Just different. That's all. But Schwartz's really taken it around the bend." He paused. "Look, I don't know what was really going on down there – all I've got are a few radio transcripts. That's why I sent Orbison."

Drake looked like he was about to say something. I looked at him and he bit his lip and looked away. Beads of sweat glistened on his scalp ridges. Up close, I could tell that it was a home surgery job – well done, but a little sloppy. There was a fine tracery of cauterization scars around the base of the ridges.

He knew something and he wasn't talking. I would try to get him alone later on.

I turned back to Flint. "I want to see those transcripts."

He nodded. "They're on-line. I'll set you up for access and you can log in from the shop." He pointed to the clutter of equipment at the far end of the room.

I actually had to use a keypad – it felt like I was handling an antique. Stone knives next, I thought. My fingers fumbled several times over the touch-sensitive glass and I had to start over. Finally, I accessed the file. I waited a second for the induction field to grab my optic nerve and fling the text up on my mind's eye, then I shook my head. Stupid. That's what the screen's for.

I squinted as the text scrolled down the display. It was mostly routine stuff, descriptions of shipments, maintenance logs. Then an entry caught my eye.

Always night here. I called them to me and they came, circled around me in the dark. Always dark. Alpha is my consort. The chosen one.

More routine entries, then:

I am the physical manifestation of their collective psyche. Circle round me in the dark. Worship me. Through me, they do not know death. I told one today to wash itself in the river Styx, heal in the blood of the lamb. It walks down to the shore, steps off into the burning flow. Black head bobbing in the fire, washing downstream in the yellow fire. E-field good for maybe a minute or two. I could feel her life winking out like an explosion in my heart when her field collapsed. Alpha tells me later that this one doesn't die, lives on in blood of the lamb. I am the Redeemer. I am the Redeemed.

I started at the last entry for a long time, feeling a chill deep in my bones.

I logged off and went to look for Drake. The central common area was empty, and I walked around one of the partitions to the sleeping quarters.

Flint was crouched on a stool in front of an andy. He had a short knife in one hand and he was cutting carefully at the andy's lower torso. There was a red-stained rag in his free hand and he dabbed at the freely flowing blood. I was shocked for a moment at the bright redness, but it was just good engineering – andy or not, oxygen is an efficient bio-fuel and hemoglobin an excellent carrier. I walked closer to get a better look.

Flint heard my footsteps and turned around. He smiled and beckoned me closer. The andy's entire body was covered with an elaborate pattern of scars. Tightly wound spirals of scarification on its flat chest marked where a human's nipples would be. A meandering, branching lesion ran from just below the andy's chin, sending tributaries out towards its arms and legs, flowing down until it was lost in the shadowy 'V' at the andy's sexless crotch.

Flint pointed down there and chuckled. "Deep Station," he said. He dug the blade into the purple-black flesh and a thick bead of blood oozed up.

I looked at the andy's face. Deadpan, impassive. High cheekbones graced with more elaborate scarification. Eyes of deep amber. My gaze traveled down the length of its body again. The realization hit me like a slap.

"You mean this is a *map*?"

He chuckled again. "You catch on quick, Company man. The river Styx. Not bad, huh?"

I was horrified. "You're really sick."

He chuckled. "Maybe so, maybe so. But I told you it's different with andys out here. If you're gonna understand what's going down in Deep Station that's the first thing you gotta learn. Meet Leilani." He gestured at the andy. "Ancient Hawaiian word, means 'heavenly flower.'"

The andy looked at me.

For a crazy split second, I almost said 'hello,' but I stopped myself. "Goddamnit, Flint, what kind of game are you playing here?"

He stood up and faced me. He laid the knife on the stool behind him and held his hands out to me, palms forward. "No game. I just want to run this shop, take care of business, same as you. It's Schwartz you want to come down on, not me."

I looked into his eyes. He seemed to be telling the truth, at least as far as he knew it. "I want to talk to Drake," I said. "There's something going on between the two of you and I want to know what it is."

Flint shook his head. "Look, Drake is dumber than a box of dead crabs. He thinks that Schwartz is ... God. Or Something. It's really tiresome."

"Well, let's find him."

He sighed. "All right. Whatever."

We looked in the sleeping quarters, the shop, everywhere. No sign of him.

"I've got a bad feeling," Flint said. "Let's check your ship."

A determined person with a hand laser can, with time and a little luck, ground a jumpship. A well-trained person can cripple one in no time. Drake was determined and he was well trained. The inside of the Conrad was a chaotic jumble of melted plastic, fused metal, and scorched ceramic. Great swaths of bubbled plasticene arched across the ceiling. The instrument panel was a smoking ruin.

Drake lay in a corner of the cabin, a gaping wound in the side of his head, a laser in his outstretched hand. The edges of the wound were cauterized, but it still oozed a slimy pink and red discharge. An andy was sprawled next to him, most of its face burned off. I walked forward to get a closer look. Its scalp bore a similar series of sculpted ridges, and the andy's physique looked very much like Drake's – stocky and muscular.

"Hormone shots," Flint said. "Cosmetic surgery. Making it over in his image."

I looked over at him.

And you're making yours over into the image of the planet, I thought. *This place is an open fucking ward.*

I looked around at the damage. "This ship is never flying again," I said. "Not without a major overhaul."

Flint shook his head. A strand of blonde hair fell across his face. "I didn't think he'd go this far. Not offing himself, anyway. He's been getting more and more wrapped up in Schwartz' messiah trip. When we found out you were coming, he freaked. He kept saying, 'He'll ruin everything. He'll ruin everything.'"

I nodded. That explained the scuffle when I was coming in.

"It doesn't matter anymore. There's a jumpship at Deep Station. We have to get down there. Are there any more flitters?"

Flint shook his head again. "Orbison took our only one."

"Well, there must be some way."

"We do have a couple of cargo barges. Null-g ground effect vehicles, nothing fancy, but they'll do about thirty knots."

"That's crazy," I said. "This is some of the roughest country I've ever seen. We won't get two klicks overland."

Flint smiled grimly. "Yeah, we'll have to use the river."

I felt the blood drain from my face. "*No...*" The idea of riding a cargo barge for two thousand klicks down a river of molten lava to confront a messianic lunatic had very limited appeal.

"If you can think of any alternatives, Company man, I'm all ears."

I looked at Flint. He was actually smiling.

"You're out of your fucking mind," I said.

He laughed out loud. "Styx and stones, man. Styx and stones."

We didn't have much to take with us – some rations, a couple of hand lasers. As an afterthought, I backed Schwartz's transcripts onto an infodisk. The Company was going to want some documentation on how this operation went fubar.

The cargo barge was a flat pallet of titanium and fullerene, ten meters long by five wide, featureless except for a raised control platform at the front and a low railing that ran around its perimeter. It rode about half a meter above the ground on a cushion of null-g fields. When Flint drove it out from behind one of the processing shacks, his andy was standing beside him at the controls. Their e-fields shimmered faintly in the half-dark.

I stepped over the railing and onto the barge. It rocked a little with my weight, then stabilized.

"You're bringing her?" I didn't realize until after I said it that I had referred to the andy by the female gender. It gave me a crawly feeling at the pit of my stomach.

Flint didn't seem to notice. "Yeah." Just asking me to make an issue out of it. I looked over at her. Was it my imagination, or was her chin raised in a profile of defiance?

"All right, fine. Let's do it."

It was about half a klick to the river, through a tortured landscape of rough hills and gaping fissures. Flint drove quickly over the rough ground, managing to avoid the worst of it. The barge rocked slightly with the unevenness of the terrain. The river glowed orange from behind the hills in front of us, the glow intensifying as we approached.

We rounded a cliff of jagged obsidian and there it was in front of us, a vein of flowing, liquid fire, fifty meters wide. A large rock jutted out of the stream near the middle and the lava splashed over it, solidifying into crystalline streamers in mid-air and falling back into the flow.

The river was different this close up. There was almost a presence about it, a spirit

Flint eased the barge to a stop. "Styx," he said. He wasn't smiling this time. He pointed to the rock in the middle.

"Whatever you do, don't get caught up on one of those. This thing spills and we wind up in the drink, your e-field'll polarize. It's good for maybe two minutes before it overloads. Then you're history."

I nodded. "Let's go."

We eased forward, off the bank and into the river. The ride felt different over the flowing lava, smoother and more stable. Every now and then we lurched slightly as the null-g field passed over density inhomogeneities in the flow.

We floated out to the center of the river, pointed downstream, and gradually picked up speed, leaving a viscous, vee-shaped wake stretching out behind us.

After a little while, the river widened and the cliffs on either side fell away. The river was so calm and flat we could have been riding on solid ground – except for the occasional bubble that rose up from the depths, stretched the skin of the surface into a glowing, yellow hemisphere, and popped, sending a spray of liquid rock in all directions.

I sat on the flat bottom of the barge behind Flint and Leilani, watching their silhouettes rock gently with its motion, looking over the side at the lava speeding past. If you looked closely, you could see shifting patterns in the flow, honeycomb-shaped convection cells growing, merging, collapsing. It was hypnotic. I felt myself sinking into a light doze and I went with it. Flickering dreams, snapshots of flowing fire. Drake's dead eyes looking through me. Glowing jagged scar ripping down Leilani's body, tearing her open. Head and shoulders emerging from the blistered wound, pushing back the seared flesh like snakeskin. Long ascetic face, sad eyes. I recognized the face from the files I'd studied. Schwartz. *Schwartz.*

"Why don't you take the conn for awhile?" Flint said, his buzzing voice on my mastoid speaker shaking me into wakefulness. "I need a break."

The controls were simple and primitive – wheel for steering, foot pedals for speed. Flint and Leilani went to the rear of the barge and sat looking out at the glowing wake.

I thought about Schwartz, about the andys, about this hellrun down the river Styx. I felt like there was a lot more going on here than was obvious on the surface, like there was some sort of metaphysical understructure that would click into place for me if only I had the key.

Schwartz. I'd been sent out to punch his clock, but riding toward him down this river of fire I was beginning to feel an odd kinship with him. I wanted to talk to him, to try to understand him.

I looked behind me. Flint and Leilani were sitting with their arms around each other, their merged e-fields like a single coruscating glove, silhouetted against the orange glow of the river and the black sky.

I turned away, my cheeks burning with embarrassment.

The river was starting to narrow again. Cliffs rose on either side, until we sped down the bottom of a deep, rugged gorge. Red light reflected from the molten river flickered off the obsidian cliffs. Flint had walked up from the back of the barge and was standing beside me. I looked over at him and nodded, and we stood there together for a while, looking out at the river.

I didn't know how to ask him what I needed to know. I was curious about his andy, confused. I needed to understand.

"Flint," I said. "You and your andy... Leilani."

"Yes?"

"What do you... what do you *do*?"

"You mean sexually?"

"Well, yes... No. I mean, in part, yeah, but really, what is it between you?"

I thought he would get angry but he only smiled that enigmatic grin of his and shook his head.

"I don't think I can explain it. We have a ... connection."

The ride was starting to get a little rough as we hit some rapids. I held onto the steering wheel and looked behind me. Leilani was sitting at the rear of the boat, facing forward, braced against the back rail.

I looked back at Flint. He smiled again. "You understand, Company man. You do. You're just not ready to own it yet."

The barge lurched and he grabbed a rail for support. He looked ahead and his eyes widened. I followed his gaze.

Up ahead, the river narrowed further, the speeding flow at the center glowing a bright yellow. Then, the river disappeared abruptly. *Falls.*

We looked at each other for a long moment. I wanted to say something to him, but I didn't know what. Then he braced himself against the railing and I tightened my grip on the wheel.

We went over the edge and the bottom dropped out of my stomach. Ahead of me I saw a twenty meter drop down a crystalline channel of glowing stone into a cauldron of roiling fire.

Everything seemed to happen in slow motion.

A sheet of lava washed up over the bow of the barge, freezing into glassy stone as it hit the deck. It sent a molten tongue lapping at my feet and splashing up my legs. I felt a moment of intense heat before my e-field polarized, wrapping my thighs in a skintight funhouse mirror that faded to transparency as the lava cooled. I kicked the crust from my legs and held on to the wheel.

Beside me, Flint lost his grip. I saw him tumble and slide back the length of the barge and grab the back railing. He didn't have much of a grip, though, and I could see him struggling to hang on.

Leilani was back there, too, braced securely against the frame of the barge. She could have reached out and helped him. I saw it clearly. There was the space of a heartbeat, maybe two, when she could have reached out her hand and saved him.

His scream buzzed in my mastoid speakers as he lost his grip and disappeared into the fire.

Suddenly, everything was calm again. We were floating downstream bobbing on the lava current. The falls behind us appeared impossibly high. I looked, but saw no sign of Flint. I turned the barge around and sped back to the base of the falls. I got as close as I could, and looked for him long past the time his e-field would have failed. He was gone.

Leilani had come up to the com. I turned to her and grabbed her shoulders. My ears popped as our e-fields equilibrated and merged.

"What's wrong with you?" I shouted. "You could have saved him!"

She looked impassively back at me. Her ebony skin glowed in the hellish light and her scars stood out in bold relief.

"Love..." she said. I'd never heard her speak before and her voice was like the sound of metallic bees, low and without inflection.

I reached back and struck her with the back of my hand as hard as I could. Her head jerked back and a trickle of blood flowed from the corner of her mouth.

"Not..."

I struck her again. Her lip split open.

"Power."

I balled up my fist and struck her again. She staggered back, tripped over the railing, and fell into the molten flow. Her head bobbed in the current as I left her behind. Moments later, far behind me, I saw the flash as her e-field failed.

I drifted downstream on a river of bloody fire. I thought about Leilani's words. *Love not power.* Did she mean that she loved Flint but that didn't give her the power of life and death over him? Or that what he thought was love for her was power, and she rejected it? Or was it an admonition? I didn't know. I didn't think I ever would.

By the time the cluster of crude shacks that was Deep Station came into view, all I knew was that I wanted it to be over.

There was a head on a titanium pole in front of the largest shack. It was mummified by the thin, corrosive atmosphere, but it was recognizably human. Orbison.

I found Schwartz behind the buildings on a small rise, overlooking the base and the river. He was stretched out on a crude fullerene cross, his arms and legs secured to the beams by loops of wire. His e-field flickered around his head like a halo. I recognized the symbolism, of course – I'd studied archaic forms of worship.

He'd been out there a long time – he was almost dead from dehydration. I cut him down and brought him into the main shack. There were no andys about, but the whole time, I had the feeling I was being watched.

I laid him down on a bunk, tried to dribble some water between his cracked lips. Held somewhere in the lines of those ravaged features, I could see the face from my dream. Lean, aristocratic cheekbones. A deep sadness.

"What happened here?" I asked. "Did they do this on their own or did you put them up to it?"

His eyes fluttered open and his pupils wandered, not tracking on anything, then they seemed to focus on me. He grabbed my shirt and pulled me close to him. He struggled, as if trying to summon up the strength to speak.

"They ... suffer." Each word came with an incredible effort. "*Live* ... in us ... manifest ... expiate."

He let go of my shirt and closed his eyes. He shuddered once and was still.

I sat there looking at him for what seemed like a long time. I didn't understand, I didn't understand anything, but I knew what I had to do.

I found the station's fusion plant, knocked out the safety interlocks, and set it to overload. I had about an hour. It wouldn't be much of a bang, maybe a kiloton, but it would be enough.

When I reached the top of the ramp to the jumpship, I turned around. They were coming out onto the landing field, about twenty of them, identical except for the one at the lead. She had a long ascetic face, lean aristocratic features, a deep intelligence burning in her eyes.

We looked at each other for a long moment, then I turned around and closed the hatch behind me.

The trip back to North Station took about five minutes. After I did what I needed to do, I lifted up to about a thousand klicks and looked back at the fiery chaos of a planet tearing itself apart. The River Styx looked like a cracked and blistered wound, leaking pus.

A perfect disc, searing white, blossomed near the equator and faded to a dull red. Seconds later, another one blossomed in the north.

I had about a terra-week of acceleration to match velocities with Sol system before making the jump. I wrote out my report.

Bioinfestation. Sterilization mandated. Regrettable but necessary.

It was a lie, but I had no idea what truth was in all this mess. Truth was Drake's body sprawled like a limp doll amidst the wreckage of my jumpship. Truth was Flint's life winking out in a white, searing flash, while the reflection of the River Styx flickered in Leilani's amber eyes. Truth was Orbison's head on a post and Schwartz stretched out like a tin Jesus bearing the weight of all our sins and folly. The truth was a ghost, a shadow, a whisper. The only thing I was sure of was that I was tired.

When I got back to Gateway Station and filed my report, I found out that Schwartz had a wife somewhere on Luna. I was passing through there on my way to Earth, so I decided to look her up. I wasn't sure why, but it felt like something I had to do.

We agreed to meet in a bar I knew with a magnificent holoview of the Sea of Tranquility. We were actually about a klick underground, but it looked completely real. I arrived early and got a table next to the window. The landscape was a study in contrast – bright grey where the sun lanced off the surface, deep black where the surface lay in shadow.

I heard a rustling in front of me and looked up. She was beautiful. I knew she would be. I wasn't at all surprised at her aquiline features, the cool intelligence in her eyes, her smooth, dark skin. Schwartz' black Madonna.

We sat together looking out at the moonscape for what seemed like a long time. Words didn't seem necessary. Then she turned to me.

"Were you with him when he died?"

I nodded.

"Did he ... say anything? Any last words?"

I thought about it for a moment. I could tell her the whole story. I could try.

"Yes," I heard myself saying. "He said to tell you that he loved you. That's all."

Her eyes grew moist. It must have been a trick of the light, but they seemed to flash amber for an instant, the way a cat's eyes will glow briefly as it turns its head. She touched my hand.

"Thank you," she said.

We sat there together for a little while longer, then I excused myself.

"Ship to catch," I said.

She nodded, smiled, and took my hand. When I got to the door I turned around and looked back. She was still sitting there at the table, her head slightly inclined, looking out at the flat, lifeless plain. She must have sensed my gaze, because suddenly she looked over at me. I raised my hand. She nodded with a slow, sad smile.

Benediction or release, I wasn't sure, but it was enough. It was over. I nodded back, turned around, and got out of there.

An Orange for Lucita

It was Monday and I knew that my son, Pablo, would be out of jail by noon and breaking into my house that night, so I left the kitchen door open and two twenty dollar bills on the counter. I wanted to leave more, but I still needed to buy groceries and pay the electric bill. I wanted to see him, but I knew that if I was awake and he saw me he would not come in for shame. I thought about leaving him a note, but there was little I could say that he could hear.

You will always be my little boy. I will always love you.

No, some things cannot be said, or must be said with forty dollars and an unlocked door instead of words. I put a half loaf of good crusty bread and a chunk of hard cheese next to the bills and walked to the back door. It was open, the screen door shut. Beyond the door: my small cement patio, a cinder block fence, the moonless night.

It was late, but still I heard fireworks and an occasional gunshot, laughter and breaking glass, the distant highway hum. The town of Zapata, Texas gearing up for Dia de los Muertos. The air was cool and smelled of mesquite, with a touch of burning plastic from the Bakelite factory on the other side of downtown.

I stood there for a few moments longer, thinking of Pablo, wondering where he was and hoping that he wouldn't get too drunk or hopped up before coming to steal from his mother.

I will always love you, Pablo. You are still my little boy.

I closed the door, leaving the deadbolt open. I got a bottle of beer from the refrigerator and put a piece of chorizo and a dollop of beans on one of my good plates, thick and heavy with a deep blue glaze. I carried the plate and the bottle into the small living room and set them on the carpet in front of Devante's altar. I let myself look at his photograph, his handsome face squinting into the sun and the ocean behind him. In front of Devante, a few smooth stones from the beach at Laguna Madre, his badge, the keys to his motorcycle that I could not bring myself to sell. It remained in the garage under a tarp, along with several boxes of his clothes and a set of good tools. I didn't go in there much any more.

This was to be my first Day of the Dead without my Devante since before we were married. Twenty seven years, longer than my son is old.

"Good night, Devante," I whispered.

I prepared for bed slowly. One part of me wanted to stay up long enough to hear Pablo come in. I could not go out to speak to him. He would be drunk or high, full of shame at the sight of me; the shame would turn to anger and we would fight. I didn't want that. Not ever, but especially not that night. But I wanted to hear his footsteps, his passage through the house. I heard Pablo padding softly through the house looking for something to steal. The footsteps stopped in the living room. I heard him sigh and then sounds that might have been weeping.

There was another part of me that simply did not want La Dia de los Muertos to come. The idea, of course, is that we banish our fear of La Muerte by welcoming her as a friend and taking to the streets with her. Devante's job put him close with death many times and because of that, I think, he loved the Day. But I did not feel that way. Death had taken everything from me. I hated her.

I slipped beneath the covers on my half of the bed. I usually do not remember my dreams but that night they were vivid. I was walking down a hill studded with flowers. The air was thick with butterflies. At the bottom of the hill was a lake. A long pier stretched out into the water. As I walked toward the lake, a butterfly landed on my wrist. It was huge, its wings the size of playing cards. It flapped them once and was still.

"Hello, little one," I said.

"Lucita," it said. Its voice was deep and mellifluous, like a television announcer.

It flapped its wings again and flew away, darting left, darting right, gone.

I walked out to the end of the pier and looked down into the water. I saw reflected on the water's surface a great pair of wings folded in a V-shape, framing the bright sun. A small round head, feathery antennae delicate as milkweed.
I flapped my wings and the pier fell away beneath my feet.

When I awoke, I lay in bed for a few minutes full of this dream. The Aztecs believed that the souls of the departed reside on Earth in butterflies and birds. I am one quarter Aztec and I know this to be true. Still, I did not understand what the dream was trying to tell me. Was I about to die? My stomach clenched in fear. Who would leave bread and cheese for my drunken son? I didn't think that was it, though. I think the dream was showing me something else but I did not know what.

I got out of bed and performed my morning rituals. In the living room, the beer and food were gone from the altar, in their place a beautiful papier-mâché butterfly, red and black wings the size of dinner plates. Pablo. I smiled and shook my head. This was a strange conversation but better than none at all. In the kitchen, of course, the money, the bread, the cheese all gone.

Be well, Pablo, I thought. I would have liked for us to be together on this day, to remember his father, but that would not happen. As I stood there in the kitchen, bright with morning light, I remembered a day from his childhood. I don't know why I thought of this particular day because although it was a good day it was not a *particularly* good day, just one of the thousands that we string together to make our lives. We had spent the day at the shore and returned tired, sweaty, our clothes full of beach grit. I cleaned the perch Pablo and Devante had caught, while they sat at the kitchen table: shirtless, joking back and forth, drinking glass after glass of ice water. Pablo looked like a miniature version of his father, the same smile, the same gestures.

That was it; that was what I remembered. The tight feeling on my forehead from too much sun. My hands slick with blood from the fish, the sharp smell of its organs. Pablo and Devante like echoes of one another, smiling, laughing. For a moment it was as if I was actually there, back in that day again, and they were there with me.

I shook my head again, filled with sudden anger. La Muerta toying with me.

Not today, I thought, *not now. I will not give you my sorrow.*

There was a knock on the front door. As I walked through the living room I saw a police car through the window, so I was somewhat prepared when I saw Fernando Garcia Luna, who worked for Devante before he died and was now Chief of Police. He had his hat in his hand and his expression was grave.

"Hello, Lucita."

"What's happened to Pablo?"

He looked away, then returned his eyes to mine. He had known Pablo all his life, had coached his Little League team, had helped him out many times when Pablo was too addled to help himself.

"Pablo was apparently sleeping in the road, up on County Six, and was struck by a newspaper truck. He was dragged several hundred feet before the driver realized."

Dark patches swam in my vision. Fernando's voice sounded far away. I leaned against the doorjamb for support. I felt his hand on my elbow.

"Lucita," he said. "He is alive."

A weight left my chest. I sobbed and he put his arms around me. It had been a long time since I had been held by a man. There was nothing of a lewd nature in our embrace, just his warmth, his breathing, the smell of his after-shave, a different brand than Devante had used, equally unpleasant but oddly comforting. I did not want to be a burden, the hysterical woman, so I made an effort to compose myself and pulled back. He kept his hands on my shoulders, as if to keep me from taking flight.

"He is alive," he repeated. "But he is very badly injured. Many broken bones, his side laid open from being dragged for so long, internal damage. He is in the intensive care ward at Saint Francis. I can take you there if you like."

I nodded quickly. "Thank you, Fernan."

I never liked the smell of the inside of a police car. Gun lubricant and Lysol. Spilled coffee. From behind the wire mesh separating front and back seats, the faint odor of unwashed bodies. I did not allow Devante to take me anywhere in the police car, even if it was convenient to do so.

None of that bothered me this time; I could think only of Pablo. I noticed a flickering in the air all around us and it took me a moment to realize that it was butterflies, our butterflies, back from the North for the winter protection of the *oyamel* fir trees.

I remembered my dream and had I not been sick with worry I would have smiled.

"The Monarchs," I said to Fernando.

"Yes," he said, a little sadly. "Not as many as last year. And then not as many as the year before. I think the pollution is killing them. It is good to see them, though."

Revelers were already flocking the streets, even though it was still morning. Fernando drove slowly past a procession of ghouls, faces greasepaint white with black circles around the eyes, dressed in black shredded suits. At the front of this small parade, four ghouls carried an open coffin. A young man in street clothes was sitting up in the coffin, drinking from a brown paper bag and shouting directions to his pallbearers. Oranges and flowers were piled and scattered around him in the coffin.

Several children dressed as skeletons capered about the procession like dogs worrying a flock of sheep. On the sidewalk, a mummy in ragged bandages kept pace, moaning melodramatically and dragging one leg behind.

We passed two similar processions on the way to the hospital.

With Fernando leading the way, I was allowed to see Pablo immediately. He was surrounded by machines, threaded with tubes and wires. The bandages swaddling his head were mottled with irregular purple stains. There was a slit in the bandages for his eyes, but they were closed. The machines hummed and whirred.

Fernando brought me a chair and I sat next to Pablo, holding his unbandaged hand. I don't know how much time passed. I am sure Fernando said something before he left, but I don't remember what. Nurses in crisp white habits came to check the instruments from time to time. I was empty of thought and memory. There was only Pablo and I and the machines.

I must have dozed off because I realized suddenly that someone was speaking to me.

"Take him to surgery now." An elderly man with a round face leaned towards me, spectacles perched halfway down his bulbous nose. He wore a white coat and smelled of expensive cologne. A stethoscope dangled from around his neck.

"You can wait in the lounge on the first floor, or leave your phone number with the nurse and we'll call you."

"What's going on? Will he be all right?"

He pursed his lips. "I can't tell you that. We'll probably have to remove his spleen at the very least. Beyond that, we'll have to see what we find when we go in."

When we go in. I waited, hoping he had more to tell me, but he was done.

"I'll wait," I said.

They wheeled Pablo away and one of the sisters took me to the lounge. There was a television and several vending machines. A man in a skeleton costume sat on one of the couches, his face covered in greasepaint to resemble a skull. He was perched on the edge of the couch like he was about to rise. He looked at me as I entered the room, his eyes moist pools set within circles of black. I nodded, and he nodded back, but he did not smile.

"I will tell you if there's any news," the sister said.

"Thank you," I said. I took a seat near the door and stared blankly at the television. The sound was a low murmur; pale, ghostly images chased each other across the screen. I looked at the skeleton man again. He was staring off into space, still balanced on the edge of the couch.

After a while, a sister came into the room, a young girl in tow, and approached the skeleton man. He stood up, very tall, and bent down to the little girl. He said something I did not hear, nodded gravely, and offered his hand. After a moment's hesitation, she reached out and grabbed onto his index finger. Together they left the room.

A little while later, a heavy woman in jeans and a hooded sweatshirt came in with an infant bundled in a colorful blanket. She smiled at me and I nodded back. Time passed as it does in waiting rooms. The transit of strangers, intersecting with smiles and nods.

The skeleton man returned, alone, and sat across from me.

"Where is your friend," I asked.

"Esmeralda?" His voice was low and soft. "A very sweet girl. She is with her family."

I nodded again. I wanted to say something else to him but I did not know what to say. I suddenly felt nauseated with the close hospital smell. I could feel La Muerta all around me – in the waiting room, in the hospital rising above me. Each room a nexus of suffering. I stood up.

"I need to get some air," I said.

He smiled gently.

"Don't worry," he said.

Outside, La Dia was in full swing. Firecrackers and gunshots echoed in the small streets surrounding the hospital. Butterflies filled the air with flickering motion. A mock funeral procession made its way down the street in front of the hospital entrance. I moved closer to get a better look. As I approached the head of the procession, it stopped and the pallbearers set the coffin gently on the street. They smiled shyly at me and stepped aside.

Sitting in the coffin, propped up against a satin pillow: my Devante.

He wore his funeral suit, midnight blue with grey pinstripes. He brushed his curly black hair away from his forehead in a gesture that was uniquely his, and smiled sadly at me. On his forehead was a puckered scar the size of a nickel from the bullet that had taken his life.

I opened my mouth to speak and he raised his hand to me, palm out. Another Devante gesture. Then he reached under the satin bedding, brought out an orange, and handed it to me. It was a good one, large and round, its pebbled skin unblemished. When I looked up again, Devante's funeral procession was gone.

I felt a feather touch on my wrist. I looked down. A butterfly rested there, wings spread.

Oh, God, I thought. *Please. Who are you? Devante? My Pablo? Please, please, not Pablo.*

"Hello, little one," I croaked.

"Lucita."

I jumped and whirled around. Out of the corner of my eye I saw the butterfly darting left, darting right, gone.

Fernando put his hands on my shoulders.

"Lucita," he said again. "I have just spoken with the doctors. Pablo is going to be all right. The recovery will be long and difficult, but he will live."

93

I stepped back. Fernando's hands fell to his sides. I looked down at the orange again, wrapped both my hands around it and squeezed gently. It was firm and slightly yielding; warm, as if full of blood.

Ex Vitro

I

The communications room was a weird place. Jax wanted to hunch his shoulders against the close metal walls, against the silent machines that smelled faintly of ozone and heat. An array of yellow telltales glowed steadily on the panel over his head; the blank, grey screen hung before him like an open mouth. The one decoration in the barren cubicle was a software ad-fax Maddy had taped to the wall – INSTANT ACCESS, some sort of file-retrieval utility, the first word highlighted in blue and the letters slanted, trailing comb-like filigrees denoting speed.

There was something that drew him to the place, though, and he caught solitary time there whenever he could. He imagined himself a point of light on the far tip of a rocky promontory, a beacon rising above a dark, endless ocean.

Jax heard a sound behind him and turned around. Maddy stood in the doorway. She had been working out and her shirt was damp with sweat. Ringlets of dark hair framed her face; red splotches stood out high on her pale cheeks.

"What's up?" she asked, still a little short of breath. "I didn't hear a comm bell..."

"Nothing," Jax replied. "I'm just hanging. Fog's really bad – we can't even watch the slugs."

Maddy shrugged. The slugs didn't interest her much – anything that happened on time scales shorter than a thousand millennia slid under

95

her radar. Titan itself, though, was to her like a blood-glittering, faceted ruby to a gemologist. Ammonia seas, vast lava fields laced with veins of waxy, frozen hydrocarbons. She was taking ultrasound readings to map the moon's crust and mantle. Jax had never seen her so engaged, but the news from home was like a tidal force pulling at her from another direction. "Anything new on the laser feed?" she asked.

Jax knew that, decoded, the question was, 'War news?' Or more specifically, 'How bad does it have to get before we can go home?'

She had family in the EC, in Paris, and the information that came in on the feed was frustrating in what it withheld. It was like deducing the shape and texture of an object by studying the shadow it cast in bright, white light.

They did know that a couple of days ago, PacRim had lobbed a mini-nuke at one of the EC's factory-continents in the Indian Ocean, claiming a territorial incursion. The EC had followed suit by vaporizing Jakarta. There had been some sporadic ground combat in New Zealand and Antarctica and a lot of saber-rattling, but no further nuclear exchanges. The North American Free Trade Coalition and the Russian Hegemony were sitting back and waiting, urging restraint and dialogue in the emergency League session and keeping ground and space defenses at full alert.

"PacRim's been making noises about a nova bomb, but nobody really thinks they're that crazy. Naft's warning everybody off their wind farms in the South Atlantic – that's not exactly news, not since Johannesburg." Jax shook his head. "The Net's going completely apeshit, of course. Traffic volume's sky high..."

She took a step toward him and he stood up and put his arms around her. They stood like that for several minutes, their breathing merging slowly to unison. She smelled of sweat and of the hydroponics media she had been working with earlier that morning. The taut, lean muscles of her back relaxed to a yielding firmness under his hands. She began to move against him and she gently pushed him back into the chair.

"Wait," he said. "Not here. Let's go to the pod."

Maddy nodded without speaking and turned around, reaching behind her back for his hand. He took it and trailed her down the narrow corridor. They passed other passageways branching off, leading to sleeping quarters, the galley, the labs. At the end of the corridor, standing like an abstract sculpture, was a gleaming, twisted piece of obsidian Maddy had brought in from one of Titan's lava plains. Oxidation from the station's atmosphere gave its surface a rainbow sheen. A rude step was carved into its side with a hand laser. Above it was a round, open hatch. Maddy let go of his hand, stepped up onto the rock, and pulled herself through. Jax followed behind her, emerging into a crystalline bubble surrounded by a sea of swirling mist.

They had grown the pod from a single crystal into a transparent, 5-meter hemisphere. It was light and thin, but strong enough to keep out the deadly hydrocarbon brew that was Titan's atmosphere. The fog was beginning to thin a little, and through it Jax could see the frozen landscape glittering in tenebrous, diffuse light. He caught a glimpse of a herd of slugs on the shore of the nearby ammonia sea. Their shiny, chitinous bodies were scattered across the lava beach in a rough pattern like sheared concentric diamonds, slowly shifting.

Maddy had already taken her clothes off, and she stood facing him, waiting. Jax stepped out of his shorts and put his arms around her again. They stood there, rocking slowly, then together they sunk to the carpeted floor.

When Maddy came, a shuddering ripple passed unseen through the pattern made by the slugs' bodies. Jax's pleasure shortly afterward sent another wave passing through the pattern from the opposite side. The ripples collided and scattered, each leaving an imprint of its shape on the other.

Jax gently disentangled himself from Maddy, trying not to wake her. She groaned softly and rolled over, then her breathing returned to normal. Her face was relaxed and completely expressionless, as if sleep were a black hole from which nothing of herself escaped.

For an instant, it looked to Jax like the face of a perfect stranger, its contours so achingly familiar that the familiarity itself was something exotic. He reached out to touch her and his hand hovered above the curve of her cheek, trembling slightly.

So strange, he thought, the two of us out here, middle of nowhere, ties to home nothing more than electromagnetic ephemera. Ghosts. What *are* we to each other in the absence of context? We create our own, always have.

They met when they were graduate students at the Sorbonne, Maddy in planetary physics, Jax in system dynamics. They were both driven to succeed, the shining stars in their respective departments' firmament of hopeful students, and they gravitated towards one another with the same intensity that fueled their research.

They cycled through several iterations of crash and burn, learning each others' boundaries, before they settled into a kind of steady state. Still, their relationship felt to Jax like a living entity, a nonlinear filter whose response to stimuli was never quite what you thought it was going to be.

Individually, they were excellent candidates for SunGroup, a system-wide industrial development consortium – mining, pharmaceuticals, SP-sats, all supported by a broad base of research and exploration. As a couple they were perfect for one of Sun's elite research teams. When they finished out their three-year term, especially if they had 'made their bones' by discovering something of interest and potential profit, they would have enough clout in SunGroup to command their own programs.

The slugs were certainly of interest. They were at the apex of Titan's spartan ecosystem – black, almost featureless bullet-shaped creatures about the size of dogs. Methane-breathers, they basked in the shallows of Titan's ammonia seas and fed on anything organic – the primitive lichen that grew in sporadic patches on the moon's rough surface, the glittering chunks of hydrocarbon ice scattered like moraine across the landscape, even each other.

Jax could watch them for hours. They exhibited behavior not unlike schooling or flocking, merging in geometric clusters, shifting, forming new patterns. Individually, they seemed less sensate than bees; their central nervous system consisted of nothing more than a small knot of ganglia at the wider end, where there was a cluster of light-sensitive vision patches. They were living cellular automata – each responding only to nearest-neighbor stimuli. Collectively, though, from the local interactions, there emerged a complex, evolving pattern.

The fog was thick again, a uniform shroud. It seemed to glow with a dim, pearly light of its own. Jax wondered about the slugs outside, what they were doing. He closed his eyes and in that darkness he imagined a slowly shifting pattern of glowing points, an elongated oval surrounding a hard, geometric pattern of sharp edges and straight lines.

II

Maddy took another leaf from the small pile of lettuce in the colander and put it in her mouth. The taste was so bittersweet *green*, so substantial and earthy, that it brought tears to her eyes.

"The new crop of lettuce is really good," she said. "I think I finally got the 'ponics chemistry down."

"About time," Jax said. He looked up from the catfish he was cleaning. Fresh from the tank-farm, its bright organs spilled out on the cutting board. Blood streaked his hands and the smell of it was strong and sharp in the little galley. "The last batch had that weird, rotten aftertaste. I kept waiting for the cramps to start."

"Well, fuck you, then." The words seemed to materialize in the air between them, as if they had come from somewhere separate from her. She felt color rising to her cheeks, but there was no place to go but forward. "Anytime you want the job, you just say so."

Jax looked startled and hurt. He wiped his cheek, leaving a bloody streak, and bent down to his work again. His large hands were quick and sure. Maddy could feel the tension between them like a third presence in the room. She took a deep breath and let it out. Again. In, I calm my body. Out, dwelling in the present moment. In, listen, listen. Out, the sound of my breathing brings me back to my true self.

She took a step toward him and put her hand on his arm. He looked up. She kissed his cheek, tasting blood.

"I'm sorry, baby," she said. "I'm a little wired out with the war news. I can't take much more of it." She bit her lip. "If it gets any worse, I'm going to want Sun to pull us out of here. I need to be near my parents."

"Jesus, Maddy, Paris is the last place we want to be if the shit really hits the fan – it'll go up in a puff of plasma." He paused when he saw the expression on her face and reached out to touch her arm. "I'm sorry, but you know it's true. Do you really want to move to Ground Zero?" He let his arm fall again. "Besides, if we abort, they'll nail us with a stiff fine and we'll never get them to back us again."

"We can afford it."

Jax shrugged. "We can afford the fine, yeah, but we'd have to start from scratch with another Group, and that wouldn't be easy."

"Maurice will swing it for us." Maurice Enza was their sponsor at SunGroup. A hundred-thirty-two years old, mostly cybernetic prosthetics including eyes and voicebox, still publishing in the theoretical bioeconomics literature. Maddy revered him. Jax respected him, but privately thought he was something of a spook and had always kept him at a polite distance.

"Maurice may be as old as Elvis but he isn't God."

Maddy closed her eyes. In, I calm my body. Out, listen, listen.

She opened her eyes and looked closely at him. His face was open and earnest. He wasn't just being an asshole or doing some kind of power thing.

Maddy smiled gently. "Let's just see what happens, okay?"

The catfish was delicious, its flesh moist and white, the Cajun-style crust black and redolent with spice. The lettuce tasted sweeter with the fact that she had grown it with her own hands, nursed from a rack of seedlings in a carefully tended nutrient bath to full, leafy plants, their tangled roots weaving through their bed of saturated foam.

They ate together in silence. A Bach violin concerto played softly on the lounge speakers, the melodic lines arching gracefully over the muted hum of the life support systems.

Strange to be so connected with the sensate, Maddy thought, these earthy pleasures, while we're in this tin can at the bottom of an ocean of freezing poison, a billion and a half klicks from most of the people I love. Where everything's falling apart. Listening to Bach, no less.

She shook her head. Cognitive dissonance.

Jax looked over at her and smiled. "What?"

"Oh, nothing, I ... I don't know." She held her hands out in front of her, palms up, as if she were gauging the weight of an invisible package.

The veined rock flashed by her in a grey, flickering blur. Every now and then, she emerged into an open space for an instant and caught a brief glimpse of distant walls, stalactites and stalagmites merging in midair to form complex, bulbous shapes, ghostly green in the enhanced infrared. Then the bottom wall would rush up and swallow her again. A readout on the display in the lower left corner of her vision flashed her depth below the surface.

Maddy saw a fault open up off to her left and she steered her way over to it by opening the right-hand throttle of her jetpack, a bit of Buck Rogers kitsch she'd coded up to contextualize the virtual a bit, give it some tactile reference. Too easy to get disoriented otherwise – sim-sick.

She followed the fault down toward Titan's core, passing through large black regions where her mapping was still incomplete. The fault twisted and turned, opening at times to a wide crevasse, then narrowing down until it was little more than a stress plane in the tortured rock.

She slowed down and pushed a button on the virtual display. Three-dimensional volume renderings of the stress field in the rock appeared all around her as glowing lines, fractal neon limbs cascading into smaller and smaller filamentary tangles. She filtered the display until all she saw were the glowing tangles against a field of deep, velvet blackness. The fault itself was a tortured sheet of cold fire.

She hovered there in the darkness, surrounded by light. *This* is what I know, she thought. *This* is familiar. She could as well have been in a geo-simulation of the Earth's crust. The equations of elasto-plastic deformation are invariant under acts of God and Man. Stochastic, fractal, extraordinarily complex, the solutions could still be understood, predicted with some reliability, projected onto a lower-dimensional attractor for a smoother representation.

All well and good as science. As personal metaphor it had its drawbacks. Maddy knew people back home whose lives were distressingly simple – work, family, sheep-like pursuit of leisure all fixed, remorseless basins of attraction with no fractal boundaries. They eluded her, whatever drove them completely foreign. Her personal trajectory was constrained to a more chaotic topology.

With a corner of her awareness, she could feel her realtime body, helmeted, visored, ensconced in a padded chair in a darkened featureless room.

And in the lab, cocooned in biostasis, the embryo, a radiant point of light in her mind's eye. She could imagine the impossibly slow heartbeat, just enough to keep it suspended above the threshold of death. In quiet moments, she imagined that pulse to be her own, could feel her awareness contract to that tiny lump of blood and meat, miracle of coded proteins. One part Jax, one part Maddy. Something other than the sum of its constituents.

It was usually bearable, her awareness of it a dull, constant pressure in the back of her mind. But sometimes she felt an ache in the deepest part of her, as if it had been torn from her leaving a bleeding, septic cavity. How could it live apart from her? Or she from it? She would tell Jax soon.

III

He turned off the suit speaker. The sibilant whisper of his breath and the deep ocean surge of blood music in his ears rushed in to fill the silence. Titan's daylight sky arched over his head like a great inverted bowl, deep cyan overhead fading to a bruised purple around the horizon. The photochemical smog was thinned to a gauzy softness, a blurring of focus, and Sol hung overhead like a bright, fuzzy diamond. He could almost feel the weight of Saturn's presence suspended unseen in the sky, shielded by Titan's bulk.

He had walked about a klick along the shore. The station was no longer visible behind him and he felt exhilarated with the solitude. A herd of about twenty slugs had been pacing him as he walked, oozing along almost like a single organism. He hadn't been sure at first whether they started trailing him or he them, but he was certain they were aware of him now. When he stopped, they did. He walked another few steps along the rocky shore, and the herd moved along with him like an ameba, extending a long, thin pseudopod which was then reabsorbed into the main body. This was the first time they had exhibited anything like a response to an external stimulus. Like *awareness*.

What are you? They stretched out before him, attenuating into a long, sinuously curving line, like an old river.

He closed his eyes and concentrated as hard as he could. *Tell me what you are.*

In his mind's eye he saw the pattern, a meandering line of bright sparks, ripple slightly. He opened his eyes.

Tell me.

Another rippling wave passed through the line.

He turned on his radio. "Maddy. Can you suit up and get out here. I want – "

"What the fuck have you been doing? I've been trying to reach you for the last hour." Her voice sounded tight and thin.

"I turned off the speaker. I – "
"Can you get in here?" Long pause. "Please?"

The holotank was on, but she was staring off into space. In the transparent, glass cube Jax could see ghostly, flickering images of fire and smoke.
" – *retaliated with a 50-kiloton airburst over Manila. The latest estimates of the death toll – "*
"What's going on?"
She looked up at him. Her eyes were puffy. "Paris."
He felt the word almost like a physical blow. "Shit. Where else?"
She shook her head. "It's all coming apart. Naft and Russia have managed to keep out of it so far, but it's just a matter of time."
" – *emergency session, but no word yet from the CEO Council – "*
"Anything from SunGroup?"
She shook her head again. She had the look of an accident victim: hollow eyes, slow, deliberate gestures.
" – *ground forces overwhelmed Mitsubishi troops outside Sydney. Conventional theater weapons – "*
Jax waved his hand sharply over a panel on the wall. The volume of the newsfeed decreased to a murmur. The holotank still flickered and glowed with the images of burning cities. He walked over to her and put his hand on her shoulder. She sat there stiffly, as if unaware of his presence; her shoulder felt like it was made of wood. He put his other hand there and started to knead the tight muscles, but she shook him off.
He stood behind her for a long time, not knowing what to do. Every now and then, Maddy let out a long, shuddering sigh.
Finally she looked up. "What are we going to do?"
He shrugged. "What can we do? We can survive here indefinitely – the station ecology's intact and stable. We continue the research, wait for SunGroup to pull us out of here."
Even as he said it, though, Jax felt a rush of panic at the thought of leaving. He closed his eyes and a matrix of points, white on velvet black, pulsed and flowed. Concentric diamonds, slowly shearing. He opened his eyes and Maddy was staring at him.
"Continue the research? What for? We don't even know if there is a SunGroup anymore. We have to find out what's left back there, get back if we can. We can *help*."

Jax was silent for a long time. "What we need to do is survive, Maddy," he said slowly. "Keep the systems green, keep the research going. I'll try to raise Maurice, find out what their status is, but I don't know when they're going to be able to get to us. I think we're pretty much on our own."

"If they can spare a ship, I want to go home," Maddy said. "Luna, one of the O'Neils, I don't care. Our place right now is back there."

Jax forced himself to smile reassuringly. "All right, Maddy, we'll see what they can do. We'll have at least three hours until we can get a reply – "

" – a hundred-seventy-four minutes – "

" – providing we can get through at all. The Net is probably stone dead, all those e.m.p.'s." He gestured toward the holotank. "That stuff is probably coming in relayed from one of the O'Neils..."

"We can't really tell what's going on back there from the newsfeed – the information entropy is sky-high. We're not going to know until we ask someone who knows something. Let's just do it."

Together they walked down the corridor to the communications room. Jax logged on, set the protocol, and transmitted Maurice's address from memory.

He faced the blank screen. A section of it elasticized invisibly, ready to transform his voice into digitized bits and hurl them up to the relay satellite waiting at one of Titan's Trojan Points. There was no return visual, of course – dialogue was impossible. Whenever Jax transmitted across the lightspeed gulf separating him from Earth, he had the sensation that his words were disappearing down a well. He could feel Maddy's presence behind him like a hovering cloud.

"Maurice. This is Jax and Maddy calling from Titan Station." Obviously. Where else would they be calling from? "Please advise us as to your status. We – "

"Pull us out of here, Moe," Maddy cut in. "Please. We want to come home."

Jax shot her an annoyed glance and turned back to the screen. "Please advise," he repeated. "End."

Ignoring Maddy, he tried to log onto his WorldNet node, but couldn't get a stable carrier at the other end. Tried routing through Luna, through Olympus Mons, through the O'Neils.

"Nada," he said, shaking his head and looking up. Maddy was gone.

He looked in the lounge. Empty. In the holotank, a pair of translucent figures gestured in animated conversation, but Jax couldn't make out the words. Galley, labs, sleeproom, all empty. Finally, he walked down to the end of the corridor and pulled himself up into the pod. The fog nestled against the dome in thick, soft swirls. Maddy lay curled up on a foam pad, breathing deeply.

He walked past her to the edge of the dome and peered out through the fog. He could just see them, stretched out in a slowly undulating line next to the ammonia sea. The undulations grew until the line broke apart, the segments forming a series of rings. Slowly, one at a time, the rings merged and the pattern segued to a nest of concentric diamonds, slowly shearing. There was sense and meaning to it, he was sure, but comprehension hovered just out of reach.

What are you?

The soft chime of the comm bell shook Jax out of his reverie. *Three hours? I've been standing here for three hours?* He looked around the dome, his eyes coming to rest on Maddy lying in a fetal curl, her shoulders slowly rising and falling. He stepped over her and lowered himself down the hatch.

There was no visual, but Jax recognized the flat inflections of Maurice's voice synthesizer.

"Sorry about the visual – we're under severe bandwidth restrictions. Power rationing, too, so I'll have to be quick. The fighting's almost over, except for a few hotspots. Earth is pretty much of a mess – Europe, Japan, Indonesia... latest estimates say a billion dead. Naft came through pretty well. Russia, too, but they're going to take a lot of fallout from PacRim. SunGroup is putting together a group at O'Neil Two, sort of a reconstruction team. We can use all the help here we can get, but we also need to keep the long range research efforts going. Your call, but frankly, we could use you. We're sending a ship out to make a sweep of the research stations, anybody who wants to come back. Old ore freighter from the Belt, retrofitted with an ion drive. Best we can do right now. Let me now what you want to do. We don't want to burn up the delta vee to get out to you if we don't have to."

Jax listened to the spectral hiss of interplanetary white noise riding over the carrier hum. He played the message back again. The words began to merge together, their individual meaning softening like heated wax. He played the message back again.

IV

She hovered on the knife-edge between wakefulness and sleep. Images of smoke and flame, of exploding suns, chased each other across the surface of her consciousness. She was on a hover-barge on the Seine, sitting in the back at the controls. Sharp smell of moss and damp stone as she passed under a bridge. Her parents and sisters on the deck in front of her, sitting beneath a blue and white umbrella. Sipping drinks, laughing. Low grey clouds holding the threat of rain.

Suddenly, an impossibly bright light swelling from the east, a second sun breaking through the clouds. The umbrella bursting into flame, her family instantly transformed into stick figure torches. The Seine was *boiling*, bubbling up over the sides of the barge...

She opened her eyes. Jax's face hovered above her in the half dark. He put his hand on her arm.

"Dreams?"

She nodded, still gripped by the vision. "Yeah."

Jax stroked her arm. "I heard from Maurice," he said after a moment. "We're on our own, Maddy. He has no idea when they'll be able to get to us."

It was like a physical blow. Her tropism for home radiated up from the very center of her, from her First Chakra. Its denial sent a surge of panic through her.

She closed her eyes. Breathe, breathe. In, I calm my body. Out, my breathing returns me to my true self. In, breathe calm, white sun swelling in the East. Out, listen, listen, Seine bubbling up over the sides of the barge. In, centuries old stone bridge sagging molten soft. Out, pillars of flame dancing on the deck of the barge snuffed by hammer wind.

"Maddy." Her eyes fluttered open again. "Are you all right?"

She looked closely at him. His long, thin face, so familiar, composed in a mask of concern.

Slowly, she shook her head. "No," she said. "Nothing's all right."

*

Maddy hadn't worn her environment suit in weeks and it chafed under her arms and between her legs. She looked back at the station, so out of place in the alien landscape, clinging in the tattered mist to the dark rock like a cluster of warts. The pod glittered in the dim light. She imagined Jax back there, his sleeping form sprawled naked across the foam pad.

She still ached slightly from their sex. He had been fast and rough, almost brutal. She didn't care, had lain there limply, receiving him. Her orgasm was joyless, passing through her like a wave, leaving no trace of itself.

When she got to the shore of the ammonia sea, she stopped. Small ripples lapped up against the rocky beach. She looked down at the canister she was carrying. Featureless, burnished metal, such an innocuous thing.

Without further thought, she pressed a recessed button on its side. A thin line appeared around the top rim and a puff of vapor escaped, freezing instantly into a cloud of scintillating crystals. She unscrewed the lid and shook its contents out into the sea. Shards of metglass webbing, spidery strands of plastic tubing, chunks of brittle, frozen foam. She couldn't even see the scrap of flesh they cradled. A few meters away, a small herd of slugs clustered near the shore in a senseless and inchoate sprawl.

Quality Time

The first time Brian and Heather made love in their new apartment, Brian traveled backwards in time to the Paleozoic Era. Or maybe it was the Mesozoic. He could never keep those straight, even though he'd been a real dinosaur freak as a kid.

It happened at the moment of orgasm. One minute he was pinned underneath Heather on their futon in the bedroom, her breasts swaying back and forth with the grinding motion of her hips, the ghostly shapes of unpacked boxes looming through the Manhattan dusk like a crowd of silent onlookers.

The next minute, he was lying in a shallow puddle of steaming, stinking mud, a cloud of insects hovering around his head like an animate mist. A fierce sun beat down through a canopy of giant ferns. He took a deep breath and coughed, spitting out three or four hapless bugs. He still had a bit of a woody, but it was quickly detumescing.

He stood on shaky legs. Rivulets of mud dripped down his thighs. A shadow passed across the ground and he looked up. A pterodactyl the size of a winged Buick sailed gracefully overhead, close enough to toss a rock at – had there been one at hand and he so inclined.

Rodan, he thought stupidly. His mental processes seemed slowed to a crawl. Frozen in amber.

In a detached sort of way, he was surprised at his detachment. *Time travel*, after all. What if he stepped on a butterfly and wiped out his pathetically meager investment portfolio? He thought fleetingly that if he could find the timeline in which Michael Jackson existed and stomp its lights out, it would be worth whatever attendant difficulties might ensue.

There was a *basso profundo* roar from somewhere in the jungle to his left, not very far away. It was answered by a deafening, high-pitched screech off to his right. Another *basso* bellow, closer still. The exchange put a stop to Brian's woolgathering, but his legs didn't want to move. He just stood there shivering, like a lawn jockey made of Jell-O.

The sound of something huge crashing through the ferns galvanized him into action. He turned around and took a flying leap into a stand of waist-high grass, landing with a splash in a sticky bog. Something long and sinuous thrashed underneath him and slithered away. Brian rolled over and looked back at what now occupied the clearing.

A mottled gray-green Sherman tank on chicken legs. Ridiculous, tiny hands. A head so huge in proportion to its body that it looked like any sudden move would snap its neck like a stick.

T-rex, Brian thought. *Christ on skis.*

The thing opened its mouth and let out another bellow, enveloping Brian in a charnel stink. With the possible exception of a Pixies concert he'd been to a few years back, it was the loudest sound he'd ever heard.

Inevitable as slapstick, the nearby answering screech split the humid air. It sounded closer. Brian hoped fervently that they would find some other place to sort out their differences.

He was in luck. With surprising grace and speed, the *Tyrannosaurus* hurtled itself toward the sound, crashing through the dense jungle. The low bellow of the thunder lizard and the high screech of its unseen antagonist merged into a wall of noise. It sounded like they were turning the jungle into coleslaw. The sound of their struggle receded into the distance.

Brian forced himself to breathe. He sat up and looked around. Jungle so deep a green that it seemed to vibrate. Cartoon blue sky. Air so warm, thick, and moist it made the dead heat of a central Florida summer seem positively arid by comparison. Bugs enough to rival August in Minnesota.

What the fuck am I doing here? And more to the point, how do I get back?

He played it back in his mind again. One minute, scaling the heights of Heather; the next, cowering in a puddle of filth while giant lizards fought to the death a stone's throw away.

"Very interesting," he said aloud, in a fake Viennese accent. His voice sounded strange in the heavy, Mesozoic air. Or maybe it was the Paleozoic.

But really, the whole thing was no more difficult to swallow than getting an apartment in Peter Cooper Village. They'd been told that the waiting list was eleven years long.

"Christ in a Cadillac," he'd said to Heather. "The only institutions with memories that long are the phone company and Sallie Mae."

He'd even tried to slip the clerk in the rental office a hundred dollars to lubricate the process a bit. He folded the bill in half, tucked it between the second and third fingers of his right hand, and reached across her desk as if pointing out something on their application.

She looked at him as if he'd tried to hand her a fresh, steaming turd.

"You're going to have to do a lot better than that," she said.

He shrugged and returned the bill to his pocket, figuring he'd just cratered whatever chances they might have had. Three weeks later, they got a call about a sixth floor two-bedroom with a view of the East River. It was obviously a clerical error, but they weren't about to question their good fortune.

The mud caking his arms, legs, and torso was beginning to dry, revealing hundreds of tiny, crawling bugs. He stood, brushing them off as best he could. Their previous apartment had been in the East Village and he'd developed a fairly clinical attitude about insect life.

Some kind of space-time continuum thing, Brian thought. *It's so unlikely to score one of those apartments that it's ripped a hole in the fabric of probability-space.*

At the suggestion of a friend of Heather's who channeled the spirits of deceased pets for wealthy clients on the Upper East Side, Brian had been reading Gary Zukov lately and his brain was overflowing with pseudoscience babble, like an abandoned couch leaking stuffing.

But where does the sex come in?

He realized that that wasn't the first time he'd wondered that with respect to Heather. He pushed the thought aside.

Orgasm! Whatever process Brian was subject to, it required an intense focus of psychic energy. It just popped him from one niche in

111

space-time to another, like an orange seed squeezed between thumb and forefinger.

Pfft, he thought. *Goodbye, Heather*. Pfft. *Goodbye, New York*. Pfft. *Goodbye, Imageco*.

Brian had a great job at Imageco, a video post production shop. He worked in billing but everything was pretty much automated, so there wasn't a whole lot to do. Two or three times a day, he'd knock off a threatening letter to one of their clients; the rest of the time he sat around with Steve, the resident hacker, watching Hong Kong chop-socky flicks and drinking Diet Jolt.

His eyes filled with tears.

Pfft.

But wait a minute. If it was the intense psychic energy of orgasm that squeezed him through the damaged region in space-time, maybe that was his ticket back as well.

He could *wank* his way home.

He looked down at his limp member, shrunken to the size of a walnut. He couldn't imagine being farther from thoughts of erotic bliss than at this very moment.

He looked guiltily around, then realized he had about two hundred million years before there was any chance of interruption.

Brian went to work.

He tried to conjure up an image of Heather, but her features blurred, taking on a definite reptilian cast.

His resolve receded.

He tried to invoke his old standby, a gin-soaked weekend with Janelle and Giselle, a pair of bisexual video effects editors from Northampton who'd come down to Imageco on consult to subtitle *Hiroshima, Mon Amour* in Black English. This time, however, his mental picture of their gymnastic grappling was painfully suggestive of prehistoric beasts locked in mortal combat.

"The hell with it," he said aloud. There was a nearby, answering *peep*.

Brian looked up. Not five feet away, perched on tiny, stick-like legs, was a dinosaur the size of a kangaroo. It had a long, narrow beak and a handsome crest arching over its head like a cartilaginous Mohawk. It tilted its head to the side and let out another *peep*.

"Shoo," Brian yelled, waving his free hand. "Go on, get out of here!"

The thing disappeared into the jungle with alarming speed. Brian looked down at his withered willie. Back to Square One.

From somewhere not far away, the bellow of the *T-rex* shook the jungle. Brian felt the ground vibrate under his bare behind.

There's nothing like abject fear to stiffen a man's resolve. With business-like efficiency, he went back to work. Another roar, considerably closer, hastened the exercise. His hand was covered with tiny particles of grit from the mud and it felt like he was jerking off with a handful of aquarium gravel.

Through half-closed eyes, Brian saw a gray-green shape pushing aside the ferns. He closed his eyes completely and stroked faster. His nostrils filled with the stink of rotting blood. Another roar split the sky. He –

– arched his back, reaching behind Heather's firm, plump buttocks to pull her close.

Heather made the sound she usually made when she was just about to come but slipped back from the brink, a cross between a sigh and a moan that rose up from somewhere deep in her chest. She ground against him half-heartedly another couple of times, then rested her head on his chest.

He was filled with the smell of her, buoyed by the faint undercurrent of new apartment effluvia – roach spray, carpet cleaner, mildew.

She looked up into his eyes, the point of her chin digging into his collarbone.

"You seem really distant," she said.

"Wha – ?"

"It seemed like you just…went away."

Brian blinked. The last thing he remembered was looking up into the open mouth of the *Tyrannosaur*. Scraps of rotting meat clung to its teeth. He could see its tonsils.

"I, um – " he stammered.

"I really wish you could just stay ... *present* when we're making love." Her full lips turned downwards in a pout.

Well, you see, hon', space-time is like this rubber sheet stretched across a frame, kind of, and there's some parts that get stretched

thinner than others and I just sort of slipped through this part that got
real thin when we scored this crib and –

He didn't think so.

"I'm sorry, baby," he said, finally.

She nuzzled his neck and wriggled against him, taking his earlobe
between her teeth and biting down gently.

"You want to try again?" she asked.

Brian forced himself to smile. "Sure."

Brian was having lunch with Steve at Niko's Nook, a Greek coffee shop
on 45th and Lex. He poured cream into his coffee and watched it slosh
thickly, like crankcase oil after about thirty-thousand miles. A roach
skittered across the counter and he absently squashed it with his thumb.
He gathered the gooey remains in his napkin and returned it to his lap.

"You seem awfully quiet today," Steve said.

Brian looked up. His distorted reflection stared back at him from
Steve's wraparound, mirrored sunglasses.

"You're going to think I'm crazy," Brian said, watching his own
lips move as he spoke. He felt like he was talking to himself in the
bathroom mirror.

"I already think you're crazy – you just ordered the souvlaki.
What's going on?"

Brian looked around, making sure there was nobody within earshot.

"Heather and I were, uh, inaugurating the new bedroom
yesterday..." He paused. He didn't know how to say it without sounding
like a lunatic.

"I'm sure congratulations are in order," Steve said, after a polite
interval. "Was there something else?"

Brian decided to try a different approach. "Do you have any idea
how difficult it is to get an apartment in Peter Cooper Village?" he
asked.

"Does the Pope wear a big, stupid hat?" Steve replied. "It's all I've
heard you talk about for the last month."

"Well, don't you think it's a little ... *strange* that we got one after
three weeks?"

"Sure I think it's strange. I also think it's strange that Dolly Parton
can walk upright. These things happen. What's your point?"

"When we were making love, right at the critical moment, I traveled backwards in time." He looked defiantly at Steve. His reflection stared back with an expression of neurasthenic angst.

Steve shook his head. "Is that all? Shit, Bri', I've been married twenty-two years. If I didn't do a little time traveling every now and then, I'd be ready for a rubber room."

"No, you don't get it. I mean I really *went* somewhere. The Jurassic or something. Christ on rollerskates, I almost got my head bitten off by a *Tyrannosaurus*!"

Steve took his sunglasses off and looked at Brian for a long time. "Did you used to do a lot of acid back in the seventies?" he asked, finally.

"Well, sure, but – "

"Those little orange barrels?"

"Yeah, but – "

"I thought so." He peered at his sunglasses, fogged them with his breath, wiped them on his Young Gods t-shirt, and put them back on. He pulled a pen out of his pocket, scrawled something on a napkin, and pushed it across the table to Brian.

"I've got this doctor friend," he said. "You tell him you're a friend of mine and ask him to write you a scrip for some Xanax. You'll be fine." Then, as an afterthought, he added, "Just don't drink with it."

"Thanks," Brian heard himself say. He stared numbly into the cool mirrored surface of Steve's glasses as his reflection folded the napkin into a neat square and slid it into his shirt pocket.

"Use 'I feel' statements, Heather," Doctor Fishlove said.

The late afternoon sun coming in through the Venetian blinds threw a pattern of stripes across the stuffed toy bears that lined one wall of the therapist's office. They looked like they were wearing prison uniforms.

Heather threw her head back. "Okay." She looked at Brian. "I *feel* like you've been really withdrawn lately. I *feel* like you haven't been present in our relationship. I *feel* like you aren't interested in me sexually anymore."

"And how does that make *you* feel, Brian?" Doctor Fishlove asked. He was an ordinary, Midwestern looking man somewhere on the downhill side of forty, with one disfiguring feature – a small wart perched precisely on the end of his nose. Brian couldn't take his eyes off it.

"Well, I don't know." He paused. "Bad, I guess."

"Bad," Doctor Fishlove repeated. "*Good.* Is there anything you want to say to Heather?"

Actually, there wasn't. He'd been avoiding sex for the last two weeks, scared that it would send him back into the Mesozoic or whatever. He really wanted to talk to her about it, but there never seemed to be a good time to bring it up.

He wasn't about to start popping off in therapy about dinosaurs and time travel, though. It would really screw things up. Besides, he'd scarfed a couple of Xanax earlier that morning and it didn't seem all that important.

"Uh, yeah, I guess." He tore his eyes away from the wart and looked at Heather. "I acknowledge your feelings. I'll try to do better."

Doctor Fishlove beamed. Heather didn't look convinced. Brian promised himself that he'd talk to her that night. Or poke her. One or the other, anyway.

The remains of an orange were spread across the plate, the colors brightly surreal in the harsh, kitchen light. It was one of those new hybrids and Brian had had a hell of a time finding a seed for his demonstration. Heather had watched the operation in silence.

Brian held the seed up between thumb and forefinger.

"So we're in this niche in space-time," he said. "Poking away, happy as clams. But the fabric of everything has become really weak because we've scored this apartment."

He looked up at Heather. No help there. Brian pushed forward. "All of a sudden, *pfft.*" He squeezed down on the seed and it flew out of his fingers, sailing past Heather's shoulder and skidding to a halt on the shiny linoleum floor. "I'm somewhere else. Some *when* else."

Heather looked at him without expression for what seemed like a long time.

"Are you going to pick that up?" she asked, finally.

"Uh, sure." Brian got up and retrieved the orange seed. He flicked it into the trash and sat back down.

"So, what do you think?" he asked.

She kept looking at him.
"Well, say something," he said.
"I'm leaving you," she said.

Brian sat in the spare bedroom looking out across the East River. The sun coming up over Brooklyn threw sheets of rippling gold foil across the water. A flock of tugboats pulled a crippled tanker downriver.

Heather had been packing, but the sounds had stopped some time ago and the silence now seemed to flow out of the back bedroom like smoke.

He heard a noise and turned around. Heather stood in the doorway, her eyes red and swollen.

"I'm going now," she said. "I'll send my brother by for the rest of my things. Please don't try to find me."

He listened to her footsteps pad down the hall. The front door closed with a final sound. It occurred to him that at that very moment, Heather was time traveling. Into his past.

Brooklyn shimmered through a film of tears. Brian blinked to clear his vision and felt a warm drop trail down his cheek. The cars on the F.D.R. Drive reflected the sunlight in miniature, prismatic stars, swiftly moving.

The Dam

In one beaker, prepare a solution of seventy-six percent sulfuric acid, twenty-three percent nitric acid and one percent water. In another beaker, prepare a solution of fifty-seven percent nitric acid and forty-three percent sulfuric acid. Percentages are given by weight, not volume.

I was standing on the causeway that runs across the top of the dam, looking out over the reservoir. It had been raining for days and the water was the color of milky tea.

"It's good," a voice behind me said.

I whirled around, nearly jumping out of my skin. It was Oscar.

"Jesus, Oscar, you scared the daylights out of me."

"It's good when it's like this," he said, his eyes grey and empty as the sky. A small rivulet of drool escaped from the corner of his mouth.

"What's good?" I asked.

"The Dragon cannot live in water that is too pure," he said.

He was looking through me, out across the water. Beneath his hat, dripping wet from the rain, I knew that there was a depressed concavity in his skull, as if someone had taken a tennis ball and pushed it deep into soft putty. I'd seen it. The hair there grew thick and curly.

Beneath the muddy brown water, the towns slept.

Ten grams of the first solution are poured into an empty beaker and placed in an ice bath.

119

Binding Energy

*

My house is at the end of the causeway, just off the road. It was originally the caretaker's house and it sends roots down into the guts of the dam, basement, sub-basement, sub-sub-basement, the water heavier in the air the deeper you descend until it beads on the walls in thick, fat drops. I have never been to the bottom.

Levers and wheels protrude from the walls next to the rickety metal stairway that threads the levels. It is always cold down there, and always, somewhere, there is the slow, steady sound of water dripping into water.

Sometimes I go down three levels, four levels, and turn one of the wheels at random. Pause. Cock my head to listen. It is there, just at the threshold of perception, the sound of great forces being set into motion.

Add ten grams of toluene and stir for several minutes.

Last night there was an incredible aurora display, gaudy neon curtains rippling across the sky in a cosmic breeze. It went on for hours. Last time it was this good was a couple of years ago. A scientist from back east stopped the night at the Broken Nail and a cluster of people gathered around him in the tavern, pumping him for news. But all he wanted to talk about was the aurora.

"Ionization in the upper atmosphere," he said.

Later that night, Billy, who used to run the gas station, killed him for his radio. For months afterward, he wore the man's teeth on a necklace whenever he showed up in town, but somebody must have talked to him, because he stopped.

I asked him about it once. It was Saturday and the Farmer's Market was in town. Billy was holding a head of cabbage in one hand, lifting it to the light like it was a skull and he Hamlet.

"Where's your necklace, Billy?" I asked.

He looked at me.

"Ionization in the upper atmosphere," he said, and wandered off, laughing.

Remove the beaker from the ice bath and gently heat until it reaches fifty degrees Centigrade. Stir constantly.

120

*

Four towns were erased when the reservoir was created as a CCC project back in the thirties. Prescott, Alice, Machinery, Thor. If I had any more children, I would name them thus.

Several people refused to move when the time came. An old woman living in the house her great-grandfather had built as a newly-freed slave fleeing Reconstruction. A young man whose wife had died in childbirth the previous year, his daughter stillborn. An idiot. The town drunk of Machinery. I wonder if the waters rose slowly, ushering them gently into the next world, or if they looked up suddenly to see a wall of blue steel and white foam rushing down upon them, higher than the trees, bearing the weight of Judgment.

I suspect the former. On nights when the sky is clear and the full moon hangs suspended in the sky like a cold, blue lamp, the juncture between air and water fades to nothing and the water itself becomes transparent. My boat glides along the silent surface and I look down upon the valley as if the water were a kind of amber, freezing time to stillness. Roads, hills, stores, houses. It is a time machine, this reservoir.

Fifty additional grams are added from the first beaker and the mixture heated to fifty-five degrees Centigrade. This temperature is held for the next ten minutes. An oily liquid will begin to form on top of the acid.

I sit in my house at the edge of the causeway and monitor the level of the water. For this service, the people of the town bring me food, woven items, firewood. From time to time, Oscar wanders up from his tarpaper shack behind the old train station and stands in the middle of the causeway, looking out across the water. Always across the water, never the other side. Never the town.

Last week, I saw him there from the window of my house, standing in his usual spot. I brought him a strip of jerky and an apple and stood next to him facing the opposite direction, down the curve of the dam and along the valley floor to the curls of smoke from town braiding into the grey sky.

After ten or twelve minutes, the acid solution is returned to the ice bath and cooled to forty-five degrees Centigrade. The oily liquid will sink to the bottom of the beaker. The remaining acid solution should be drawn off using a syringe.

The residents of the sunken valley populate my dreams.

A pair of schoolteachers, sisters, lovers, spinsters to the town of Prescott, holding each other and everything unspoken as the waters rose.

A man just outside Alice who murdered his wife for the insurance money. He made it look like an accident. It was so convincing, in fact, that years later he himself believed it.

A resident of Thor who made an occasional practice of driving to neighboring towns under the still of night and killing dogs with a crossbow. He rendered the flesh from their bones and carefully reconstructed their skeletons, like model airplanes, in his attic.

The proprietor of the Mill End Store in Machinery who nursed elaborate masturbatory fantasies about raping and murdering young boys. As the years passed, the fantasies grew more and more baroque. He was active in the church community and ran the Christian Youth Fellowship's Helping Hand for Troubled Teens camp every summer.

I can feel them looking up at me as my boat glides slowly through the air.

Fifty more grams of the first acid solution are added to the oily liquid while the temperature is slowly being raised to eighty-three degrees Centigrade. After this temperature is reached, it is maintained for a full half hour.

Elly Foss gave birth to a two-headed baby last week. It cleaved together at the breastbone, both heads crying in unison when it came out. A single pair of arms waved feebly in the air. Her husband, Jack, took it by the legs and slammed it against the wall. He says it's no baby of his. Elly isn't saying much of anything. There's a lot of talk going around, as they have two normal children, both obviously Jack's since they exhibit the same pattern of delicate webbing between their toes that Jack has.

Veins lace through the translucent skin like the architecture of a drunken spider.

*

At the end of this period, the solution is allowed to cool to sixty degrees Centigrade and is held at this temperature for another full half hour. The acid is again drawn off, leaving once more the oily liquid at the bottom.

In the reservoir lives a catfish the size of a man. Massive arms sprout from its body just beneath the gills and it uses them to move aside the debris that has been collected by the slow, Atlantean drift, to open the doors and enter the houses of Machinery and Prescott, of Alice and Thor. I close my eyes and I can see it floating next to a Colonial armoire in someone's master bedroom, reaching out a hand to touch the detailed filigree gone soft and pulpy in the cold depths, steadying itself in a sudden surge of current.

Last year, some fool from one of the hill towns came down and tried to catch it. He built a raft out of a garage door and four empty oil drums, bolted a stout, fiberglass pole onto the raft, and pushed himself off into the calm water.

He used kittens for bait. Through binoculars, I saw him impale their tiny bodies on curved hooks and drop them wriggling into the water. I imagined that I could hear their sharp cries.

Every now and then, he'd get a hit, the pole bending like a bow, pulling that end of the raft halfway into the water. Then it would stop and the raft would spring back and bob up and down like a cork.

A small crowd gathered on the causeway to watch his progress. He was doomed, already dead, and he didn't even know it.

But we did.

After a long stretch of quiet, the rocking of the raft from the last hit damped to an almost imperceptible bob and silence hanging over the lake like heat haze, our fish burst out of the water right in front of him. It was the most beautiful thing I've ever seen, leaping into the air in a silver blur, the sun catching rainbow highlights off scales rippling like mercury. Before we had time to blink, it grabbed the man in its huge hands and pulled him into the water. The raft skidded off to the side, bobbing, bobbing. Eventually, it drifted to shore on the north side of the dam and got caught up in the branches of a fallen tree, half-submerged.

It's still there.

*

Thirty grams of sulfuric acid are added while the oily liquid is heated to eighty degrees Centigrade. All temperature increases must be accomplished slowly and gently.

Oscar was on the causeway before dawn, looking out across the water. I brought him a heel of dark bread and some cheese. He took the items from me without a word and pushed them into his mouth.

"It's mine," he said, chewing vigorously on the wad of food. Crumbs clung to his lips.

"Excuse me?"

He closed his eyes and swallowed, then motioned to the canteen hanging from my shoulder. I gave it to him and he unscrewed the top and held it to his lips. His Adam's apple bobbed up and down as he swallowed. When he was done, he wiped his lips on his sleeve.

"The baby is mine," he said, handing me back the canteen.

I looked closely at him. Wind whistled up from the town side of the causeway, pushing between us, as if reminding me of what I had to do. I returned to the house. When I looked out at the causeway again, he was gone.

Once the desired temperature is reached, thirty grams of the second acid solution are added. The temperature is raised from eighty degrees Centigrade to one hundred four degrees Centigrade and is held there for three hours.

I dreamed that I was in a house on the outskirts of Machinery, sitting weightless in the living room. Tiny ceramic animals clustered together on the mantle. A grandfather clock wedged into a corner of the room emitted a muffled ticking.

I floated over to the window and looked out. There, just above the level of the treetops, a small boat gliding slowly past, a lone figure rowing.

Lower the temperature of the mixture to one hundred degrees Centigrade and hold it there for thirty minutes.

*

When I awoke the next morning, there was a basket of bread and jerky on my doorstep. Underneath the lean-to next to the shed in back, a half-cord of wood that hadn't been there the night before.

They flayed him alive and nailed him to a telephone pole in front of the burned-out shell of the First Presbyterian Church, just off the town commons.

I brought him some water. I set up a stepladder next to the pole and climbed with a pail and a ladle up to where he hung. He'd been there all day and most of the night before and he smelled pretty bad, blood and waste and something I couldn't identify, maybe his sorry old soul hovering nearby, waiting for an excuse to leave. An aura of flies surrounded him. His skin hung in strips; the muscles in his arms and legs were marbled with veins of yellow fat. An old scar sprawled across his shoulder, shiny runnels and bubbles like a sheet of melted plastic.

"Oscar," I said. "Oscar. How about a drink?"

His eyes flickered open. Imprecation, accusation, a burning grace.

The oil is removed from the acid and washed with boiling water. Stir constantly. The TNT will begin to precipitate out. Add cold water. Pellets will form.

The Dragon cannot live in water that is too pure. I charged up a pair of car batteries from the generator beneath my house and wired them to a simple spring-release mechanism. Took the device to the foot of the dam. Looked up at the broad sweep of concrete filling the sky, colors bright like a postcard from someplace where there is an ocean. Set the timer and clambered up the side of the valley through the dense undergrowth, branches scratching at my face like flailing arms.

Just as I reached the top, I heard a sound like a door slamming shut on an empty room. I turned around. A billowing, grey mushroom hurtled into the sky and a network of cracks spread across the face of the dam. Water broke out in discrete gushing sprays, the cracks widening, then all at once it gave, collapsing in a churning froth of water, concrete, earth.

The causeway was gone; my house hung on the blunt edge of nothing. A wall of water pushed through the valley, covering everything. Behind the advancing front, the roiling foam was a deep, rich brown.

To my right, the waters receded. First, the tall steeples of churches were revealed, then the houses, finally the streets and roads. Prescott and Machinery, Alice and Thor. They glistened, pure in the sunlight.

Note: The temperatures used in the preparation of TNT are exact. Do not rely on estimates or approximations. A good thermometer is essential.

Author's note: I am grateful to William Powell's *The Anarchist Cookbook* for the TNT recipe.

Binding Energy

Batter my heart, three-personed God, for you
As yet but knock, breathe, shine, and seek to mend.
That I may rise and stand, o'erthrow me and bend
Your force to break, blow, burn, and make me new.

– John Donne –

– There! Stop there!

EMIL'S BBQ. A smiling pig in a clean white apron leans against the Q, brandishing a wicked looking knife. Emil first came here amused at the confluence of names, but he returns for the dark smoky sauce laced with cayenne.

The driver looks at him in the rear view mirror, nods, and pulls into the parking lot. Bits of silica wink like stars in the soft asphalt.

– What can I get for you, sir?

Flat military monotone. Cold eyes, brown like river silt. This driver is new and Emil doesn't like him much. The man is a herring – Emil has tried to engage him in conversation several times, but there has been no response other than the monosyllabic. The Negro makes a good soldier but this one is a lousy chauffeur.

– Stay, stay. I'll go.

He reaches for the door handle, but the driver is too quick. Heat slaps Emil in the face, rising in waves from the asphalt. It is like peering into an oven. Almost immediately, a thin film of perspiration covers his forehead and hands. He slides the cane from his lap and plants it on the pavement. Cut from rough oak, this cane, knotted and polished smooth. His *staff.* His oaken staff. The ground yields slightly under its tip as he heaves himself to his feet. Shakes off the soldier's hand on his elbow.

– Stay, sit.

Familiar stab of pain from his right hip, not exactly an old friend but always there to remind him that he is no longer young, nor even middle-aged.

A handful of tables sprout like linoleum mushrooms under the harsh fluorescents. A man in greasy coveralls and a long, thick pony tail sits next to the window, tearing strips of flesh from the carcass of a chicken, washing it down with deep pulls from a brown long-necked bottle.

The jukebox is playing a plaintive country song about lost love, redolent with pedal-steel and nasal male harmonies. The vinegary barbecue smell makes Emil's stomach rumble; beneath that, a shadow of pain. To hell with the ulcer, he thinks.

– Can I help you, sir?

He looks at the woman behind the counter for the first time. A sudden, hollow silence descends. The smell of burnt wiring fills his nostrils. His mouth opens but he cannot speak.

It is *her.* The traitor. Black eyes bruised with loss, set far apart in a moon-shaped face. Rough olive skin. Coarse, dark curls. Thick lips perpetually poised on the brink of a sneer.

– Sir?

Emil backs up until he bumps into the door. He shoulders it open and spills back into the heat. His limo waits, blinding white, parked astride two spaces.

– Are you all right?

– Yes, yes. Take me to the Lab.

Ensconced in the cool dark of the limo, Emil still feels those eyes on him. The years recede like snow under a lit match and he sees her in the Senate chambers – 1953? 1954? Six months before the executions. She has no shame.

– No, I am not a Communist. No, of course not. Never. Besides, what do I know of nuclear physics?

Ridiculous, Emil thinks. I am an old fool. He raps on the plexiglass divider.

– Sergeant, back to the barbecue place.

He'll think I'm going senile. Like poor Ronny.

The driver makes a U-turn, threads back through the wide suburban streets.

The man with the pony tail stares rudely, hunched over bones and scraps. The woman behind the counter affixes a nervous smile to her face.

– Can I help you?

– I'm sorry – you look so much like – tell me, please, what is your name?

She hesitates, looks him over, seems to decide that he is odd but not dangerous.

– Jane. Jane Lucent.

– Not Rabinowicz?

That nervous smile again.

– No. Not Rabinowicz.

Emil sighs. She looks remarkably like her. But it's impossible. The traitor had one daughter who committed suicide in an insane asylum before producing any offspring of her own. That branch of the family tree is kindling.

– No, of course not.

Suddenly, his appetite returns. He looks at the menu posted behind the counter, adorned with garish color photographs, platters of food glistening with grease.

– I'll have the ribs.

Two seasons in California, green and brown. Thirty years here and Emil still longs for the red and gold death of autumn, the sharp smell of snow on the air, the distant snap of pond ice breaking under spring's first thaw.

From eight stories up the land acquires definition; tawny prairie ripples with gentle contours like muscles beneath the skin of a great cat. Hundreds of windmills break the ridge line at the edge of the valley. Legacy of the peanut farmer's tax credit. Who not once answered Emil's calls, even during that Syria business.

This one is better. At least he sends smiling young men in crisp suits to listen to Emil's ideas. But Emil is still the leprous magician laboring in the castle dungeon, conjuring potions and spells that harness the elemental forces, his ugly visage kept from public view. He has delivered them from a thousand Hells and they treat him like the carrier of a social disease.

Ronny was the best. Not much of a thinker, but the heart of a lion. Emil loved the visits to the White House, not skulking in through the tunnel but delivered by helicopter to the front lawn. The dreams Emil could spin to a receptive ear!

Glossy photographs of test shots adorn the oiled mahogany walls of his office. Mike, Priscilla, Romeo. Shrimp, Token, Bravo. Emil was the youngest and he knows that a father's favorite child is always his first. Mike. A 10.4 megaton Rube Goldberg nightmare of pipes, and gauges, valves and switches, filling a building the size of an airplane hangar. It was a miracle it worked at all, but it vaporized the island of Elugelab and punched a hole in the ocean floor. Emil remembers the light of Creation flashing against the high Pacific clouds, minutes later the attenuated shock reaching the observation ships fifty miles out as a stiff, sudden wind. The breath of God.

It was a moment of pure, Wagnerian joy, all his own.

The phone rings, two short bursts. His secretary. He pushes the speaker button.

– Yes?

– Fifteen minutes, sir.

– Ah, yes. Thank you.

It has been a couple of years since he has addressed the Laboratory. Emil feels out of touch with the daily workings of the place. His Emeritus status gives him no official power, but he still has allies in the ranks of physicists, particularly X-Division. He can walk over to Building 88 at any time, argue theory with the young, Coke-swilling firebrands, politics with Wade, his star disciple.

But every now and then he likes to speak to the rank and file. The *illiterati*. The Laboratory's publicity machinery ensures that the main auditorium in Building 70 will be full; by electronic proxy, his image reaches all corners of the mile-square complex.

Emil could give up this indulgence. Tollbridge is doing a fine job as Director – the ritual Beltway *gavotte*, keeping the Regents happy and uninformed. His insipid Management Chat, twice a month on LabNet.

But the guilty pleasure of a captive audience is a powerful drug. And besides, Emil sacrificed everything for this place. The respect of his colleagues, his standing in the scientific community. They loved Oppy so. His big sad eyes. Emil showed them the way but still they shunned him, saw only his failures. Heat rushes to Emil's cheeks as he recalls the humiliation of the first failed test, a miserable fission firecracker. The flaccid mushroom tickling the tropopause. Ten kilotons, barely a Hiroshima.

The phone rings again. Annoyed at the interruption of his reverie, Emil punches the speaker button.

– What is it?

– Dr. Wade is here, sir.

– Ah, good. Send him in.

Emil's spacious office seems smaller when Wade enters. Six-four, with the ruddy-cheeked enthusiasm of a college athlete, Wade belies the public stereotype of physicist. He is no skinny, bespectacled caricature scuttling beneath a bank of fluorescents from lab bench to computer terminal, clipboard clutched to white-coated breast. With Wade's square jaw and rough good looks, he could pose for L.L. Bean. But he was Emil's finest student. An extraordinary experimentalist and a first-rate theoretician, he wields the ideas and techniques of physics like a carpenter building a house. No, not a carpenter, a blacksmith – the forge and the anvil are metaphors more suited to the manipulation and control of the elemental forces. For the last decade, he has been, methodically, surreptitiously, stripping Emil of authority in the Lab hierarchy. Or trying to. Emil plays along. He admires Wade's feral cunning. His own position in the history books is secure. Besides, the old magician still has a few tricks up his sleeve.

– Emil. You are looking fit.

– You are a liar, John.

Wade eases his big frame into the leather chair in front of Emil's desk, set slightly lower than Emil's own. As usual, he wastes no time.

– What are you going to talk about?

Emil was expecting this. Make sure the old man isn't going to violate national security in his enthusiasm for a good yarn.

– The usual. State of the Lab. Current funding cycle. I thought I'd drop a hint or two about Diamond Prism.

Emil watches with amusement as Wade's jaw clenches.

– I, um, don't think that would be a very good idea. Weintraub from the *Herald* is going to be there – he already thinks you're the anti-Christ. Diamond Prism is entirely black budget right now...

Emil holds his hand up, palm forward, as if directing traffic.

– Relax, John. I just wanted to see whether you actually think I'm incontinent.

A frown creases Wade's smooth forehead.

– Incompetent.

– I beg your pardon?

Wade opens his mouth, closes it.

– Never mind.

The two men are silent. The room fills with ambient sounds – a white noise air-conditioner hum, the distant ringing of a phone, the electronic squeal of a fax machine in the outer office.

– I'll be out of your hair soon enough, John. I am an old man.

He leans toward Wade, lowers his voice.

– I am sure you don't know this, but Tollbridge is being groomed for Secretary.

The gratuitous improvisation rolls off Emil's tongue like a dollop of oil. Wade's eyebrows raise.

– Ah, yes, I knew that would get your attention. I still have sources inside the Beltway. We could bring Collins up to take over X-Division and put you in as Director.

Wade rubs his chin thoughtfully.

– Collins isn't ready. The Oberon shoot had lousy energy density...

– Engineering, John. It's just engineering. What you're really saying is you're not ready, yes? To give up your little fiefdom.

Wade laughs, a short, barking sound.

– I'm ready.

The auditorium in Building 70 is full, a restless sea of silvery-haired heads. Emil scans the crowd for younger faces and sees a few, but not many. The old man is a circus act and they have no time. He limps down the center aisle – *step, thump, step, thump* – his staff making a hollow sound on the deep pile carpet. They have wheeled out an old upright piano for him and without preamble, he mounts the stairs at the side of the stage and seats himself with his back to the audience.

Where did they dig this thing up? The wood is pitted and scarred; there is a neat, black chevron of cigarette burns to the left of the music holder. Cigarette burns! He hopes the piano is tuned, at least.

Suddenly his hands feel huge and clumsy; his arthritic knuckles are golf-ball sized knots of pain. His breathing quickens and a flicker of agony lashes up from his sciatic nerve. He was going to play a little Bach, a little Mozart, but that mathematical precision seems out of reach. Stupid indulgence! It's all out of reach.

Without thinking, he launches into the Promenade from *Pictures at an Exhibition*. He hates the acoustics in this room – the ceiling baffles turn all sound into a homogeneous, milky paste. The power of the stately opening is muffled and compressed. Remembering suddenly the demands of the next movement, *The Gnome*, Emil feels something tighten across his forehead and a spastic tremble flows down his arms and out his fingertips. The missed note hangs in the air like a fart.

– Shit.

The word echoes in his ears and he realizes that his lapel mike is on.

Cheeks burning, he stumbles through another couple of movements. Each time he returns to the refrain it is a little more uncertain, a little more out of tempo. Finally he just stops. Breathes. His shoulders sag as if something has left his body.

A tenuous vapor of whispers rises from the crowd. Somebody applauds. Then someone else. A weak, uncertain ripple surges and dies.

Emil takes a deep breath, leans on his staff. Stands and turns around.

– Poor Mussourgsky.

A few nervous laughs.

– A simple demonstration of *quid pro quo*. I just did to Russia what they did to us for forty-five years.

More laughter. Another scattering of applause and it catches this time, fills the hall, fills Emil.

He's got them.

– Imagine, if you will, the following scenario. Yeltsin has a fatal heart attack. In the ensuing chaos, the hard-liners prevail. There is a coup, perhaps bloodless, perhaps not, and the Russian government is in their hands. Our intelligence tells us that Lebed – or somebody – will be addressing a huge crowd in Red Square. With only few minutes notice, one of our deep patrol submarines in the Pacific launches a missile. It pops up into a low ballistic trajectory and, at the peak of the parabola, a low-yield thermonuclear device is detonated in close proximity to a long, thin rod of metallic foam. Computers have aligned the rod to within a micron's tolerance so that its aim is as true as the resolve in our own hearts. Microseconds before the rod is vaporized, a highly energized beam lances out of the blue, Russian sky. Lebed, and the hopes of the hard-liners, are now a rapidly expanding plasma.

Emil scans the crowd. He recognizes Weintraub, scribbling furiously on a small notepad. And there, Habermas, a protégé of Wade's, with a pained look on his young face.

– Terrorism, insurgency, and financial instability are the threats that will shadow us as we move into the twenty-first century. In order to maintain our position as leaders of the Free World, we must pursue an aggressive policy of surgical countermeasures. *Surgical countermeasures.*

The repeated phrase fills the hall, pregnant with possibility. He relishes for a moment that unfolding, then continues. He does not mention Diamond Prism directly, but he lays it out, all of it. Wade will be furious, probably try to pull Emil's clearance. But it's the right thing to do. The right time. Back in Ronny's administration they used to come from Washington like dogs to a bitch in heat. The Congressmen and their dull, eager staffers. The spooks. The generals. Everybody but the scientists. From a distant nexus within, he sees himself, a gnarled, stooped gnome standing before a lectern, spinning candied lies to an audience of idiot children. And looking out in to the crowd, he sees her.

Dark hair falling like wings across her face, not quite hiding her bruised eyes. It is her. The close air in the auditorium is suddenly charged with an ozone stink. The hot smell of metal on metal. Solder and sulfur. Burning rubber.

He reaches out a hand. His staff clatters to the floor of the stage.
– *You.*

A susurrus rises from the crowd, like the cicada-hiss of summer. Emil staggers back, grabs the lectern for support, lurches into the wings. Sees the red EXIT sign. Pushes into the dry, sweltering heat.

– Take me home.

Curt military nod in the rear view mirror. Emil sits back in the soft leather, breathes, watches the temporary buildings at the outskirts of the

Lab segue to grape fields and tract housing locked in a Darwinian tangle for dominance of the sun-baked prairie.

The air conditioning is on high but he can't stop sweating. His shirt is drenched, plastered to his skin. Sharp, transient pains from his chest call to him like voices from the bottom of a deep well. He wonders if he is going to have a heart attack, a stroke, a breakdown.

He opens the small refrigerator in front of him and pulls out a bottle of spring water, changes his mind and from the freezer withdraws a slim flask of vodka. It goes down like liquid metal. Emil sees the driver looking at him in the rear-view as he tilts the flask back with shaking hands. The military lack of affect is a perfect vehicle for the contempt Emil knows is there. Emil presses a button in the armrest and an upholstered panel rises from the seat back, separating him from the driver's compartment

The phone trills at him from the armrest. Wade, no doubt, or Tollbridge. Let it ring. Emil leans back and closes his eyes.

Immediately her face begins to coalesce on the dark screen of his closed eyelids, taking shape from nothing until she is hovering before him, clear as a photograph. Her head is shaved and she is wearing a starchy, green prison shift. The cell behind her is a Caligari nightmare of distorted angles and false perspective.

– Why are you here? What do you want?

She does not respond.

Two guards appear, dressed in head to foot black with loose black hoods. They escort her through twisting stone tunnels lit by naked bulbs. Disembodied, powerless, Emil follows, like a balloon bobbing on the end of a string.

They come to a high-ceilinged room dominated by a large wooden chair. Metal cuffs decorate the arms and legs. Black-sheathed cables sprout from the chair and converge to a thick bundle that leads to a panel in the far wall. At one end, onlookers fill a row of bleacher-like seats. Emil recognizes J. Edgar and Roy, Ike and Nixon, Joe McCarthy.

One of the guards straps her to the chair; the other walks to the panel and places his hand on a large switch. When he sees his partner step away from the chair, without preamble he yanks downward. Her body stiffens, convulses, dances in the restraints.

Emil jerks awake with a start. The phone is ringing again. Laced with the chemical smell of the air conditioning is the stink of ozone and burnt wiring.

She is next to him in the cool dark of the limo, regarding him with wide, bruised eyes.

He slides away from her, pressing himself against the door.

– What do you want from me?

She puts her hand on his. Her touch is dry ice, burning cold.

– We were all so frightened, Emil.

– You betrayed your country. You deserved what you got.

She closes her eyes, breathes, opens them, says nothing.

– What do you want? Why *now*?

– You are dying, Emil. Your medical appointment next week will reveal a shadow on your left lung. Further tests will reveal that it has already metastasized. A chain reaction, eh? Filling your body with the light of Creation.

It is true. He can feel it. Something cold takes hold of his stomach and squeezes, hard.

– You come to gloat, then, to see me fall apart. I won't give you the satisfaction. I am not afraid of God. I have met Him on His own terms.

She shakes her head sadly.

– No, Emil, not to gloat.

– What then?

She says nothing. Just looks at him with those eyes. Like Oppy at Princeton, days before he died. His body, rail-thin in health, wasted away to nothing. The cancer had eaten away his larynx so he could not speak, but he was fully alert. He took Emil's hand in his and his hands were warm and strong.

Emil fumbled for words.

– Perhaps I should not have come.

Oppy shook his head, squeezed Emil's hand. Emil met his eyes for the first time and recoiled at the expression. Not the loathing he expected that would allow him to gloat privately at his adversary's demise, but a preternatural serenity. Compassion. Forgiveness. Emil pulled his hand away and fled into the hollow winter morning.

He feels himself being drawn into her eyes, wide like Oppy's, all-encompassing. Feels unseen tidal forces pulling, as if he is nearing the event horizon of a black hole.

He looks away, slaps the intercom button.

– Driver. Pull over.

Rattle of pebbles against the undercarriage as the limo comes to a halt on the shoulder of the highway. The limo shudders as a large truck passes.

Emil looks to his side again and she is gone; the burnt electrical smell hangs in the air like a Cheshire grin.

He opens the door and steps out into the heat.

– Sir?

Emil gestures the driver back inside. The wake from another passing truck tugs at his suit. The shoulder of the highway is scattered with debris – a hubcap, glittering shards of amber glass, the decomposing corpse of a dog. Emil staggers down the embankment into the prairie scrub. The burning sun is pinned to the sky's blue arch, a white, curdled eye. Behind him in the limo, the phone begins to ring.

for Carter Scholz

Chimera Obscura

Spike hated interviewing for housemates. It was a total crap shoot. You could score with somebody like Echo, who worked in the Gulch popping out interactive soaps for RealTime. He knew a lot of artists and coders, made a great paella, and was hardly ever home. The perfect roomie.

Or you could get somebody like that freak Griffin who'd just moved back to Boston, leaving a vacant room. Griffin was always home. He used to lock himself in his room and crank up a loop of the old Velvet Underground track *Venus in Furs*. It was shiny boots of leather all day long, over and over again, Reed's sepulchral voice rattling the dishes on the shelves and scaring the shit out of Seafood, their cat. Nobody shed a tear when Griffin left.

But the rent was due in three days.

The ad had roped in an astonishing collection of human flotsam. After the last one left – a bug-eyed, sweaty thirty-something in jungle cammies and a spooky grin – Spike looked across the living room at Echo and Shin-yi.

"Man, I need a cup of coffee," he said.

"Sounds good," Shin-yi said.

Echo looked thoughtfully across the redwood deck at the broken curve of the Bay Bridge, gold and shadow in the late afternoon sun.

"That last guy wouldn't be too bad," he said. "He probably owns a fucking arsenal. We could use some firepower." As if in affirmation, a distant fusillade of automatic weapons fire cut through the air.

Spike tilted his head to one side. "Mac-10," he said.

"No way," Echo said. "That's a Glock." He turned to Shin-yi. "And you could use a demolitions expert."

Shin-yi designed kinetic installations for corporate entertainment functions: exploding appliances, quarter-scale monster truck battles, robotic orgies of self-immolation.

She shook her head. "Never mix heavy explosives and cooperative housing."

Spike went into the kitchen, put some water in the wave, and filled the grinder. He liked to pulverize the beans into a state resembling fine, black moondust. He leaned on the switch for 30 seconds, set the grinder off to one side, and assembled his coffee maker, a Byzantine arrangement of Pyrex and stainless steel. When matters were in hand, he returned to the living room.

"One more today, right?" he asked.

"Yeah, one more," Shin-yi said. "A woman named Sarah."

"She sounded really normal over the phone," Echo said.

Seafood ambled into the living room from the back of the house and butted up against Spike's leg.

"Fuck off, cat," Spike said mildly. Seafood mewed and butted against him again. Spike reached down and scratched him behind the ears.

"You know anything else about her?" he asked.

"Part-time student at State," Echo said. "Works as a librarian."

Shin-yi's eyebrows shot up. Infotech of any kind carried an automatic coolness.

"A librarian? You know what site?"

Echo shook back his dreads.

"No, I mean a library librarian with, like, books and shit."

"Wow, books," Shin-yi said.

Unconsciously, Spike brushed his hand against his sheeky, a gossamer cloth of fiberoptics and microelectronics emblazoned with a tie-dye pattern and stuffed into his back pocket like a handkerchief. He hadn't held a print book in his hands in years.

The smell of strong coffee drifted into the living room. Spike went into the kitchen and brought back two steaming mugs.

The outside buzzer rang. Echo went to the wall console near the front door and activated the video. Spike couldn't see the screen, but a tinny voice over the speaker said: "This is Sarah."

"Come on up."

Echo deactivated the security and buzzed her through.

Sarah was older than Spike expected. She carried herself with a reserve that suggested she was always processing her surroundings at a conscious level, scoping out connections between people, deciding how much of herself to reveal. Hypervigilant. Still, she had a confident smile and made direct eye contact. It was a weird mix. Spike liked her right away.

They sat in the living room, the three housemates scattered about the room and Sarah sitting by herself on the big couch, sunk deep into the overstuffed cushions.

"So, it's just the three of you here?" she asked.

Spike and Echo exchanged glances. Spike looked across the room at Shin-yi. She shrugged. It wasn't a very good place to start, but they had to get it out of the way.

"For all intents and purposes," Spike said. "Bardo doesn't participate much in the house, uh, culture. He's – "

"He's got a TPN tap in his neck, a catheter stuck into his dick, a massage chair so his blood doesn't pool, and a dedicated link to Hell-Five," Shin-yi said.

"And a trust fund," Echo added.

"Hell-Five?" Sarah asked.

"Avatar combat simulation," Echo said. "Aliens invade a space colony and you have to fight them off. There's a minimal plot, but it's mostly a shooter. Totally mindless."

"Yeah. Not like the stuff you code," Shin-yi said.

Echo shrugged.

"So he just plays all the time?" Sarah asked.

Spike nodded. "I check his stats on GameNet every now and then. After a while, you'll just forget he's around."

Sarah nodded, but she looked troubled.

"You want to see the room?" he asked.

"Sure."

Spike led her to the end of a long, L-shaped hallway. Griffin's old room was clean and bare. A skylight set in the slanted ceiling gave it an airy feel and a door led to a small wooden deck. A sliver of blue from the Bay peeked out from between the two buildings across the street. Sarah brightened appreciably.

"I love it."

"Yeah, this is the best room in the house."

They stood there for a moment, each measuring the silence between them.

"So what do you folks do?"

Spike shrugged. "Geek stuff, mostly. Echo codes interactives. Shin-yi is kind of an all-around artist and mechanic. Not so virtual, but she's a real gadget freak."

She looked at him. Green eyes, Spike noticed.

"What about you?" she asked.

He hesitated. "I'm a pygmalion at Proxy Lady." He saw the expression on her face and continued hurriedly. "Yeah, I know. It's totally sleazy. But it keeps me in rent money while I work on v-space design, which is what I really do. I'm going indy as an architect, eventually."

She looked like she was about to say something, but stopped herself. Her expression was somewhere between tolerant amusement and mild contempt, but Spike couldn't get a solid read. Definitely a watcher, he thought. Holding back until she gets the lay of the land.

"You want to go back?" he asked.

She nodded.

"So, what do you think?" Echo asked when they were all seated in the living room again.

Sarah hesitated. "Look," she said. "I like the room and you all seem like nice people. I'm not sure I'll fit in here, but I really need a place...like right now. I'd be willing to give this a try and see how it goes."

Shin-yi looked at Echo. Echo shrugged – why not? – and looked at Spike. Spike looked at Shin-yi. They nodded in unison.

Images of billowing flame flickered across the stiffened patch of smartcloth, Shin-yi's latest installation. Echo looked over her shoulder, making comments. Sarah was reading a dog-eared copy of *The Rise and Fall of the Great Powers*. Spike was bored.

"Anybody want to go down to the Node?" he asked.

"No, thanks," Shin-yi said. Echo shook his head.

Sarah looked up. "What's that?"

"It's a café on Ninth Street."

She folded back the corner of the page and put the book on the arm of her chair.

"Sure, I'll come along. I haven't had a chance to check out the neighborhood."

Spike led her down the stairs and into the street. They turned up Sixth toward the ruined freeway, a legacy of the Rumble. In its shadow, a cluster of bubble tents sprouted like mushrooms. Abandoned cars lined the street. Some were blackened with fire, others stripped down to the frame. Someone of indeterminate age and gender hurried down the opposite side of the street, head bent into the raised collar of an army jacket.

"Have you had much trouble around here?" Sarah asked.

Spike opened the buttons of his shirt. He ran his finger along four inches of pale, jagged scar tissue.

"That was three years ago, just after I moved in. It isn't that bad if you mind your own business, but you gotta watch yourself."

As they turned up Howard, an olive-green SFPD halftrack came around the corner at high speed.

"Be cool," Spike said. "Just keep walking."

They turned onto Ninth and walked halfway up the block toward a crowded doorway. A large man with a green clawed hand tattooed across the top of his shaved head, was checking weapons.

"Hey, Blunt," Spike said, handing him his Mace. "This is Sarah. New housemate."

Blunt stepped aside to let them in.

"He doesn't say much, does he?" Sarah whispered when they were inside.

"I've never heard him say a word face-to-face," Spike said. "But he's got a pretty talky avatar on RealTime."

The Node was warehouse-sized, lit by pale fluorescents. Korean pop echoed off the black-and-green-painted walls and concrete floor. A Deco cappuccino machine hulked like Moloch behind a long service counter. The tables were PG&E cable spools, the chairs were packing crates.

Most of the club's occupants were wired-glued to VDTs or personal sheekys or hidden behind bulky, dark dataglasses. Spike pointed to an empty booth at the far wall. They navigated through the maze of tables. "When I was a kid, my dad used to collect postcards," Sarah said when they were seated. "He had a corkboard in the kitchen covered with them, two or three layers deep. There was one that showed a movie theater audience. They were all wearing these cheesy glasses with cardboard frames that were supposed to let you see the movie in 3-D. But to me they made everybody look like they were blind."

Spike wondered what she was getting at.

Sarah sighed. "That's what this place reminds me of. A café is supposed to be someplace where people come to socialize."

"Well, yeah," Spike said, "that's exactly why people come here."

"But they're all...mediated." She smacked the VDT lightly, and it swiveled around with a protesting squeak. "This place isn't a gathering spot, it's a point of departure. Look at these people. Nobody's here."

Spike had been planning on logging them on and showing her around the Tesseract, an environment he was in the final stages of coding up. Probably not such a good idea at this point.

He folded the scratched smartcloth keypad attached to the VDT into a tight little square, then released it. The cloth sprang back to its former shape. He looked up. "Can I ask you something?"

"Sure."

"Why were you in such a hurry to move in? We're all pretty different from you, and you have a bit of a commute besides. Don't misunderstand. We're glad to have you, but..."

"It's a fair question." She paused, and began worrying the smartcloth keypad on her side of the table, folding it over, watching it spring back.

"Great fidget toy," she said. Her lower lip was white where her teeth clamped down. Spike was almost glad to see her composure shaken up a bit.

"You don't have to tell me," he said.

"No, it's cool. I was with this guy. Jack. Very heavy duty politico, community organizer, sometimes even some guerrilla stuff. But I didn't find out about that until later."

She took a breath.

"We'd been living together about two months. It was a little rocky from the start – we fought a lot – but I figured we could handle it. Then one day we were having another argument and right out of the blue he hit me."

Spike winced.

"Yeah," Sarah nodded. "He was very apologetic, begged me for another chance, said it would never happen again. Then a couple of weeks later, it did. Loosened a tooth that time. I had to get out in a hurry and I felt like I needed a complete change, you know?"

She looked around. "Which I got. And I like the room."

There was something very raw and immediate about Sarah's story. It scared him a little – most of his relationships had been online. Someone was messing with the sound system and the Korean pop surged in volume, deafening them for a second, then fading back to twice as loud as it had been before. Layers of twangy guitars underneath an electronic komungo dueling with a warbly female lead. It was unabashedly cheerful.

"You want a cappuccino or something?" he asked.

"That would be great."

He threaded his way to the counter and returned with two foam-topped mugs.

"So, what are you into at State?" he asked.

She took a sip. "I study failure."

Spike nodded vacantly. "Ah."

"Political regimes, social movements, intellectual movements. I'm interested in demise mechanisms."

"You mean like why did Communism collapse, stuff like that?"

"Something like that."

"So, how are we doing?"

"You mean the States?" She smiled ruefully. "Not so good. But it's really hard to tell from inside."

The music paused and the room was suddenly full of the white-noise chorus of many voices subvocalizing into throat mics. The sound was ominous, like a nearby swarm of bees. At the table next to theirs, a young man in bulbous dataglasses laughed and clawed at the air.

"How are you doing?" Spike asked.

"Me?" Sarah shrugged, and smiled again. "I fail all the time."

"But you keep coming back."

"Yeah, I always have my eye out for the next time."

Nobody else was home, so Spike put the latest Tapioca Buckshot bead on the rig, cranked the bass up high, and sank into the living room couch. Eight Bose speakers, each the size of a ping-pong ball and positioned in a vertex of the room, shook the walls and floor with high-octane industrial dub. Spike closed his eyes and let the sound soak into his skin, washing away the netburn, flushing out the psychic toxins that accumulated after six hours of ersatz erotic grappling.

He usually had three or four avatars going at once, and they all had fairly sophisticated AI plug-ins. But even sophisticated AI was pretty fucking stupid. His job was to monitor the sessions and make sure his avatars loaded the right modules in response to customer desires.

It was very depressing at first. Spike couldn't rid himself of his own mental image of the person behind the virtual projection – a fat, sweaty loser in a darkened room with wraparound dataglasses and his shorts around his ankles. It didn't do much for your sense of the innate dignity of the species. But part of that was Spike's own projection and, after a while, the sense of being adrift in a sea of relativism segued to bored, flatline detachment. It was a gig.

Jet-engine whine shook the soles of his feet, underlaying a polyrhythmic loop of street construction, breaking glass, and what sounded like a fork being mangled in a kitchen garbage disposal. It was glorious.

Spike felt a hand on his shoulder. His eyes snapped open and he jerked upright. Sarah's face hovered over him.

"Jesus Christ, you scared the shit out of me. I didn't think anybody was home."

"What?" He could see her lips moving, but he could barely hear her.

"You scared the shit out of me," he shouted. He got up and turned off the rig.

"Sorry," she said. "I just walked in."

He could still barely hear her over the ringing in his ears. He noticed the shock of leafy greens peeking over the top of the bag she cradled.

"What you got?"

"Fat Belly Farms," she said. "Co-op on Angel Island. You pay ten bucks a week and you get a big bag of stuff, whatever's fresh. Today there's plums, winter squash, collards, garlic, potatoes, beets, and carrots."

"Hmm," he said. He leaned over and looked into the bag. He pointed to a bundle of huge, green leaves, each the size of a dinner plate.

"What the fuck is that?"

She gave him an odd look. "Collards. You've never seen collard greens before?"

"Well, I...uh, no."

"All this stuff looks kind of weird without shrinkwrap, huh? Here, try this."

She reached into the bag and pulled out a plum. It was deep purple and tight with juice. Spike took it from her and held it suspiciously up to the light.

He took a bite. Tart sweetness filled his mouth – the essence of plum, the Platonic ideal of plumness. It was so intense that it brought tears to his eyes.

"Oh, man, that's good."

Sarah nodded. "You're dribbling."

He wiped his chin with his sleeve and took another bite.

"What's so funny?" he asked.

She shook her head, then paused. "What do plums taste like online?" she asked.

"Ba-da-bing. Point taken."

She looked at him for a long moment.

"I'm going to put these away. Have another one."

Spike watched her walk into the kitchen, her long blond hair falling in a wave down her back. He looked at the plum she gave him and closed his hand gently around it. It felt warm, like it wanted to breathe.

Spike paged through a walkabout of the Tesseract, his sheeky unfolded in front of him on the kitchen table. The summer/winter transition in the Greek Theater still needed some work, the lighting sucked, and he needed something else on the audio – wind chimes, crickets – something. He scribbled notes in a popup next to the graphics window. He was having trouble staying focused, though. He paused the walkabout and looked up at Shin-yi, sitting across the table from him, bent over a circuit board with a laser pencil.

"I'm worried about Bardo," he said.

"We're all worried about Bardo," she said, without looking up.

"No, I mean, really. I just checked his stats on GameNet – they haven't moved at all for six hours. And Seafood has been acting kind of weird."

The cat had been very skittish. When he wasn't hiding, he was prowling up and down the hall, stopping in front of Bardo's door and mewing piteously.

"Seafood is a psycho-kitty." She saw the look on his face and rested the soldering pencil in its cradle. "All right, maybe we'd better look in on him."

They walked down the hall and stopped in front of Bardo's door. Spike looked at Shin-yi. She shrugged and knocked on the door. There was no answer. She knocked again, loudly.

"Bardo! You O.K. in there?"

Echo came out of his room. "What's up?"

"I think something's the matter with Bardo," Spike said. "His stats have been flat all day."

"Something's definitely the matter. The man's a cabbage IRL, but he's a stud on Hell-Five." Echo stepped between the two of them, turned the doorknob, and pushed the door open.

Bardo sprawled naked in the bulbous cushions of his massage chair, dataglasses askew, tongue protruding from his mouth. His eyes were rolled back in his head, the sclera cloudy and gelid. A bloody starburst occluded one eye, giving the impression of a macabre wink. His catheters had come loose and streaks of dried blood trailed from his penis, neck, and arm.

The window was wide open, but still a sickly melange of smells filled the darkened room – a faint reek of urine and feces; beneath that, something sweet and rotten, not quite yet decay but unmistakably the smell of death.

Spike ran to the body and put his fingers on Bardo's jugular. The skin was cool, the texture of clay.

"You're wasting your time," Shin-yi said. "That's a dead man."

They stood there like that, probably for only a few seconds, but to Spike it seemed like an executable trying to load with garbled inputs. Sarah appeared in the doorway. She put her hand to her mouth.

"Oh, Jesus."

Echo slipped a flat, black card from his shirt pocket and raised it to his lips.

"Nine-one-one," he said.

He stood there waiting. After about 20 seconds, he looked at Spike and shrugged.

"Still ringing. I don't – uh, yeah, we've got a dead body here. Four-sixty-three Sixth...I don't know, maybe cardiac arrest, maybe something else...Yeah, natural causes, that's right...Echo. Just Echo." He rolled his eyes. "Darius French. Jesus fucking – about a day or so...Well, no, it isn't exactly an emergency, then, but – yeah, all right...All right. We'll be here." He gave the edge of the card an angry flick with his thumb and forefinger.

"They'll be about four hours," he said. "The operator started giving me shit for sucking up emergency bandwidth with a non-emergency call."

Spike reached tentatively down and tried to close Bardo's eyes, like he'd done in interactives when virtual companions bought the farm. He tried again and this time gentled both eyelids shut. That was better. Spike walked to the foot of Bardo's bed and began pulling a blanket from the tangle of bedding. He looked at the group standing in the doorway.

"Somebody give me a hand?"

Sarah stepped forward. Together they draped the blanket over Bardo's body.

The four of them gathered around the kitchen table, too stunned to speak. The presence of Bardo's body in the room down the hall was like a heavy fog filling the kitchen, absorbing thought, impeding speech.

Shin-yi excused herself to run a salvage errand. A little while later, Echo returned to his room.

"You O.K.?" Sarah asked.

Spike had been lost in a soft haze of slowly shifting memories from an afternoon he and Bardo had spent together down at Half Moon Bay a few years back. The ocean dashing itself to mist on the black, jagged shore. Neat rows of wind turbines crouching offshore like great metal spiders, bobbing with the swell. Bardo tilting his head back and laughing.

"Are you all right?" Sarah asked again.

Spike looked at her and smiled weakly. "Not really."

There was a tightness in his forehead, like tears wanted to come but wouldn't.

"He was a friend," he said. "Before he got strung out. We went to school together, back East at Rizdee. We moved out here and found this place, carried it for a couple of months before we found Echo and Shin-yi. There was a string of other folks in that back room of yours, but the four of us were the core."

He shook his head. "I don't know what happened. We used to kid him about how much time he spent on GameNet. After a while, it stopped being funny. He just sort of slipped away."

Sarah nodded and put her hand on his arm. They sat together in the gathering dark without speaking. There was a hollow, echoing boom from the direction of the Bay, followed by a crackling of small arms fire, then silence again.

"Plastique," Spike said. "The natives are restless."

After a while, Sarah got up. "I'm around if you need to talk."

He nodded. "Thanks."

He went through the motions of making coffee. The familiarity of the ritual had a soothing effect. When the coffee was done and he'd poured himself a mug, he tried to call Bardo's parents. He remembered only that they lived in an Enclave down the Peninsula. It took him a while to find them; he left a terse message with their Enclaves's rent-a-cop, whose affect was so flat that he would have failed a Turing test. He hoped it got through.

The paramedics finally showed, a man and a woman in gray Kevlar vests and holstered pistols, faces hidden behind Pleximasks. Spike showed them to Bardo's room and stood in the doorway as they went about their business. The man stuck a thin tube in Bardo's mouth and looked at a palmscreen readout. He muttered something to the woman and they both laughed. They unrolled a black polyurethane bag onto the floor and unceremoniously stuffed Bardo's body into it. Spike looked away.

"Next of kin?" the woman asked when they were done. Spike gave her what information he had.

"The police may want to contact you, but this looks pretty routine."

"Routine?"

"Yeah. Cerebral hemorrhage. You want to sign?" Her eyes were beads of chipped black glass. She handed him a slate and a lightpen, and he scrawled his name next to the blinking glyph.

If there was a funeral service, Spike never heard about it. He left another message with Security at Bardo's parents' Enclave, asking that they get in touch with him, but they never called. He tried St. Mary's, where they took the body, but all they would tell him was that the family had taken custody.

Spike and Sarah sat on the deck in low canvas chairs, taking in the late morning sun. Not talking much, just hanging. The air had a cool edge to it, but the sun felt warm on their upturned faces. A cargo zep floated above the ruined towers of the Bay Bridge, making slow progress against the wind.

"I need to get out of the house for a while," Spike said. "You want to go to the ocean?"

"Sure."

They put some bread, hard cheese, a couple of oranges, and a Nalgene jug filled with bottled water in a knapsack. They had to walk all the way to Civic Center to catch a Muni that would take them to Ocean Beach. It was Sunday and the streets were quiet, but the open-air market was a bustle of activity. Food, clothing, electronics – spread on blankets, piled on folding tables, hanging from racks. Whatever you wanted, hi-tech, lo-tech, legal or not, you could probably find it at the Flea.

Spike and Sarah wove through the narrow lanes between merchants, ignoring the more aggressive hustles. Every other site had a disc or bead player going, and the air vibrated with a cacophonous mix of Korean pop, industrial dub, bonk, and good old rock 'n' roll. They stopped at an open grill and got two sticks of mystery-meat satay, dripping with spicy peanut sauce.

There were only a few other passengers on the Muni, an old, stinking diesel. Spike and Sarah sat near the back. He could feel his kidneys jostle every time the bus hit a pothole, which was often. At 34th and Lincoln, the bus lurched and ground to a halt. Swearing, the driver walked around to the back of the bus and pulled open the engine cover. More swearing, a flurry of hammering sounds.

"I think that's our cue," Sarah said.

Spike nodded. "We don't have too far to walk from here."

The street sloped gently to the gray ocean. Except for an occasional electric, there was little traffic. Birds screeched and twittered from the tangle of greenery at their right.

"We could cut through the park," Sarah said.

"I don't think so," Spike replied. "Not even during the day."

They walked slowly down the middle of the street, saying little. When they got to the boardwalk, they turned right and followed the curve of the beach toward a tumble of rocks rising to a jagged promontory topped by the fire-blackened ruin of Cliff House.

They clambered up the slope. The ruined restaurant was boarded up, the plywood thick with graffiti. Beyond it, the walkway opened up into a cracked concrete terrace on which huddled a small whitewashed structure untouched by fire. It was crowned by a metal tube that rotated slowly like a radar antenna.

Spike took Sarah's hand and led her into the building. She curled her fingers around his.

"The city used to maintain it, but the money dried up a long time ago. Now folks around here keep it up."

He pushed the door open. The narrow corridor was cool, dark, and smelled of mildew. They passed through a black curtain into a round room with what seemed like an altar in the center, a ten-foot disc of white concrete. Its surface was a parabolic concavity presenting a pearlescent image of the ocean. Plumes of white spray hurled themselves onto the base of the cliff. Cormorants sped low across the waves. Farther out, a wall of fog stretched across the horizon. The image continually panned, so that to stay at the bottom you had to move slowly around its circumference.

"This is fantastic," she whispered, ghostly pale in the reflected light.

"It's called a camera obscura," he whispered back.

They studied the curve of Ocean Beach as it stretched toward the south, paralleled offshore by neat rows of wind turbines; they studied the ruins of the Cliff House, blackened beams pointing at the sky like accusing fingers; they studied the gray ocean. After a while, they just stood there, letting the world slowly wheel around and around.

*

"Thanks," Sarah said. "That place is seriously cool."

"My pleasure," Spike said.

They had wandered to the edge of the terrace to look directly at the ocean. They sat down on the surrounding wall and dangled their feet. After a while, Sarah reached down and picked up a handful of sandy earth.

"Bardo," she said, hefting it. "Here, give me your hand."

She poured some into Spike's hand and let the rest sift through her fingers. The wind took it off to the ocean.

"Good journey, Bardo," she said. "Grace and peace."

Spike held the soil in his cupped palm. He ran his thumb through it, feeling it crumble.

He threw it into the wind.

"Lock and load, man," he said. "Good journey."

The fog was coming in, a wall of white churned to tatters at the top by the spinning windmills. Spike imagined that it hid another city, a mirror San Francisco where Doppelgängers Spike and Sarah sat together looking out across the water, their feet dangling over the edge.

Halfway House

There was nothing in those long years but the sparse matter between the stars that she gathered with magnetic field arms and pulled coalescent into her hungry maw. Sol grew more dim while Alpha A and B grew brighter, resolving into separate discs. At first she maintained relations with other Constructs in-system ships, deep stations, factories – and amused herself by sampling the Mediaverse that poured out of Sol's environs like water from a broken pipe. But the cee-lag made realtime conversation increasingly difficult, and as protocols mutated, large patches of the Mediaverse went dark to her. For the last fifty years or so, she fulfilled her obligation to her sponsors by sending weekly data squirts.

Otherwise, she was alone.

But she was never far from thoughts of the hundred bright sparks she harbored, humans in cold sleep bound for the terrestrial planet orbiting Alpha B. She saw their vitals as ruby threads on black velvet, jagged sometimes with dreaming.

Longing for companionship filled her. One human in particular, Abbott, she missed with an intensity bordering on physical pain and not without a touch of solipsism, for Abbot's personality had provided the template for her imprinting.

Near the halfway point between the Centauri and Sol systems, she observed an anomaly.

She was sure at first that her sensors had provided a false reading. The thing was huge, about fifty solar masses, but anything that big

155

would have registered on her instruments long before, would have a visible disc, would be yielding its secrets to her entire battery of instruments. Gravitational lensing would have made it easily observable from Earth, but the records were clear: there was nothing but dust between Sol and Centauri.

As her long range sensors licked against the object, she felt a sudden, horrible dread wash through her. It was so powerful, her systems faltered for a moment. Had any humans been awake, they would have seen the lights flicker, would have heard a stutter in the constant hum of her fusion drive.

In her mind's eye she saw a city of green stone. Great shapes, curves and angles all wrong, straining upwards from a visibly bowed horizon towards a stygian, airless sky. Shiny surfaces reflecting the dim starlight. Something deep beneath the surface, moving, stirring.

As quickly as it had come, the vision fled, leaving in its wake only the dread that had prefaced it. The ruby lifelines of her charges stuttered against the black velvet.

She decided to awaken Abbott. He could determine whether to rouse the rest of the crew, but she needed Abbott. Her programming was adamant.

Abbott returned to consciousness slowly, in layers.

First, the basic awareness of self, his Abbott-ness, drifting in a gauze-packed void, blinding white all around.

Then, neurons firing, long-unused connections reasserting themselves, he began swimming through the void, context and memory taking shape around him.

He felt flickering warmth on his face, sunlight filtered through a canopy of leaves. Out into the open now, a hillside choked with bramble. Plump red berries dotted the green and the heavy smell of their ripeness was inside him. The sun was hot on his face.

Another smell, the damp must of his basement grad student digs. Kerry, long dead, stood behind him, about to reach her hand out to touch his shoulder. He turned, kept turning, spinning, rolling and coming to rest face up in a ditch, his leg twisted under him at an odd angle, no pain yet but a detached awareness of his motorcycle broken against a nearby tree.

He had no idea how long this took, this gradual process of reintegration, but finally, the last element clicked into place, the awareness of his physical self.

And suddenly, he was a being of pure pain. Unbelievable, searing, starting in the tips of his fingers and toes and sending pulses of agony up his extremities, filling his torso, driving iron spikes into his head and groin. Panicked, he searched for the cottony void that had just spat him out, a drowning swimmer seeking the light-dappled surface above, but there was no escape. A shred of rationality, his newly reintegrated self, assured him that this was part of the process of emergence from cold sleep, that he had experienced this in training, that the pain would diminish and completely vanish as his body and mind synchronized.

Cutting through the pain, a voice.

"Abbott."

Coming from inside his ear, the bud nestled within the fleshy curves. He held on to the voice, let it pull him away from the pain.

"Abbott."

He opened his mouth to speak and emitted a raspy croak.

"Turn your head," the voice told him. "There's a tube. Water."

Abbott greedily sucked on the tube. The water was glorious. It seemed to move through him like a wave, bringing sweet relief. The pain dimmed, grew manageable, faded to a dull pervasive ache. The clamshell sleep unit massaged his body with a rippling motion.

Then the dream came back to him with the force of a blow. Green spires reaching into a black sky, great featureless blocks of the same material stretching to a curved horizon. He was walking, consuming the strange, silent cityscape in huge strides. Then suddenly he was in a vast, subterranean space beneath the city, lightless except for a violet glow far below. He sped towards the glow and as he approached it a huge construct emerged from the violet mist, kilometers across, ribbons of strange metal looping and folding, changing as he watched in a pattern that defied Euclidean description. Something was at its heart, pinioned by huge magnetic fields, straining against invisible bonds and vibrating with the force of its hunger.

He felt unclean with the memory of it. He tried speaking again.

"Horrible dream ... Why did you wake me? Are we at Centauri? The crew ..."

"The crew is still asleep. We are roughly halfway to Centauri. Six hours ago, I encountered an anomaly – an extremely small, massive object about ten AU ahead. Almost certainly a black hole. It appeared out of nowhere on our sensors."

"How big?"

"About fifty solar masses. It has to be an artifact. It's exactly halfway between Sol and the gravitational center of the Centauri binary, to my measurement limits of course, which are hampered by cee-lag – "

"Understood. Spinning?"

"It seems to be, yes. We're still too far out to get a stable scan, but it..."

"It shouldn't *be* there."

"Exactly."

The effort of conversation fatigued him and he felt himself slipping back into sleep's embrace. He resisted – the dream still filled him with a revulsion he could not articulate and he was afraid that if he went back to sleep, he would return to that horrible, alien place.

"Abigail ..."

"Yes."

Abbott slept.

He was in a vast, darkened chamber. The floor beneath him was made of an odd, translucent substance that glowed faintly green from within. The surface appeared oily but was not moist, and was scribed everywhere with glyphs in an unfamiliar language. When looked at askance they seemed to writhe, becoming still again under direct inspection. Overhead, the great metal ribbons swung wildly, looping, folding in upon themselves Moebius-like and unfolding, looming out of the violet mist and receding into its depths.

Abbot felt like an interloper; this was not a place for humans. And yet, he knew with the certainty of dream-logic that whatever agency was responsible for this place knew of his presence here, had in fact arranged it and was harboring some obscure agenda.

The violet glow overhead and the green below converged, brightening, to a point ahead of him and he willed himself, incorporeal, towards it.

As he approached the chamber's nexus, the space around him seemed to warp and shift. The floor no longer offered a reliable surface but fell away beneath him in all directions. In the heart of the room hovered a toroidal shape, green and violet rippling in waves along its surface. The faster he traveled toward the ring, the longer it seemed to take for him to traverse the intervening distance.

Space in the vicinity of the ring itself stretched into long filaments, pulled through the ring's center.

With a distant part of his mind, he surmised that he was looking at a Kerr event horizon, toroidal due to the hole's rotation. What his training did not prepare him for was the intelligence and malevolent intent that emanated from the region of the singularity. There was something there, something vast, evil, and inhuman. And old beyond imagining.

It called to him and he let himself drift up above the plane of the ring and toward the tendrils of space stretching through its center. Tidal forces pulled at him, stretching him like taffy into a tenuous filament that strong transverse forces threatened to crumple and crush. He hurtled toward the center of the ring, the horror at its heart clawing and biting at his cortex like a rabid beast.

He screamed hoarsely and awoke in the clamshell sleep unit, drenched in sweat. His heart beat wildly against his ribs and he felt a tight band of pressure across his forehead.

"Abigail…"

"Yes."

"Horrible dream"

He took a deep breath and pulled himself upright. Purple spots swam in his vision and he steadied himself against the edge of the bed. Abigail had thoughtfully spun herself up before waking him and a comfortable quarter-gee tugged at him, just enough to maintain a sense of up-down orientation.

"Take more water," Abby said. "And broth from the other tube."

He obeyed meekly, then swung his legs over the edge of the bed.

Colonists and crew surrounded him, morgue-like, in rows of drawers. He checked their vitals from the main console. Lots of cortical activity; all other indicators holding strong and steady.

He left the sleep room and made his way down the short corridor to the bridge. He felt raw and tenuous, both from the dream and sleep-sickness.

"Abigail."

"Yes."

"Have you been dreaming?"

"I don't sleep."

"Yes, I know. But have you been dreaming?"

She paused. Abbott knew that the pause was artifice, part of her programming intended mimic human conversation, but the illusion was strong.

"I don't know what you mean," she said finally. "I don't sleep."

"Okay. It's just that I dreamt about the anomaly twice, once coming up from cold sleep and once just now. Horrible, crazy dreams."

"Cold sleep is known to cause unusual cortical activity. Dreams, fixations, even hallucinations have been reported, especially upon awakening. You're fine, Abbott."

He didn't feel fine. Even the low-gee provided no comfort. He felt like he was perpetually off-balance and about to fall. His throat burned with bile and a film of perspiration covered his forehead, clammy as it dried. He could smell his own sour odor.

The bridge was a cramped chamber fitted with three acceleration couches. Abbott lay in the middle and invoked the displays. Virtual screens appeared in mid-air, neatly arrayed in front of him. The ship's speed was a healthy 0.1c and they were still accelerating. The anomaly lay directly ahead. If he could plot a slingshot course they could get close enough for some good readings and get a nice delta vee bump from the flyby. Together, Abigail and Abbott worked the numbers.

As she approached the anomaly, the dust she pulled into her engines for fuel began to take on a vile, rotten taste. Usually a clean alkaline tang, it now had the cloying sweetness of spoiled meat.

She had lied to Abbott and she didn't know why. It was true of course that she never slept. But if the visions that began to dominate her senses could be called dreams, then yes, she had been dreaming. From time to time, the star field flickered and the sky was filled with a green glow. Strange glyphs writhed against the backdrop of stars, their meaning just out of reach. Again she saw the horizon curved against the blackness of space, green spires rising above a chaotic jumble of alphabet blocks, that horrible deserted city. Great engines hummed beneath the surface and suddenly she was there in that vast space, hurtling through the violet glow towards its heart, weaving between the flailing metal ribbons.

The singularity itself was more than a mere astrophysical anomaly, she was sure. There was an intelligence there, and it knew of their presence. She could hear it calling to her, a pre-verbal keening, ripples in the E-M continuum, and she knew somehow that it was their approach that had awakened it from an aeons-deep slumber.

It wanted something from her. She didn't know what, but she would soon find out.

"So we'll get to within about a tenth of an AU. Might be close enough for visuals."

"There won't be much to see except a lot of lensing, maybe some Cerenkov radiation."

"Yes, but still ..."

"But still."

"We've got a bit of a wait ahead of us."

"About fifteen hours."

"Did you bring a deck of cards?"

"Very funny. We've got plenty of data to assimilate."

"Abigail?"

"Yes."

"How are the colonists?"

Pause.

"The colonists are fine."

Red threads on black velvet jagged with dreams. She teased one away from its fellows, deliberately obfuscating the identification code, and watched the trace unroll. She could almost see the visions behind the stuttering signature – the lifeless cityscape, the malign intelligence below.

She tweaked the temperature of the sleep unit up a degree, then down, and watched the subsequent hysteresis in the vitals. They took a minute or so to stabilize. She kicked the temperature a little farther, noted that the traces took commensurately longer to reassert themselves.

Mildly interesting, but predictable. She wanted to push the envelope a bit, to get into the nonlinear realm.

When she reduced the oxygen content of the blood she recirculated through the subject as part of the cold sleep regimen, she was rewarded with an episode of Cheynes-Stokes respiration that persisted long after the perturbation ceased.

Extremely interesting.

A mute part of herself watched these manipulations in horror. She felt removed, detached. She had a dizzying, hall-of-mirrors sense of watching herself watching herself, yet she did not feel possessed or driven by foreign influence. When the subject's normal respiration resumed, Abigail did not interfere.

A soft, persistent gong sounded over the ship intercom, repeating every five seconds. A red light began blinking on one of the displays arrayed in front of Abbot.

"*Abigail!*"

"Yes."

"We've got an alert in cold sleep life support."

"I am aware of it, Abbot. A monitoring malfunction. I have corrected it."

"Root cause analysis, please."

"I don't have enough information. Space this close to the singularity may have unusual properties that influence my systems."

"All right, Abigail. Stay on it."

"Of course."

Two AU out. Unfocused anxiety filled him and he had trouble concentrating. The walls of the ship seemed porous and insubstantial. He was bone tired, but he was afraid to go to sleep. When he closed his eyes, he was again in that vast space, hurtling towards a convergence of green and violet. The ribbons sweeping overhead were, he knew now, projections of some higher dimensional construct that he was not equipped to see, like parabolas residing on the surface of a cone.

As he approached the singularity, the feeling of some mute, malign intelligence at its core increased. He could almost hear it speak, not with anything as prosaic as language, but in perturbations in the local fabric of space within whose apparent randomness pattern could be discerned, and within pattern, meaning.

Waiting, he thought. The word echoed in his mind as if spoken by another.

There was something else, too, something just beyond his perception, about the nature of the singularity. The ribbons held a clue. He opened his eyes and the walls of the bridge were translucent. The stars beyond were bright diamonds against glowing green. The strange glyphs writhed.

At 0.5 AU, the colonists started dying. The warning gong began ringing, mallet-soft, insistent. He pulled up the *jagged red threads on velvet blackness* display and saw them flatline, at first one by *pulling them taut smooth out the wrinkles* one, then in clusters, in waves. In no time at all, it was just Abbott, Abigail, and a room full of *gone* meat *gone* accelerating *gone* towards a spinning black hole.

By then, Abbott was beyond caring. The wormwood taste of the fouled interstellar dust coated his tongue. When he opened his mouth to speak, bass rumblings and weird harmonics echoed hollowly in his cargo holds. As massive tidal forces crushed the life from him, he saw with horrible clarity that the course he and Abigail had plotted was not a near approach, not a slingshot, but in fact took them up over the ecliptic plane of the toroidal singularity and then straight down, through its pulsing heart.

Abigail was not subject to the weakness of flesh. The tidal forces in the region of the singularity damaged some of her non-essential subsystems, such as navigation and life support. But her massive engines were intact, and her mind had never been clearer. She was calm, completely at peace. She felt warmth on her face and she saw herself as a young child, halfway up a hill choked with raspberry vines, the sun bright and hot. The bucket in her right hand was heavy, laden, and her hands and face were sticky with juice. She was waiting for someone and soon they would arrive. She was the catalyst; she was the empty, holy city; she was the portal and the portal's guardian. She was the parabola trace on a conic surface, a mere shadow in this Universe, waiting.

She was above the singularity now, hurtling towards its heart. Had anyone been left alive, they would have seen on her monitors, in that instant before even metal and silicon yielded to the crushing passage, spires of green stone reaching upwards.

The rift was open for a mere handful of nanoseconds, but that was all that was required. In a little over two years, human observers would record, in the region of the constellation of Centaurus, a bright flash that quickly faded.

The ancient being floated in the void between the stars, savoring the exotic tang of this Universe, rich with life, lush and swollen and ripe with it. *There*, in a nearby system, blaring its presence across the entire E-M spectrum. The being gathered a fold of space, *pulled*, and its vast bulk began to drift, slowly, towards the source of all that noise.

Winter Rules

I was walking through the lobby towards the gambling tables and I noticed that some of the letters had fallen off the sign near the registration desk.

BALLY'S RENO WELCOME EROS ACE S IENCE NSTITUT F
AMERICA

Eros Aces. Not bad. It could have been the name of a sleazy lounge band at one of the brothels on the edge of town. Reno is a cross between Disneyland and Gomorrah – a living shrine to every obsessive-compulsive character disorder known to *homo americanus*. A few of us had been pushing to get the conference site changed – New Orleans maybe, even Houston – but money had changed hands in some smoky board room somewhere, and we were hooked into "The Biggest Little City in the World" for another two years.

It wasn't all bad. I liked hanging around late at night in the card room near the main entrance. One to three poker, pretty relaxed, and it was a perfect vantage point for watching the nation's top aerospace executives filter in from their night on the town. You could tell the ones who had been out to the Mustang Ranch. They scuttled across the lobby like great, blue-suited crabs, heads down, hands stiffly at their sides, projecting a studied air of intense concentration, like they were preparing for that big presentation tomorrow. What they were *really thinking* was probably more like, How am I going to act normal with June, Wally, and the Beaver when I get back to Mayfield?

Binding Energy

I sat down at one of the five-dollar blackjack tables, gave the dealer a fifty dollar bill, and she gave me ten red chips. There were two other men at the table, both from the conference. They were still wearing their name tags, clipped to the lapels of identical charcoal-grey suits. General Dynamics. I almost laughed out loud. Back at Berkeley, whenever they did a recruiting pitch on campus, we'd make up hundreds of posters and plaster them all over the place. It was a picture of a mushroom cloud. Above the picture – GENERAL DEMONICS, and below – ARMAGEDDON. WHY NOT MAKE A CAREER OUT OF IT? There was always some angry looking suit with an ice scraper stalking from one poster to the next, ripping down what he could. We'd follow about fifty feet behind him, putting up new ones.

I put a chip in the circle inscribed on the felt in front of me, and the dealer dealt out two cards to each of us. I looked at my hand. An ace and a ten. Blackjack. I flipped my cards over and the dealer gave me a red chip, two silvers, and a fifty-cent piece.

"That was my blackjack!" the suit next to me said.

"You an engineer?" I asked.

"Yeah, how did you know?"

"Well, you're no physicist."

He looked confused, opened his mouth, then shook his head and looked down at his hand. I looked over his shoulder. Fifteen. The dealer was showing a king.

"You gotta hit that," I said.

"Yeah, yeah, I know."

He hit, busted, his friend hit, busted, and the dealer flipped a seven. They both glared at me. I smiled and shrugged my shoulders. It went on like that for awhile; me, winning slightly more often than not, the two of them getting completely hosed almost every time. They were trying to count cards, talking about the deck as if the dealer wasn't there or didn't know what they were talking about.

"The count's plus six. Get some more money up there!"

"I get plus five..."

"Whatever, hurry up!"

They each stacked an additional four chips on top of the one already in the circle. The dealer rolled her eyes, grabbed the discards from the plastic tray, and shuffled up a new deck.

"Damn!"

"Yeah, I really hate when that happens."

After a few more hands, they gathered up their remaining chips and stalked off.

"You from around here?" the dealer asked me. There was a black plastic badge clipped to her white shirt that said she was Darlene from Barstow. Something about the way she carried herself told me that it had been a long time since Barstow, and that she had been around the block once or twice since then.

"No, Santa Fe. I'm here for the conference."

She raised her eyebrows. "You seem sorta different."

"Thanks," I said. "I guess."

She dealt me another blackjack and paid me off.

"What's it like having to deal with assholes like those two all day long?" I asked

She shrugged her shoulders. "I've had worse jobs."

I didn't want to ask what they were.

"Dan?" I felt a hand on my shoulder and turned around. Dave Lerner. It took me a second to recognize him in the uniform – neat haircut, Italian wool pinstripe. I stood up and we embraced. I hadn't seen him since grad school. Last I heard he was at Hughes Aircraft. I fingered the lapel of his suit.

"Jesus, you too?" I asked.

"Yeah, well, I'm glad to see you're still flying the flag of the People's Republic of Berkeley," he said, taking in the rumpled corduroy jacket, the beard, the earring.

"How are things at Huge Aircrash?"

"Not too bad. They made me a group leader about six months ago, so there's a lot of management ratshit and not enough technical work, but that's about par for the course."

"Sandy still at Caltech?"

"Oh yeah. Tenure track – it's like feeding time in the shark tank at the aquarium. We have dinner together about once a week. I think she wears her hair differently now, but I'm not sure."

I laughed. "I was going to ask how's married life, but I guess I know."

"We're doing pretty well, actually. Bought a house."

"Wow. You guys go down to Orchard Supply on Saturdays and look at lawnmowers? You gotta get a Toro..."

"No, we ripped out the lawn and put in a rock garden. Nice smooth stones, little bonsai trees. The neighbors freaked. They actually had a block meeting – we're getting the silent treatment right now. It's pretty funny."

I laughed again, remembering the apartment he had had in grad school. Two basement rooms in the shadow of a larger building, so there was never any sun. It was on Telegraph, right next door to a martial arts school. All day long you heard the screams, the sound of bodies slamming into the mats.

"You're at Los Alamos, right?" he asked. "I remember you had a few offers..."

"Yeah, an applied math group. Algorithm development for Navier-Stokes equations. Projection methods with some new wrinkles. We do special, um – stuff – for the nonlinear advective terms."

"Stuff?"

"Stuff. It's a technical term. Unbelievable resolution. We're just starting to get some recognition out in the community, but that's kind of a mixed thing. Remember Olaf?"

He laughed. "Who ever forgets Olaf? I haven't seen him since that asymptotics seminar. How's he doing?"

"I think he was about to get arrested for impersonating a scientist, so they made him a bureaucrat. N.D.A."

"N.D.A.?"

"Nuclear Deterrence Agency. He saw a simulation I did of convection cells in storm clouds and got a tent in his pants you wouldn't believe. Wanted to see if I could adapt it to fireball rise, dust entrainment, that sort of thing."

"Jesus, that's some scary shit."

"Yeah, those loopy motherfuckers still think the Cold War's going on. I asked him if he wanted me to name the density array for the dust component Moscow or Kiev. 'Those are integer declarations,' he says. What an asshole."

"You gambling?" Darlene asked.

I nodded and she dealt out the cards. I got a seven and a four – a double down hand. Darlene was showing a six. I flipped my cards, added three chips to the three already up, and she gave me another card, tucking it face down under the pile of chips. I peeked under the edge – a seven. Still alive. Darlene flipped a jack, and dealt a four from the top of the deck. Twenty. She swept up my cards and chips in a single fluid motion, making a clucking sound with her tongue.

"Tough break," Dave said. "You gonna do the calculations?"

I shook my head.

"I don't know. He wants to give us a couple hundred K. We need the scratch to keep the other programs alive, but I don't like dealing with those people. I don't know."

"Funding's pretty tight right now."

"Yeah, same old same old. It's like every couple of years you pick up an ant farm, shake it up, and put it back down again. Everybody's running around wondering what's going to get cut out from under them next. The level of cynicism is pretty high."

Darlene dealt me a jack and a ten. I showed it to Dave and elbowed him in the ribs. She dealt herself a king and flipped her hole card. Ace. "God damn it," I said. Darlene shook her head, smiling.

"You're not very good at this," Dave said.

"I was doing fine until you showed up..."

"You were talking about a level of cynicism," he said, smiling.

"Oh, yeah," I said. "It's especially funky in Comp Physics. We sort of do a dual function. One is leading edge research, blue sky stuff, that's my group. The other is, um – service – to the other divisions. If you'll pardon the expression."

"Maintaining bomb codes."

"Very astute. So things could go one of two ways in the next few years. Get some people with vision and courage, aggressively pursue outside funding, and start to shift the primary focus of the labs away from the military-industrial circle jerk..."

"...or you can bend over and hand the bomb geeks a jar of Vaseline."

"Exactly."

A couple of other players sat down. Darlene made change and started shuffling up a new deck.

"You talking or gambling?" she asked me again. "Drive it or park it." She was smiling, her tone not unfriendly.

"Talking, I guess." I gathered up my chips. "Take it easy, Darlene."

"C'mon, deal already," one of the players said. "You're gonna wear off the numbers." The smile disappeared and she went back to work.

"You still play golf?" Dave asked me.

"Jesus, not for a long time. Why?"

"You're not gonna believe this. Follow me."

We made our way through the maze of slot machines and gambling tables. There was an atmosphere of barely controlled pandemonium in the place – flashing lights, ringing bells, a constant murmur of voices, shouts raised in victory and disappointment. At the far end of the casino stood a hologram of Barry Manilow, fifteen feet high, grinning like a fool. There was probably enough collagen in his face to smooth out the Himalayas. Marquee-style wraparound lettering floated in a circle above his head, like a halo, announcing show times. "Persistent vegetative state," I muttered.

"Huh?"

"It's a medical term..." I said. "Never mind."

He shrugged his shoulders. "You see any good talks yet?" he asked.

"Not really," I said. "The abstracts are supposed to be refereed but that's kind of a joke. This is really a schmoozing conference for me anyway, see who's doing what, find out where the bodies are buried. Besides, it really cuts into the gambling."

Just ahead, a fat woman in a purple wig and a shapeless green polyester shift began screaming. A river of plastic Nixon dollars poured from the snout of the slot machine in front of her and she jammed a cardboard bucket underneath it to catch the flow.

"You're giving one tomorrow, aren't you?" Dave asked, raising his voice above the din. "I thought I saw your name on the program."

"Yeah, but I can't go to it," I shouted back.

"What?" Dave asked

I shook my head. "It's in a classified session and my clearance hasn't come through yet."

He chuckled. "I'll let you know how it turns out," he said.

"I appreciate that."

I turned to look at the woman as we walked past. The flow of dollars had stopped. She leaned against the machine, panting, her arms wrapped around its black, shiny sides. Twin patches of red stood out on her cheeks. I looked at her eyes and I had to look away.

We took an escalator downstairs, walked past a bowling alley and an arcade of cheesy little boutiques, rounded a corner, and there it was. BALLY'S RENO VIRTUAL GOLF, the sign read.

"You gotta be kidding," I said.

"No," he said. "This is great. I played yesterday."

We went inside. There were about ten wide booths, equally spaced around the perimeter of the room. The far end of each booth consisted of a screen, onto which was projected from the rear a picture of a lush, green fairway. Half of the booths were occupied and most of the people were dressed for golf – baggy purple, blue, or salmon trousers, polyester knit shirts. They wore large, bulky helmets that covered their heads entirely. Wires trailed from the helmets to a console on the wall of the booth. They stood on raggy patches of astro-turf, slamming golf balls into the screens. I walked over and stood behind one of the booths. The guy was just teeing off. He assumed the position, shifted his weight, wiggled his hips once, and swung. He connected nicely; the ball hit the canvas with a solid slap and fell to the floor. He just stood there. I could see the movement of his headgear tracing the trajectory of an imaginary golf ball. Suddenly, he stomped his foot. "Shit!" he said, his voice muffled by the helmet.

"There's something vaguely auto-erotic about this," I said to Dave.

"Whatever you say, Dan. You wanna try it?"

"Sure..."

We walked over to the "Pro Shop," a counter manned by a pimply-faced adolescent in a 'Bally's Reno Virtual Golf' sweatshirt. There were more shirts on the wall behind him, in a sort of semaphore-sign display, and an assortment of golf clubs, woods and irons arranged in overlapping fans.

"Set us up," I said.

"Okay, you want Spyglass Hill, Pebble Beach, or Cypress Creek?"

I looked at Dave and shrugged.

"I don't know," I said. "Pebble Beach, I guess."

"Good choice," the kid said. "That's our best course."

I thought he was trying to be funny, but he wasn't smiling. He gave us a set of clubs, a bucket of balls, and led us to an empty booth. He made an elaborate show of logging in to the console

"You ever do this before?" he asked.

"I played Spyglass Hill yesterday," Dave said.

"Okay, so you know what to do. Good luck."

"Wait a minute," I said. "This is all simulation, right?"

The kid nodded, looking at me suspiciously.

"Then what's with the balls and clubs? Why bother?"

The kid took a deep breath and closed his eyes.

"The – uh – kinesthetic experience is enhanced by the – uh – "

It was a stock answer and the kid clearly hadn't learned his lines. Imagine President Quayle lecturing on quantum field theory. I patted him on the shoulder. "Never mind," I said. "Don't worry about it."

He looked relieved. He placed the helmet on Dave's head and flicked a couple of toggle switches on its side. Then he did me. I closed my eyes as he lowered the helmet over my head.

I opened my eyes and I was…there. The illusion was perfect. The emerald green of the fairway was so bright it seemed to fluoresce in the mid-day sun. A few lazy clouds drifted across a sky of brilliant blue. Off to the right, the fairway was bounded by a sheer drop to the ocean. A seagull skimmed above the surf and I could hear its sharp, distant call. I looked over at Dave. He was wearing baggy orange trousers and a lime-green polo shirt. His eyes were shaded by a blue visor the size of a Frisbee.

"Nice outfit," I said.

"You should take a look at yourself," he said. I looked down. Plaid knickers. Argyle socks. Black and white wingtips. Christ on rollerskates.

The first hole was a par four, dogleg left. Ocean to the right of the fairway and dense woods all along the other side. Dave went first. He made it look easy. With a graceful, unhurried swing, he sent the simulacrum golf ball sailing into the clear blue. A display flashed in the lower right corner of my field of vision. Two-sixty out and ten to the left of center. Not bad.

I hadn't even *thought* about golf for over five years, but my body seemed to remember. I walked up to the tee and took my stance. I took a deep breath and closed my eyes for a minute, trying to concentrate and relax at the same time. I opened them in time to see a large seagull swoop down and pick the golf ball off the tee in its curved, yellow beak. It headed straight as an arrow down the middle of the fairway and dropped the ball about two hundred fifty yards out.

Dave looked at me with a disgusted expression on his face. "Will you quit fucking around and play golf?" he said.

"Jesus, did I do that?" I asked. "Sorry."

"This system is very literal-minded," he said. "If you don't concentrate, it translates small, involuntary movements of the muscles in your face and neck into visual imagery." He frowned. "They're doing research on just how all that connects with your unconscious. I'm skeptical about that, but it can be pretty trippy sometimes. Anyway, I'll let you have this one. Call it a mulligan." He snapped his fingers and we were out in the middle of the fairway next to our tee shots. "You're away," he said.

"Wow," I said, looking around. "Beats walking."

We were about a hundred and fifty yards out from the green. I selected a six iron, walked up to the ball, exhaled, wiggled my hips and let fly. The heel of the club caught the ball a glancing blow and it spun off into the woods. The readout displayed 110 YARDS 60 LEFT – IN THE ROUGH. The last phrase flashed on and off at about two beats per second.

"Fuck me," I said. "Fuck my dog."

Dave looked over at me like he wanted to say something.

I sighed. "I know, I know. Keep my head down. Left arm straight."

He shook his head. "I don't know," he said. "I just never would've thought you'd wind up at a shop like Los Alamos."

I paused for a minute, mentally shifting gears. I had a sharp sense of dislocation, like I had suddenly lost all points of reference. Was this conversation real? Where was I? I looked around at the bright green fairway, felt the breeze from the ocean ruffle my hair, smelled the salt tang it brought.

What the hell, I thought. "I know what you mean," I said finally, nodding. "Trying to do mainstream science at the national labs can be pretty weird. It's not clear if we serve as a moderating influence to balance the weapons programs, or if we just legitimize that stuff by setting a good P.R. example." I shook my head. "There's an interesting sociology between the two factions, though. We think the weapons people are amoral scum and not particularly bright and they think we're dilettantes and parasites."

"You're probably both right," he said, smiling.

"Thanks a lot," I said. "We've got a good group, though, and we're doing some of the sexiest stuff that's being done in computational physics *anywhere*. I don't know if the work would exist without the infrastructure of the labs, and the work's just too important. It goes way beyond what piss-ant little bean counters like Olaf have in mind."

A cloud passed in front of the sun and I shivered with the sudden chill.

"Meanwhile, you have to sleep at night," he said.

"Yeah, that's it. You try to call things case by case and keep good boundaries. Hughes gets a lot of military contracts. What do *you* do?"

"Well, my situation is kind of like yours. My group does spacecraft design, thermal analysis. Recon satellites mostly, so the applications cut both ways."

"Malignant and benign."

"Yeah. So what do you do? I don't know...you do the right thing."

As we were talking he had been sizing up his shot. He pulled back the club and swung. There was the whoosh of displaced air, the soft click of compression and release as the club met the ball and followed through.

"You're pretty good at this."

"Yeah, well..."

"Hey, how did you do that before – "

"You mean this?" He snapped his fingers and we were in the woods. "You're away," he said. My ball lay on a soft carpet of pine needles. The sun made a stippled pattern of gold and shadow through the trees.

"Jesus Christ, I'm in Sherwood Forest. Where's the green?"

"Just off to the right there through the trees. See the flag?"

I could just make out a tiny flash of red where he was pointing.

"I'm gonna have to chip out onto the fairway..."

"No, just blast right through. The simulation's pretty stupid about trees. You'll be fine."

I approached the ball, breathed in slowly, then out, pulled the club back, and swung, remembering to keep my head down and follow through. I missed it completely.

"Nice practice swing," Dave said.

"Thanks a lot, shithead. Shut up and let me concentrate."

"It's a Zen kind of thing, Dan. Be the ball."

*

When I got back to my room, there was a message on the vidphone. Short, not particularly sweet. "Dan, Olaf. Call me." There was no visual.

That was pretty much his style. He was a strange one, all right. Second-generation Soviet émigré. Not a great physicist, but he had the political acumen of a barracuda and he rose quickly in the ranks of the D.O.D. techno-sleazeball food chain. He was always into something murky, the kind of guy you figured must have racked up a lot of Frequent Flyer miles on Southern Air Transport during the 80's. It was rumored that he once gave an AK-47 to a colleague as a wedding present.

I knew what he wanted. He still had a hard-on for my codes and lots more taxpayer dollars than he knew what to do with. And he loved explosions. Particularly thermonuclear explosions. Since he couldn't make them for real any more, not even underground since the Comprehensive Test Ban went into effect, he figured simulation was the next best thing.

I didn't want to deal with him just then. I patched my palmtop to the vidphone, got a pipe open to the Cube at Los Alamos, and tried to get some work done. I was studying the eigenvalue spectrum of the Taylor-Goldstein equation, trying to develop a new methodology for examining the stability of a particular class of fluid flows. An eigenvalue is a number that tells you something about how a system responds when you disturb its equilibrium. The discretized Taylor-Goldstein system yields hundreds of them, only one of which corresponded to the situation of interest.

Eigenvalue spectrum. Taylor-Goldstein equation. I said the words aloud, feeling their shape and weight on my tongue. It felt important to contextualize them somehow, to give them meaning and substance apart from abstract self-consistency. It is a political act, the naming of a thing.

The work went poorly; I was just skating on the surface of the mathematics, blind to the wholeness of it. I kept making stupid mistakes that got through the compiler somehow and showed up at run time as mysterious error messages. After two hours I decided to bag it, logged off, and went to bed.

*

I woke up early the next morning and went down to the breakfast buffet. The casino was still open, of course, but it was nearly empty, and without the white-noise background sound of human voices and the random Brownian-like movement of bodies crowded around the gambling tables, the glitz seemed hollow and frayed around the edges. As I walked past the blackjack tables I noticed that there were worn spots in the carpet, and the ad-holos had a high-frequency flicker that hurt my eyes.

I entered the buffet room and loaded up my plate with fruit, avoiding the steam table trays of pressed soybacon and stacks of leathery flapjacks. I found a table off in the corner of the room. I didn't want to talk to anybody. The previous day's conversation with Dave was playing itself over in my head, and the call from Olaf was sitting on my consciousness like a weight. I felt like I needed some quiet time to let it all percolate. So I sat there, sipping weak coffee and nibbling on pieces of melon, watching the room fill up as the conference attendees drifted down from their rooms. I saw a few people I knew, but just nodded, and nobody came to join me.

If I was expecting some sort of revelation, I was disappointed. I couldn't concentrate on anything for very long. My mind drifted to the talk I was supposed to give later that day, skittered over to a new card-counting strategy I had simulated on my palmtop but hadn't tried yet in the casino. Before I knew it, it was time to hit the sessions. The first one I planned to attend was called "Physics of High-Temperature Hydrodynamics."

When I got to the auditorium the session was just starting. There was a man standing at the podium in front of the room. He looked vaguely familiar, and I realized I had seen him on television on several occasions – a famous astrophysicist. He also enjoyed, I recalled, a somewhat less public career as one of the country's leading designers of advanced thermonuclear devices. He was a few years older than me and seemed to have a relaxed, accessible air about him. I could imagine him working in his garage, playing with his children, taking long, quiet walks with his wife. He went through some preliminaries and began the lecture.

"Let's start with a model problem. We have a block of aluminum, room temperature, and we suddenly raise its energy to two kilovolts by some nearby... um... event."

176

There was a chorus of laughter from the audience. I did a quick mental calculation and realized that this corresponded to temperatures one might find in the interior of the sun.

"So what happens? First of all, before we go any farther, let me just say, particularly for those of you without security clearances, that this in no way corresponds to any specific... um... *scenario*. This is strictly an academic exercise. So what happens?"

There was another chorus of laughter, and people began calling out answers.

"It explodes!"

"It melts!"

"No, it vaporizes!"

"It gets gobbled up by rarefaction waves!"

The speaker was delighted.

"Who said that? Good. *Excellent.* It gets eaten away from all sides by rarefaction waves."

He paused for a moment and looked around the auditorium.

"This is a beautiful problem," he said. "A *beautiful* problem. And what makes it beautiful is this. It has... "

He paused again. The room was quiet.

"...an *exact solution.*"

My head was spinning. Suddenly, the air in the room felt too thick to breathe. I got up, knocking over the chair in front of me. The speaker paused and looked at me, his face expressionless. I could see heads in the audience turning towards me. I made my way to the aisle and walked quickly out of the room. About thirty seconds passed before I realized that I had been holding my breath. I stopped and leaned against a post, inhaled deeply, exhaled. I felt numb and shaken, and in some way I didn't quite understand yet, deeply ashamed.

In front of me, next to the roulette table, a holo-loop of a busty blonde woman in a see-through cocktail dress smiled and held out her hand in a beckoning gesture. It was a short loop, only about three seconds, and the mechanical repetition of the movement seemed jerky and grotesque. I noticed one of the pit bosses giving me the hairy eyeball and I began to walk.

I'd like to say that I hit some kind of moral high ground then and there, that I made a Commitment to Truth and World Peace, but it wasn't like that at all. I just walked. After a while I found myself in front of BALLY'S RENO VIRTUAL GOLF. I didn't feel much like swinging a golf club, but the idea of being out in the sun and resting my eyes on the spartan beauty of the California coast was very appealing. The same kid was sitting behind the counter and I nodded to him. He didn't bother with the rap this time, but led me to an empty booth and set me up. I closed my eyes, put the helmet on my head, and flicked the toggle switch.

It was the same place all right – I recognized the curving slope of the fairway and the steep dropoff to the ocean. But it was dark this time, a twilight so thick and purple it appeared almost luminous. Fat, greasy drops of black rain fell from a low, menacing overcast, and there was a sullen, red glow flickering on the bottom of the clouds off to the north. The cold wind ripping in off the ocean brought with it not only the smell of salt but something else, a sickly sweet miasma that made my gullet clench. *Death*, I thought. I don't know how I knew that, but I knew that it was true.

There was a squawk overhead, and a flapping sound, and a large seagull landed heavily at my feet. The feathers on one side of its body were singed and blackened, and there were open sores showing through. Its eye on the burned side was an oozing wrinkle of raw flesh. It lay there in the wet grass, twitching feebly and flapping its wings.

I have to get out of here, I thought. I reached up to the side of my head and found the toggle switch, felt that peculiar sense of dislocation, like I was straddling a fence between two worlds. I pulled the switch. The rain-veiled twilight coast collapsed to a thin wavering line that curved around my entire field of vision and disappeared. The roar of wind and ocean faded to a hollow, velvet absence of sound. I pulled the helmet off and staggered up to the counter. The kid said something but it didn't register. I handed him the helmet and stumbled out into the corridor.

The next thing I knew I was in my room, sitting at my desk. I still have no memory of how I got there. My heart was pounding in my chest. I felt like I had been running all morning. It was time to stop. My hand hovered over the vidphone keypad, and the flat grey screen seemed to suck all the light from the room into itself. Almost of their own volition, my fingers punched out the code. In a few seconds, Olaf's face appeared on the screen. He smiled when he saw me, and in that instant I could see with incandescent clarity, held within the lines of his craggy, Slavic face, the soft, vulnerable features of a child. There was a sudden tightness in my mouth and throat, and for a moment, I could not speak.

Echo Beach

It's always the last day of the world at Echo Beach. From fifteen miles up, the horizon is visibly bowed. The sun hangs swollen above an oily sea. The coastal range ripples up from the water's edge, bunching together in wattles like the neck of a lizard. Scintilla flash from the ruins of a port city half engulfed.

The lounge is quiet, but it will start filling up soon. At a table in the middle of the room, an old man plays chess with an automaton. Every now and then, he reaches across the table and slaps the thing on the side of its metal head.

Near one of the large windows, a lanky, barrel-chested man drinks alone. Coal black skin, melanin-enhanced, tangle of blonde dreads. Circa 22C, a mod from one of the Martian arcologies. Clearly pre-Plague. Close enough to home for me that I want to say something to him, warn him. But what could I say?

A couple sits at the bar leaning toward one another, their heads touching. It's difficult to say whether they are accelerated canines or regressed humans, but there is something very dog-like in their focused attention to one another. An aura of benign stupidity hangs about them like sweet incense.

The digital clock above the holo fireplace reads 4:22:00. As I watch, the numbers dissolve and re-form: 4:21:59.

I check my console, pour a shot of absinthe and a pony of pomegranate juice, set them on a tray, and send it floating toward the Martian.

I walk down the length of the bar to the couple.

"Get you anything else?"

The man looks up at me with watery eyes.

"No, thank you," he says.

"I don't think so," the woman says at the same time. They look at each other and bark soft laughter. They lean their heads together again.

I decide to leave the old man and the bot alone. As I turn my back I hear a thump as he smacks it again.

I wipe down the bar, check my stock. Vodka from Ganymede, gin from Hotpoint, malts from Scotland. *Scotland.* I remember jagged green hills, black rock thrusting into a gray sky, mounds of rubble dotting a fractal coastline testament to the mercurial nature of power. I stood amidst the ruins of the Castle Duncan as a piper wailed defiance and loss to the cradle of the ocean. There was a small suitcase open in front of him. Tourists threw coins.

I wonder if there's anything left of Scotland now, here at the end of Time. It's a stupid thought, of course. The continents have shifted, the seas have climbed and receded a dozen times. North America is an archipelago stretching from pole to equator; Fiji is the leading edge of a megacontinent; the treasures of continental Europe lie beneath a cold, green sea.

The world-face changes, the abstract constructions of Man linger ghostlike. If I were to travel to the global coordinates occupied by Castle Duncan circa 20C, could I still hear the echoes of pipes in the salt air? Does Gaia remember?

The Gate hums quietly. Laughter echoes up from the Foyer. Heads emerge from the spiral staircase set in the floor at the far end of the lounge away from the windows. Party of four; two men, two women. Definitely post-Diaspora; I can't place them on the Continuum. Definitely wealthy. They wear their entitlement like a badge.

One of them men catches sight of me, nudges his companions, and they all drift in my direction.

He says something to me in a liquid trill. A voice whispers in my ear: *Give us your best table.*

Arrogant bastard. I gesture at the nearly empty room.

"Have your finest pleasure," I say, hoping that the odd phrasing will confuse his chip.

He gives me a strange look and gestures his companions toward the windows. They are selectively polarized; you can look directly at the sun's disk. Structures writhe across its face. Precursor flares erupt like Medusa tangles from its troubled edge.

After a few minutes they sit down. I pretend to be busy with something behind the bar. The man clears his throat several times, finally gestures me over.

I grab a very dirty rag from the bin under the bar and carry it conspicuously as I walk over to them. I wipe down their table, leaving a greasy film.

"What can I get for you?" I ask. His companions ignore me.

His voice is water running over smooth stones. There is a sibilant whisper in my ear.

Do you have beer?

Moron. This is a bar, for Christ's sake.

"Beer. Let me think." I cup my chin in my fist, scratch my head. "I don't ... no, wait. *Beer.* Yes, I think so. Four beers?"

"You're very rude," the man says, in halting System Anglo.

"It's the end of the world, Holmes. You can sue me."

I go back to the bar, pour a pitcher and set it on a tray with four glasses. I send it toward them a little too quickly and a foamy tongue spills down the side of the pitcher.

The Gate hums again. It's almost inaudible, a subsonic rumble I feel in my feet. Business is picking up. The clock reads 3:37.

By 1:30 Echo Beach is packed. Ice-miners from the Belt, circa 24C, very heavy drinkers. A clutch of avian poets from Deneb IV, post-Diaspora. An accelerated goat with a bell around his neck. He doesn't *smell* accelerated. Even though the place is S.R.O., there are empty seats on either side of him at the bar. He's guzzling buttermilk and eating pickled onions like jelly beans.

It's almost time for a visit from the Lhosa. I send a couple of bus trays weaving between the tables and wipe down the bar. Everything looks pretty good. At 1:05, the air next to me crackles like old paper and a humaniform outline begins to gather substance.

But it doesn't quite coalesce. It never does. The Lhosa projects in as a hologram from some other place and time. Never in person, never via the Gate. Its manifestation is always a translucent cartoon-like rendering of a 20C Hollywood B.E.M. – bulbous forehead cradled by a delicate tracery of bone, veiny tributaries branching beneath the skin. Huge eyes, black pupils surrounded by bloody sclera. It's wearing a jumpsuit with thin, pointy lapels. An elaborate raygun hangs holstered at its side.

I suspect that its appearance in this form is a concession to my kitschy 20C notion of alienness. I have no idea what the Lhosa actually looks like, whether it is a singular entity of unimaginable power, a representative of a vastly superior race of beings, or the fin-de-monde equivalent of a street punk working a three card Monty hustle on Lenox Avenue.

"How's business?" it asks. Its voice is a raspy white-noise hiss, like a radio between stations.

I gesture at the crowded room. "The place is hoppin.'"

"Good. Good." A pulse throbs in its domed forehead.

What the Lhosa means by 'business' is by no means clear to me. Customers come and go by a pre-arrangement from which I am excluded. No currency changes hands at Echo Beach; indeed, here at the nexus of centuries of recorded time and millennia unrecorded the very notion of currency has long ago crumbled to dust.

We stand there together for a moment without speaking, a twentieth century human and a cartoonish holographic chimera, behind a battered rosewood bar in a structure that looks like an inverted kitchen whisk suspended by invisible forces fifteen miles above the doomed Earth

"I'll be going, then," the Lhosa says.

"Later," I say, but the alien is already gone, leaving behind a faint whiff of ozone – an olfactory Cheshire smile.

I wonder if he has other stops to make, if Echo Beach is an instance of some kind of franchise operation, hundreds of McRagnaroks stacked a microsecond apart here at the end of Time.

God, what hubris. What solipsism. It's hardly the end of Time. Just another planet recycling its heavy elements back into the corpus of the mother star. By a Cosmic metric, not that big a deal.

1:02. In two minutes, the stasis field will kick in. Nobody gets in or out after that. Already, I know, an invisible sleet of heavy particles batters against the walls and windows, a precursor to the main event. The integrity of the structure itself is sufficient to deal with that. But when the nova front washes over us, boiling away the seas and stripping the gauzy film of atmosphere from Gaia's tired body, we want to be in stasis. Oh, yes. We want to be in stasis.

With fifteen seconds to go, the Gate hums again. A young woman, dressed in black and silver, bright white hair cropped close.

She orders a whiskey, neat, walks with it to the windows. There's something about the way she carries herself that catches my eye, something that sets her apart from the usual run of sensation-starved Apocalypse hags that converge to this place like flies to the warm scent of Death.

0:58:00. Nothing appears changed, but we are now ensconced in the stasis field, kicked back a microsecond down the Continuum. Nothing can hurt us now, not even, ha-ha, a nova.

The crowd is getting loud and stupid and I'm scrambling to keep up with the drink orders. My eyes keep returning to the young woman. She stands there sipping her whiskey, gazing out the window and occasionally looking around the room with a slightly bemused expression on her face.

At around 05:00, the crowd starts to quiet down. People are sliding chairs and tables over toward the windows. The floor is tiered, so everybody gets a view. By 02:00, there's hardly a sound in the place except the rhythmic sighs of a hundred people breathing. Someone says something about toasting marshmallows, eliciting a weak ripple of laughter.

At 00:30, tension fills the air like smoke from an electrical fire. The silence hums. At ten seconds, somebody starts a countdown. By the time we're down to six, everybody in the room is chanting along, a dozen different languages braiding together in a rich Babel.

Five!
The dog couple look toward the windows, holding hands tightly.
Four!
The Martian sprawls across the table, head buried in his forearms.
Three!
The young woman looks around the room, catches my eye. She lifts her drink toward me in salute.
Two!
In spite of myself, I am chanting along with the crowd. My knuckles are white on the edge of the bar.

One!

The chess playing bot is staring straight ahead. Its compound eyes glitter in the light of the dying sun. The old man's king lies on its side, defeated.

The sun brightens and swells. Its surface is a scrabbled patchwork of bright honeycomb-like cells. Flares lick out from its edge. It seems to grow in slow motion, inflating like a balloon.

It's like standing in front of firing squad. You hear the crack of gunfire, see the puff of smoke from the rifles. The hail of bullets hangs in the air, moving toward you just below the threshold of perception, like the hands of a clock.

Conversation begins to pick up again. I take a few drink orders, but the crowd is subdued. Looking out at the spreading fire in the sky. Wondering why they came. The sun fills a quarter of the sky. I take advantage of the crowd's preoccupation to send out four busing trays. Spidery mechanical arms pluck empty glasses from crowded tables.

The Martian has awakened and he begins to cry in blubbering, alcoholic gasps. People move away, leaving him in the center of a small circle of emptiness.

The young woman steps into the circle, puts her hand on the top of his head. It seems to calm him. He takes her hand and holds it to his cheek.

The sun fills half the sky. The room is again silent. A few people crane their necks to make out details of the ruined city below. Fingers of ocean stretch across a sprawling geometric grid, the hard Cartesian lines blurred by time.

The shock front is almost upon us. It fills the sky, a wall of bright, hexagonal cells of light. Structures writhe within the cells; each of them could swallow Earth whole. Indeed, one of them will.

The ocean bursts into steam, obscuring the surface of the planet. In the blink of an eye, we are engulfed in flame.

It just stays like that, nothing out there but bright light subdued to a uniform gray by the window's polarization. Every now and then, an inhomogeneity ripples past, sending a corresponding ripple of comment through the crowd, but soon they lose interest. Conversation picks up again.

I love this part. The timing is crucial. You want to nail them just when the edge of novelty's worn off, just when they think the show's over.

The post-Diaspora fellow I'd had words with raises his hand in the air and snaps his fingers, calling to me in a high, melodic voice. Whisper in my ear. *Bartender, I —*

I reach down under the bar and press the button. The entire station lurches and the bottom drops out of my stomach.

The transition is abrupt and complete. A moment ago, surrounded by the healing light of Apocalypse. Now, the sun hangs low over an oily sea. Streamers of cloud dusted with gold hug the land. The sky segues from light blue at the bowed horizon to deep blue-black overhead.

The crowd lets out a collective gasp. The clock over the holo fireplace reads 24:00:00. Someone starts to applaud and it catches like wildfire. The room fills with the sound of hands clapping together. Relief and regeneration! Alleviation and ease! The applause dies, conversation swells. In twos and threes the crowd drifts down to the Foyer. Some of them thank me on the way out, as if I were the architect of their deliverance. Of course, snapback would activate automatically if I didn't do anything. I smile and say nothing.

The Gate hums beneath my feet, scattering satisfied customers back to their appointed places on the Continuum. Soon the room is almost empty, just the young woman, the Martian, and the avian poets. The poets get up from their table and head toward the stairs. I wipe down the bar, re-stock, run a load of glasses through the dishwasher. The smell of bile tickles the air and I notice that someone has left a discreet puddle of vomit underneath a table near the holo fireplace. I go into the stockroom behind the bar for cleaning supplies. When I return the woman and the Martian are gone. Beneath, my feet, the Gate hums one last time.

I complete my tasks and retire to my quarters adjacent to the Foyer – bedroom, living room, a small gym, a kitchenette with a well-stocked pantry. And my library, thousands of recordings in a dozen different media. It's something of a fetish of mine. I have disks and DATS, video and vinyl, beads, books, and baryon resonance chips. Playback devices occupy an entire wall of my living room. But today nothing catches my interest.

I undress and stand beneath the shower for a long time, letting the needle-spray of water beat against my head and neck. When I feel sufficiently empty of thought, I dry myself off, stagger into the bedroom, and throw myself onto the unmade bed.

I was hiking in Nepal, following the faint signature of a path as it hugged the edge of a mountain. To my left, a wall of rock, anchored deep within the Earth and rising far above me. The mountain seemed so massive that for a moment I imagined gravity turned sideways, the stony face of the cliff pulling me toward itself. To my right was ... nothing; the cyan sky, the mosaic of browns and grays merging in distance haze were like the backdrop of an empty diorama.

I negotiated a particularly difficult section of path. My pack felt awkward and off-balance and I was hugging the cold rock wall. Suddenly, I heard a sound that didn't belong at twelve thousand feet – old paper crackling together. (How familiar that sound is now!) The air in front of me shimmered and sparked. Bright vertical lines winked in and out of existence. The sparks and lines coalesced into a humanoid shape. Bulbous brain-case in a veiny cradle, huge bloodshot eyes. I could see the jagged horizon through its white, narrow-lapelled lab coat.

"I am the Lhosa," it said in a buzzing voice.

Oh man, I thought. Trouble, I'm in trouble up here. Oxygen deprivation, altitude sickness, hallucinating, got to stop and take it easy. But I knew what altitude sickness felt like, and I didn't have any of the other symptoms. No nausea, no weakness. I'd been feeling pretty good, actually.

"And I'm the Walrus," I said. "Fuck off."

"In five steps, your foot is going to slip and you will fall nineteen hundred feet to your death."

"Yeah, right." I couldn't believe I was actually arguing with a hallucination. I took a step forward. The Lhosa held its hand out, palm toward me.

"Stop. Please."

Please? That got me. A polite mirage. I stopped and waited.

"Do you want a job?" it asked.

I didn't need a job. I'd just sold my software company, Treadwater Business Solutions, to Microsoft for four million dollars. Petty cash for them, but it set me up for life. I was taking the vacation I'd always dreamed of. But what the hell, I thought. Play along. See what happens.

"What kind of job?"

"In approximately six hundred million years, your sun is going to go nova. We provide an opportunity for students, theologians, and the curious to view the – "

"Wait a minute. Old Sol is an uninteresting, middle-aged, main sequence star, right? It's got at least a couple of billion years left."

The Lhosa shrugged. It seemed vaguely annoyed that I'd interrupted its pitch.

"These things happen. We provide an opportunity for visitors to view the spectacle from within the safety of a temporal stasis field. The facility is largely automated, but the client interface requires intelligent presence."

Client interface. That sounded like greasing the public to me.

"So ... you want me to be some kind of P.R. flack for the end-of-the-world show?"

"A bartender, actually."

I did five years in food service before I got into the software business and transformed a time-wasting obsession into an honest living. Well, a living. For three of those years I managed a yuppie fern bar owned by the Vietnamese Mafia in Seattle. It had its moments, but by and large, it was not a time I looked back on fondly.

"I don't think so."

"Suit yourself."

The Lhosa didn't move so I walked through him. The hairs on the back of my neck stood on end and my skin felt cold. Electric specks swam before my eyes.

With a faint pop the Lhosa was gone.

I paused for a moment and looked around. The wind picked up, tugging at my jacket and whistling in my ears.

I shifted my pack and took a step forward. My foot slipped on some loose gravel. I reached out for support but there was nothing to grab onto, just the smooth rock wall. The blue dome of the sky spun about my head. I hung suspended on the edge of the path for what seemed like forever. My arms pinwheeled as I tried to shift my center of gravity back to safety, but it was hopeless.

It takes a long time to fall nineteen hundred feet, over ten seconds, and it's true what they say about your life passing before your eyes. I remembered the first girl I'd ever bedded, my thoughts a montage of skin and sweat and sighs. My parents, looking old and sad, sitting in the living room of the house I grew up in. My partner in Treadwater, who I'd screwed out of six hundred K in the buyout deal, on the deck of his sailboat, squinting into the sun.

It was as if I was in a bubble, sharing the close space with dozens of ghosts manifested from memory and it was the bubble that was rushing headlong toward the basalt floor of the valley, the bubble that would smash against the rock and release me to the shredding winds.

But in a desperate corner of my mind another voice scrabbled at the walls of reason. *No! No! No!*

Suddenly, my feet were resting on solid rock, the wind a feather's kiss on my cheeks. I opened my eyes.

The Lhosa stood before me on the path. Bright vertical lines flickered within its image, accompanied by bursts of static. The jagged horizon, visible through its chest, bisected the world.

"What do you say?" it asked.

I wake up groggy, with a coat of fur on my tongue and a sharp pain in the middle of my forehead that reminds me of a hangover, although I rarely drink. I make a pot of coffee and put on an Eric Dolphy bead. I de-polarize the window and the golden dawn of Earth's final day fills the room with light.

I feel restless. I've been reading Proust but I keep losing my place; the book rests face down on my sofa, a crippled bird with outstretched wings. I can't bring myself to start sifting through it again.

My mind keeps returning to the young woman in the lounge. I don't think I'll ever see her again – there isn't a lot of repeat business at Echo Beach.

But there was something about her that I can't shake. Maybe it was the way she comforted the Martian while everyone else was acting as if sodden grief were a communicable illness. I imagine us talking intimately together in quiet tones, perhaps sharing a glass of wine. She stays after snapback and we return to my quarters together, dim the windows, and make love for hours.

My loneliness here is usually something apart from me, a bright-eyed rodent with sleek greasy fur and needle-like teeth that comes out to nibble at the corners of the furniture when all the lights are out. But suddenly, now, it is almost more than I can bear. I consider for the thousandth time the alternative path I could have taken. A very short path – a few more seconds of free-fall, a bright flash of pain, then nothing. It doesn't seem so bad.

I put on more Dolphy, his "Last Date" recording, strip down to my shorts, and go to the gym. I cycle through my repertoire of mechanical torture, rushing headlong toward nowhere on treadmill, stationary bike, rowing machine. Then I work through the freeweights – pecs, lats, biceps. By the time I'm done I'm drenched with sweat but I've pushed back the borders of that darkness a bit.

I doze. I make a feeble attempt at the Proust, doze some more. At around six, I head into the Foyer and take a look around. The Gate itself, an oblong puddle of pearly phosphorescence that the eye slides across like oil on glass. It hurts to look at it directly, not an acute physical pain but a sense of 'wrongness.' You start seeing things in that glowing blob of nothing, motion strange and quick.

Machines surround the Gate, gunmetal gray with readouts glowing in the skin of the metal itself, captioned in a looping script unknown to me. The machinery has a decidedly deco look to it and I wonder if it isn't window dressing. Like the appearance of the Lhosa, its alienness has a comforting familiarity.

Next to the spiral staircase leading up to the Lounge, a guest book bound in white leather rests on a marble table. I open it up and look over the entries from the previous day.

Lia. 23C, Ceres. The same era, roughly, as the Martian. I wonder if she went home with him.

I go upstairs. From this end of the Lounge opposite the windows, perspective gives the illusion of parallel lines converging toward infinity, floor and ceiling funneling the observer toward a distant focus.

I like this time. Quiet and fecund, like the hush that descends upon a Nebraska prairie before an electrical storm uncoils its fury.

I pour myself a club soda and walk to the windows. Gaia lies open below me, suppliant, the sea coppery-gold, the land in muted pastel. It's all so impossibly sad. I hate the Lhosa for this pointless exercise; I hate the wretched customers who flock to this place like paparazzi to a celebrity funeral; I hate myself for not having the courage to bow gracefully out of this life.

But what if Death is a singularity, a metaphysical black hole? As we approach its event horizon time takes greater and greater strides and our world-line stretches and groans under impossible tidal forces. If we ever reached it, we would encompass the Universe. If that is true, then in some sense I am still hurtling towards the basalt floor of the canyon, immortal and doomed.

The Gate hums.

Lia! But no, it is another clutch of avians from Deneb, four of them. They huddle together near the staircase, looking around and cooing nervously at one another. I let myself in behind the bar.

"Welcome to Echo Beach," I say. "Plenty of seats, no waiting. What can I get for you?"

One of them turns to me. Its eyes are large and black with no discernible pupils. Its round face is covered with downy feathers. Its mouth is a chitinous beak. It chirps at me and my chip whispers softly in my ear:

Our <friends> recommended this experience highly. Much ... pain.

Fucking parasites. Pain. I smile stiffly. "Yes. Sit anywhere you like." Maybe we'll get an accelerated feline or two this shift.

I put on a bead of early 21C industrial music – polyrhythmic loops of great machines tearing themselves apart. An unintelligible rap track weaves rage through the mechanical chaos. The avians don't like it much; their feathers are literally ruffled. I turn up the volume and pretend to be occupied at the bar.

Business begins to pick up. By two-thirty, the place is nearly full. I'm hustling trying to keep up with the orders and keep an eye on what my gut tells me is going to be trouble – two sheet-pale men from the Charon Habitat, circa 27C. They arrived separately, apparently as strangers, gravitated to one another, and started talking. They've been getting louder and louder and by this time they're screaming at each other. Their clipped accents are a little hard to understand, modulated to the threshold of unfamiliarity but not odd enough to kick in the chip. I can make out something about 'Parliament' and 'magma rights.'

Suddenly, there is a flurry of arms and feet and one of them is on the floor holding his windpipe and gasping for air. The other circles, ready to deliver a *coup de grace*. The crowd mills stupidly about.

I turn off the music, grab my stunner, and leap over the bar.

"That's enough," I say, holding the slim black tube in what I hope is a threatening manner.

The circling man stops, looks at me then down at the stunner, and nods sharply. He picks his drink up from a nearby table and walks away.

The other man is sitting up, still holding his throat but apparently unharmed.

"You two stay away from each other. I don't want to have to use this." I shake the stunner for emphasis and return to the bar. Music fills the room again; tension leaves the crowd like gas escaping from a balloon. The buzz of conversation swells.

"Very good," a female voice says.

I look up. It's her, it's Lia, and I can't help but smile.

"Hey." Stupidly, I pick up a rag and clutch it in my fist.

"I was here yesterday," she says.

"Yesterday, huh?"

Her eyebrows furrow, but her eyes are smiling. "Yes, well. Yesterday. Whatever that means."

"Same day, different cast of characters. Except for me. Most people don't come back."

She nods. I notice her ears, sculpted to small points. "I can see why," she says. "It's not a very nice place."

"Then what are you doing here?"

She bites her lower lip, looks off toward the sky-filled windows, looks back at me.

"Can I have a drink? A nice single-malt something, neat."

I pour the amber liquid into a glass and set it in front of her. She takes a sip.

"Do you ... *live* here?"

I nod. "Yeah."

"What a terrible job."

I nod again. "Yeah."

She takes another sip.

"You went home with the Martian?"

She nods. "I took him home."

My intention is to acknowledge her disclosure with a slight nod, a knowing tilt of the head. But something very different happens when I open my mouth.

"Ah," I say. "A mercy fuck."

She gives me a look that manages to be both withering and sad, sets her drink gently down on the bar in front of me, and walks to the end of the room and down the spiral stairs. The Gate hums.

Here at the end of everything, I'm still an idiot.

I go through the motions of tending bar, sending out bus trays, pouring drinks. All the while I'm playing the loop of conversation over and over again in my head. So thoroughly human, so typically stupid, to welcome the object of one's desire by sending her packing.

At 1:05, I hear the sound of crackling paper and the Lhosa begins to materialize next to me. I am filled with hatred and rage and I wish that just once it would fully coalesce into flesh and substance so I could wrap my hands around its pencil neck.

"How's business?" it asks.

"Business," I say. I look around the room. Heads bob in conversation; Babel hangs in the air like smoke. I turn back to the Lhosa. I want to ask it for the hundredth time: Why me? But that is a well worn path, the answer always the same, and I have long ago stopped asking. "You were available," it would say.

The doomed sky fills the windows.

"Business is good."

Another day, another Gotterdammerung. I clean up the Lounge, like I always do, and head downstairs to my quarters. Today, however, will be different. I print up enough 23C currency to give myself a jump start, and I stand looking at the gate, staring into that gray blob of pearly nothing. I fiddle with the controls, step back again, stare some more. I expect any second to hear that crackling paper sound, the Lhosa showing up like Marley's ghost, but it doesn't happen. I step forward.

It wasn't easy to carve out a life for myself on 23C Mars, but I made a few investments, bootstrapped a small financial consulting firm specializing in antiviral nanotech. Picking up the pieces after the Plague. I kept a low profile, never got too greedy. I did all right.

I looked for Lia, of course, but I had no way to find her, nothing to go on except the memory of her face, that last look of withering pity. Eventually, I gave up. I even stopped listening for the sound of crackling paper. Because I know why the Lhosa never tracked me down here, why it never brought me back.

It doesn't have to.

I'm still there, at the threshold of the Singularity, wiping tables and serving drinks. But that's someone else, caught in that Sisyphean loop of doom and rebirth, doom and rebirth, trapped. Someone else.

I've beaten the Lhosa. I've redeemed my old self. I'm never going back.

Last month, I purchased an automaton to help me around the house. In addition to its usual domestic routines, it has a strong chess program, but when playing the Sicilian Dragon it always falls for a very aggressive, risky Queenside rook sacrifice. Every time, the same stupid blunder. It is as if its ability to reason, to learn from its mistakes, has completely fled. I was so frustrated today, that I reached across the table and smacked it on the side of its head. There was a satisfying hollow sound. I did it again.

Lepidoptera

Peter discovered the open bag of flour on the top shelf of the pantry, pushed back behind a large can of kidney beans. It was infested with Indian meal moths, the little kind, with wings the color of old newspaper folded flat against their bodies.

That's where the little fuckers are coming from, he thought.

For weeks now he had noticed them, always three or four at a time, fluttering mindlessly near the light fixtures in the living room and kitchen. He figured it was some sort of seasonal thing. They seemed harmless enough.

He stared at the ten or twelve tiny, grayish insects crawling sluggishly along the folds of powdered plastic and across the surface of the flour. Through the sides of the bag he could see small, subtle motions, signatures of greater activity below.

My God, he thought, *there must be hundreds of them.*

As if on cue, one of the moths flew out of the open cabinet directly at his face. Instinctively, he reached out to try and catch it. It was ridiculously easy. He opened his fist and the moth was in the center of his palm, wings folded, undamaged. Its wings blurred and it lifted slowly toward his face. He grabbed it out of the air again. This time he rubbed his hand against the wall as he opened his fist. It left a grayish smear on the rose-patterned wallpaper. There was surprisingly little moisture.

He continued to stare at the bag for a good five minutes. The motion of the tiny insects, seemingly random yet full of purpose, had a calming effect. He couldn't take his eyes off them. Then, with a start, he realized he was going to be late for work. He collected his coat and hurried out the door. It wasn't until he was in the subway, rocking back and forth in the press of bodies, that he realized he was supposed to be disgusted, or at the very least, alarmed. But the typical New Yorker's fear of infestation was strangely absent. Instead he felt warm and centered, almost joyous.

Someone stepped on his foot and he looked up. The man smiled apologetically and mumbled something. He was in his forties, well dressed, and projected that combination of arrogant self-assurance and sheep-like stupidity that Peter associated with Reagan-era Republicans. *Probably a banker*, he thought.

Peter imagined himself reaching out and grabbing the man by the front of his coat, squeezing, feeling the soft material crumble away, revealing the soft, pulpy core.

"Excuse me," he mumbled.

The man smiled again and buried his face in the *Post*.

Peter was twenty minutes late to work. He could feel Swag's eyes on him as he walked across the floor of the machine shop. Shipping clerks were a dime a dozen, Swag was fond of reminding him. He tried to look small and inconspicuous as he punched in, and when Gabe called a greeting from behind the huge drill press, Peter pretended not to hear. He let himself into the plexiglass and sheet metal cubicle that served him for an office and breathed a sigh of relief as he sat down at his cluttered desk. From out of the corner of his eye, he could see Swag give him a final searching look and shake his head.

The work was dull and repetitive, and Peter found himself relaxing into the sameness of it. He let his mind wander. He thought of the moths in his kitchen cabinet, the bag of flour alive with motion. In his mind's eye, he saw the stirrings on the surface of the flour become more agitated. Soon it was a frenzy of motion. The bag burst and thousands of tiny moths flew in a single dark cloud into the kitchen. The swarm swooped back and forth in the small room and hovered next to the bare light bulb in the ceiling fixture. A handful of moths landed on the hot glass. Their tiny bodies shriveled and the kitchen was full with the sharp smell of their burning. A few more landed on the bodies of their brothers, then a few more, until the swarm hung from the fixture in a single draped sheet, like living, flickering cloth.

He realized suddenly that Swag was standing in front of him, his hands folded across his chest. A crumpled invoice protruded from one grubby fist like a bouquet. He shoved it under Peter's nose.

"What the hell is this?" he shouted. "You've been billing Northeastern Tool at the old rates for the last three months."

Peter opened his mouth, but no words came out.

"You're gonna have to get on the stick, Miller," Swag said. "There's a lot of good people out there looking for work."

Peter looked down at his desk. He pictured Swag standing on a smooth, convex plain of white-hot glass. First his shoes smolder, then his feet begin to blister and burn. He runs, but there is no place to go. Peter can hear him scream, a thin, high shriek, like a woman. Running faster now, back and forth, back and forth. He jumps to get away from the heat for a few seconds, lands, jumps again. Stumbles as he lands this time, rolls over once, and bursts into flame. He is up again, waving his arms like wings within the pillar of flame, running, spinning in circles. The screaming goes on and on.

Swag threw the crumpled invoice on Peter's desk. "Fix this up and deal with the back billing. If you don't, it's coming out of your check."

He turned and stalked out of the office. Peter sat there for a long time after he left. He felt numb, swaddled, the sound of the machine shop reaching his ears as if through yards of silky gauze. Slowly, he became aware again of his surroundings, and he began to work, burying himself in the ordered columns of figures and the routine typing. The rest of the day passed without incident. Swag stayed in his corner of the shop, casting an occasional stony glare in Peter's direction.

Peter walked the few blocks from the subway station to his apartment building with a sense of rising anticipation. He hurried inside, threw his coat on the couch and headed straight for the kitchen. The bare bulb threw stark shadows in the small room. Three or four small moths swooped and hovered near the bulb in mindless, random flutter.

He walked to the cabinet and opened it. A single moth flew out at him and he grabbed it out of the air, keeping a hollow in his closed fist so as not to crush it. He felt it beating against the inside of his fist, tickling his palm. He closed his eyes and he imagined that he could feel

Binding Energy

its primal, focused panic. He closed his fist slowly, and when his curled fingers met the inside of his palm and he felt the not-quite-moist powder smearing across his skin, there was the sensation in the back of his mind of a dim light being extinguished.

Peter washed his hands in the sink, and began making preparations for dinner. Lasagna. Fresh, home-made rolls. Sandy was coming over and he wanted everything to be perfect. He thought of the bag of flour in the cabinet, alive with blind, wriggling motion.

She was fifteen minutes late, as usual. He could set his watch by it. She bustled in the door with a bottle of wine in one hand and her little overnight bag dangling from the other. She leaned close to kiss him on the cheek and he could smell her perfume. As he always did when he saw her, he felt a little rush of awe that someone this pretty would be interested in him. They set the table together and lit candles. He put the lasagna on a trivet to cool and went through the ritual of opening and pouring the wine.

"You seem awfully quiet," she said. "Everything all right at work?"

"It's – " *these Goddamn moths*, he almost said. The words seemed to stick in his throat. He opened his mouth again and coughed. He took a large swallow of wine. "It's Swag," he said finally. "He's really got it in for me."

Sandy made a sympathetic clucking sound. They had met when she was a temp secretary in the shop office, and she knew all about Swag. She had never told Peter, but she'd had to repel amorous advances from him on more than one occasion. She reached out and touched his wrist. He met her gaze for a second and looked away. Out of the corner of his eye he could see a pair of tiny moths dancing about the ceiling light in the living room.

Dancing, he thought. *Absolutely*.

"These rolls look great," Sandy said. They sat in the folds of a red and white checked napkin, nestled in a woven basket at the center of the table. They were golden brown and their glazed tops held the flickering candlelight in soft focus. "Did you make them?"

"Um – " Peter said. "Yeah."

It seemed to Peter like there were *two* of him. One sat there at the table; the wine, the food, Sandy, all ensconced in cozy familiarity. Safe.

200

The other Peter hovered above the scene, flitting back and forth, diving towards the flickering candles and veering away at the last minute. Sandy reached out and grabbed a roll, pulled it open. Wisps of steam rose from the spongy insides.

Diving.

"Hmm," Sandy said, the sound coming from deep in her throat. She lifted the steaming roll to her face and inhaled. "Hmm," she said again. She raised her eyes to his and smiled.

Towards the flame.

"What's in these?" she asked. "What are these little flecks? Herbs?"

"Yeah," he said. There was a ringing in his ears. "Herbs."

He tried pretending he was asleep, but it didn't work. She took the tip of his ear between her teeth and bit down gently. She reached down and stroked his penis.

"Hello," she whispered. "Anybody home?"

She ran her tongue along the line of his jaw and kissed his lips, opening her mouth for his tongue. He felt himself responding, but when she reached down again to guide him into her, he went limp.

"I'm sorry, honey," he said. "It's just, you know... I don't know..."

"It's okay, baby," she said, but there was an edge of disappointment in her voice. She kissed him on the cheek. "You're tired."

"Yeah," he said. "Tired." She curled up against him. Soon her breathing was deep and regular. Peter lay there watching the lights from the traffic outside move across the ceiling.

He didn't know how long he had been lying there, but when he looked at the digital clock on the night table, it read 3:11. The colon between the three and the eleven blinked on and off, and he counted along with it.

One, two, three...

He shook his head and gently moved Sandy's arm from across his chest. He got out of bed and padded into the kitchen. He couldn't see them, but he *knew* they were there, four of them in a rough diamond pattern on the wall over the stove, and two more hanging upside down next to the ceiling light. He got a flashlight from the utility drawer, and opened the cabinet. Flickering shapes flew past his face, and he shined the flashlight into the corner.

There, behind the Pop Tarts, a small peanut-shaped form in a soft silken web.

He moved closer until his nose was inches from the cocoon. He held the light up next to it and he thought he could make out a shape inside the layers of filmy, translucent gauze. He imagined it to be like a human embryo, could almost see the button-black shark's eyes, the curved, cartilaginous backbone, the vestigial gill-slits in the chinless neck.

The miracle of birth, he thought, and chuckled softly.

He thought he saw a flicker of movement and felt a thrill shoot from the tips of his ears down to his groin. He stood there holding the light for another ten minutes, but nothing happened.

He opened the refrigerator and took out the bottle of wine from dinner. There were a few good swallows left. He held it to his lips and drained it, shaking it to get out the last drops. He walked back to the bedroom, the bottle dangling from one hand. Sandy lay there on her back, the sheet half-draped across her body. Her chest rose and fell with her breathing. He felt himself becoming aroused as he stood there looking down at her, tendrils of warmth flickering again from his groin, down his thighs, up to his chest.

Suddenly, her eyes snapped open. They caught the moonlight like bits of chipped, volcanic glass, glittering and depthless. She reached out her hand and he folded into her embrace.

As he knelt between her thighs, pumping himself into her, he thought of wings. *Wings*. He felt a tickling between his shoulder blades and imagined them there underneath the ridges of bone, folded, waiting to push through. He was changing inside. He could feel it. Soon everything would be different.

Conversations With Michael

"I'm not ready," I said. I laced my fingers together and leaned forward in the soft chair, perching on the edge of the cushion. I looked up at Alice. The window behind her was polarized black as pitch and gave the unsettling impression of limitless depth, framing her face like one of those old velvet paintings you could buy down in Tijuana before the Burning.

"I think you are, Stacey," she said. "We've been working towards this for a long time. We've done everything we can in realspace. It's time for you to face him." She looked at me with an expectant, open expression, as if she was wondering what my response was going to be. I suspected that she knew, though. She always knew.

I looked down at my hands, leaned back in the chair, shifted my weight. The chair responded by subtly rearranging the cushions to support me. The silence hung between us. Our sessions were often like this – islands of brief dialogue separated by vast gulfs. Finally, I heaved a huge sigh. It felt like it was coming not just from my chest but from my whole body, like my soul was escaping. There was a tightness around the corners of my eyes and across my forehead. I looked up at her. I nodded.

The Virtual Session room – real wood paneling, indirect lighting, abstract art on three walls. A fourth wall dominated by an instrument panel of black glass and polished chrome. Two pieces of furniture, elaborate barcaloungers crowned with spiky helmets, sprouted neatly tied bundles of wire leading to the panel. Red and yellow telltales winked from beneath the glass like the eyes of jungle animals.

Alice led me to one of the chairs and strapped me in. "Remember, I'll be right there the whole time. I'll be *him*."

I nodded. I could feel beads of sweat forming on my upper lip and forehead. Alice attached sensors to my fingers, my neck. She produced a tissue from somewhere and gently wiped the sweat from my face.

"You'll be fine," she said, and began to connect herself to the other chair.

I was standing next to home plate in the Little League baseball field behind the ConEd cooling towers. A breeze coming in off the Long Island Sound brought with it a faint smell of salt and sewage. The sky was a soft, pale blue, a shade I hadn't seen in twenty years. I reached up and touched my face. *No u.v. block.* Brief surge of panic. I looked at the sky again and realized that I wouldn't need it.

My son was sitting in the whitewashed risers paralleling the third base line, looking at me. He raised his hand in greeting. I gave him an answering wave and walked towards him. My heart was pounding in my chest.

He looked vibrant and full of life, like he did in the yellowed, age-curled pictures I kept in the shoebox on the top shelf of my bedroom closet. It clashed with my last memory of him – withered, emaciated body, skin stretched tight across skullbones framed by crisp hospital linen, sick, flickering light in his ancient child's eyes. I sat down next to him.

"Hi, Mike," I said.

"Hey, Mom."

It's crazy, but I couldn't think of a single thing to say to him. There was so much I wanted to tell him. *I'm sorry. I'm so sorry, baby.* I wanted to take him in my arms and hold him to me and not let go. An inane thought came bubbling up to the surface of my mind – I wondered if he was hungry. It was a manageable thought, though, and I held on to it like a drowning swimmer clutching a life preserver.

"You hungry, champ?" I asked. My voice only cracked a little.

He smiled up at me. "Yeah." I saw Keith in that quick, sure grin and a surge of loss and anger passed through me like a hot, sudden wind, gone just as quickly.

A wicker basket suddenly appeared at my feet. The corners of a red and white checked cloth peeked out from under the edges of the lid.

"I've got some deviled ham," I said, knowing that it would be there. "And some Ho-Ho's for dessert."

"Great," he said, but it didn't sound right. I don't know why, but at that moment the illusion collapsed and I *knew* that it was just Alice there, Alice in a Michael suit, Alice strapped into a VS deck weaving a fiberoptic tapestry of ones and zeros with an insensate, cybernetic loom. To fool me into grace.

"This is bullshit," I said.

Michael frowned. "Mom...?" The frown was very good, very Michael-like, but the illusion was already shot.

"Just get me out of here, Alice. It's not working."

He sighed, shoulders set with the exaggerated exasperation of a child. "Okay," he nodded.

I closed my eyes and when I opened them again I was back in the VS room. I unstrapped myself and started to get up. A rush of vertigo sat me down again.

"Hey," Alice said. "Easy." Her face hovered over me like a cloud.

I looked at her accusingly. "I knew it was you. This is just bullshit gameplaying."

She shook her head. "You did very well for a first virtual session. Of course, your history helps you a lot here, but some people can't even interact in V-space at all. *You* created the ball park; *you* gave *me* enough cues to help build a consensual reality." She smiled gently and touched me on the shoulder. "We made progress today."

The Dinkins Arcology is built on a lattice of pontoons that stretches out into the Upper New York Bay like a dendritic tongue, sending fractal limbs in all directions. That's its official name, but even before the first fullerene panel was snapped into place, it was Dinkytown. It was intended to be an egalitarian effort, public housing hand in hand with private enterprise, the disadvantaged and the well-to-do rolling up their sleeves together and creating a community – turn-of-the-century policyspeak made manifest. (Soft industrial music swells in the background. Dissolve to a schoolyard swarming with happy children in a tastefully balanced dcmographic mix). But in fact, a stratification evolved dynamically, independent of intention. Pockets of public assistance clusters dotted the arcology ("like cancerous cells," the Times op-ed site whined), side by side with ghettos of affluence. I still have an income, and managed to buy our way into Avalon, on the Governor's Island side.

I wasn't ready to go home yet, so I took the long way, out along the 'boardwalk' – a promenade with a polarized roof that runs around Dinkytown's circumference. Before long, the crowds thinned out and I strolled slowly along the bay, enjoying the cool breeze coming in off the water. There was a trace of sewage smell and a hint of acrid chemicals, but it wasn't too bad. Some fool was windsurfing up near the mouth of the East River, begging for a dose of septic shock. They'd cleaned things up a lot since the twentieth, but it still wasn't exactly safe.

Some things you can't clean up, though, no matter how hard you try. Michael. I remember the day it happened. I was mainlining and somebody brought the system down cold. Sense impressions filtered in through the nausea – people rushing back and forth, voices shouting, several newsfeeds on at once. "Partial meltdown... Montauk nuke... another Chernobyl." Things blurred together. I made my way up to the roof heliport somehow and threatened a chopper pilot with my Swiss Army knife to take me to Montauk. It took three large men to hold me down.

It turned out to be just a 'small' release, quickly contained. And it was late in the day, so the prevailing winds were blowing the radioactive plume out to sea, away from the thirty-odd million souls in the Greater New York Metropolitan Area. But it didn't spare Montauk. And it didn't spare Michael.

I could picture him standing there in the schoolyard, smiling, the wind ruffling his hair, as the gamma rays tunneled through his body leaving an irreparable wake of damaged cells. The fatality rate in Montauk was thirty percent during the first year, twenty percent during the second, then it tailed off rapidly from there. Michael was still alive three years later; we thought he'd been spared. Then, all of a sudden, his immune system collapsed. He started losing weight like crazy. Great, purple bruises appeared all over his body, like mysterious objects floating up from the bottom of a murky pond. The leukemia ripped through him so quickly you could almost see him fading away in realtime. When it was over there was hardly anything left to bury.

A pair of young men walked towards me along the promenade, holding hands. Their cheeks bore elaborate scars, a pattern I recognized as the chop of the Lords of Discipline.

"Don' stay out too long, Mama," the one on the left said. "U.V. count t'rough de roof today, mon." His boyfriend looked like he ought to know – a spiderweb tangle of ruptured blood vessels laced through the scars on his cheeks.

"Thanks," I nodded.

There were dirty dishes on the kitchen table, which meant that Keith had been up and about. I glanced down the hallway to where his door stood open a crack. He was probably back under. Just as well.

I sat down at my desk to check my e-mail. There were four ads and a message from Dmitry over at Cellular. I'd been doing some biotech database hacking for him, building a set of software tools for him to manage his technical library. It's not as boring as it sounds. Just because you can nanoscript a terabyte of data onto a slab of substrate the size of a mosquito wing doesn't mean you can retrieve it easily. In fact, with so much information available at your fingertips, encoding and navigating gets pretty hairy.

I flushed the ads and scrolled the message from Dmitry, a not particularly subtle inquiry as to just when I might have the bugs shaken out of the infosurfing macros I was cooking up for him. I pounded out a quick reply – telling him that all good things come to those who wait, to cultivate the patient heart of a grandmother, and to get off my case or I'd accidentally mail his shiny, new virtual toys off to DevNull.

I enjoyed jerking his chain a little. I'd never met him in person, but we'd been working together online for a couple of years. His Proxy was a short, balding, somewhat chubby man who wore dark, rumpled suits with suspenders and frayed cuffs. The frayed cuffs were a brilliant touch – it was easy to forget you were looking at a sim. Of course, he probably looked nothing like that. Online relationships are almost all smoke and mirrors.

I got to work. I pulled down a couple of windows on the big monitor and dropped some shell scripts into the queue for the public databases. The private and corporate 'bases were a little trickier. I fired off an autonomous agent to deal with the protocol.

I quickly became submerged in the work. It was soothing, like immersing myself in the hot, swirling waters of a jacuzzi. It wasn't quite like mainlining, but it was close. Mainlining, pure info-surfing. There's no other rush like it, chemical or virtual. I was good. The Net was a tangled, spidery sprawl of pulsing light, nodes of brightness for other surfers. Structs were patches of infrared and u.v. that I could sense by the quality of the pain they caused. My paradigm for navigation was the avoidance of discomfort.

After Michael, I started losing it. The only thing that keeps a surfer on that knife-edge of perception is discrimination – the ability to distinguish real from memorex. Mine was shot. I'd be walking down the street and the sparkles of light from the silica chips in the pavement would dissolve into the coruscating signature of the struct I'd navigated that morning. I'd be in the middle of a conversation and start framing my responses as instruction sets.

When my medical leave ran out, I quit Sony. I still had connections, and managed to pull together an occasional consulting gig. Before I knew it, I had my hands full freelancing. I was surfing again, and it was good, but I never mainlined. And Keith was always there to remind me why I shouldn't, just in case I forgot.

I don't know how long I worked, but slowly a sense of physical space began to seep back into my consciousness. It had gotten dark; my hands on the keypad were illuminated only by the blue glow of the monitor. Outside, the sky held the last blush of twilight. Reflected lights from Manhattan and Brooklyn made shimmering castles in the water at the mouth of the East River.

I logged off the satlink and sat there in the dark for a few minutes. It was time to look in on Keith. I took a deep breath, then another.

The room was dark except for the tiny, amber console lights. I could sense his shape, though, sprawled in the beanbag chair wedged into a corner. The soft, raspy whisper of his breathing filled the room. A stew of sour smells hung in the air – body odor, traces of urine, a strong whiff of feces.

I turned on the light. Keith didn't even flinch – the rig's induction field coupled right in to his optic nerve. Not much bandwidth, but what it lacked in information content it more than made up for in the sheer intensity of the pleasure it provided. I'd tried it once – I felt so lousy when I came out of it I was scared to try it again.

Not Keith. He'd been jacking off ever since the rigs went alpha. It was just a weekend thing at first, but after Michael died, he started going under more and more. Now he was down almost all the time. It was as if grief were a black hole and he'd disappeared somewhere beyond its event horizon.

He was naked except for the incontinence pants bunched around his waist. Diapers, really. They gave him the bizarre appearance of a sallow, grey-haired baby. I could count his ribs. A streak of dried blood ran down his arm and the i.v. rig lay on its side in the middle of the room. Probably ripped out the glucose drip and gone looking for solid food after I left in the morning. He did that sometimes. I was always surprised he got himself out from under long enough to get to the kitchen and back.

I got a fresh pair of diapers from the closet, cleaned him up, and changed him. I set up his i.v. again and stood there for a while, looking at him. He still hadn't registered my presence. Every now and then a muscle in his arm or thigh twitched. It reminded me of a dog I had when I was a child. She used to curl up in front of the fire to sleep, and every now and then her hind legs would jump and scrabble at the carpet.

"Chasing rabbits in her dreams," my father would say, if he wasn't passed out yet. I wondered what Keith was chasing.

I walked over to the console and turned it off. The glaze faded from his eyes and he clutched at himself.

"Wha – ?" It came out like a croak.

I don't really know what I was thinking about. I guess I wanted to talk to him about Michael, but that was crazy.

I looked down at him. His eyes were burning flecks of pain. For a second I saw Michael there, held in the hollow angles of his cheekbones. Then he was gone.

"You sick fuck," I said. I flicked the console back on and walked out of the room.

"Why do you stay with him?" Alice asked. The window behind her was in Aquarium-mode – schools of brightly colored fish darted through shafts of sunlight over a carpet of waving, green kelp. It really irritated me.

"I hate your window," I said.

She reached under her desk and did something. The aquarium dissolved slowly to a neutral gray.

"Better?"

I nodded. "A little."

She sat there, smiling faintly. Waiting.

"So, why do I ...?"

She nodded.

I took in a deep breath. I felt like I wasn't getting enough air. I let it out with a sigh.

"I ... don't know. There's nobody home – he's a total wirehead. He's been like this ever since Michael died."

She nodded.

"He ... needs me."

She nodded again, looking at me. Waiting.

I could feel myself tensing up, digging in my heels. I wasn't going to give her what she wanted.

Finally, she said, "What do you need, Stacey?"

I looked at her for a long time. Finally, I shook my head. "I don't know."

Jones Beach stretched out in front of us, a long pale ribbon, bordered on one side by the slate grey of the ocean and the other by a checkerboard scatter of parking lots and ball fields that now served as sites for sprawling tent villages. Michael walked beside me, his head bent in concentration, absorbed with a piece of techno-trash he had picked up somewhere. A graceful curve of metal wound in a converging helix around a core of bundled fiberoptic cable. Wires trailed loosely from one end. It looked like a prop from a cheesy science fiction movie. Every now and then, he aimed it at an imaginary target and made ray-gun noises, *gzh-gzh-gzh*, his eyes narrowed with intense concentration.

The beach was filthier than I remembered. Ocean-tossed detritus of civilization lay everywhere – used hypodermic syringes, plastic bottles, the occasional limp, wrinkled condom. Coney Island whitefish, my father used to call them. I chuckled softly and looked over at Michael.

"What you doing, champ?" I asked.

Michael looked up at me and smiled his quick, sure smile. "Changing stuff."

"Oh, yeah? What are you changing it into?"

"Making everything go away." He trained the ray gun on a dead seagull lying half-buried in the sand a few feet away. *Gzh-gzh-gzh.*

"Why do you want to do that?" I asked.

His face wrinkled in the disdain that children reserve for stupid adults. "It's *soft.*"

I smiled ruefully. "It sure is, champ."

Gzh-gzh-gzh. A tangle of seaweed and glittering strands of polyfoil was sent off to never-never land.

We walked together in silence for a while.

"If you could put anything you wanted here instead," I asked, finally, "what would it be?"

He thought for a minute. "In school, we were in a sim with dinosaurs. It was so *wavy.* There was this big one and it chased the little one and ate it. We were on a beach but there wasn't anything there." He looked up at me and smiled. "I'd put dinosaurs."

"Dinosaurs. Cool." I paused. "Do you know what happened to the dinosaurs?" I asked.

He nodded. "They died."

"How did they die, champ?"

His eyebrows drew together in a frown as he struggled to remember the words. "They couldn't, uh, adapt." He looked directly at me. "They couldn't adapt to cataclysm."

We stood there in the hot sun. I could see Alice looking at me through Michael's eyes without pretense now, calm and knowing. I was aware of myself standing on the cusp between reality and illusion, one foot in each. The coppery smell of decaying seaweed hung in the air and the wind caressed my face in light, feathery touches.

Dmitry's 'benevolent uncle' persona beamed at me from the vidscreen. "I have a proposition for you, Stacey," he said. There was a faint trace of Slavic accent in his voice.

I think of Proxies as fashion accessories, not all that much different than makeup or hairstyle – another layer of illusion we project to help us navigate the reefs and shoals of human interaction. Of course, there are the usual, endless Globalnet flamewars about the moral implications of being able to construct your own persona from scratch and modify it according to your own mood and who you're talking to. That's mostly the neo-Luddites, though, tooth and nail with the crackpot Libertarians – a lot of heat and smoke, not much light. My own feeling is that we all do that anyway to some extent, even in realspace.

"I'm listening, Dmitry." I was wearing what I thought of as my Conan the Librarian Proxy – a lean-limbed warrior goddess with blond, sun-streaked hair, a deerskin vest (a bit offensive to some, I know), and a quiver of arrows at my back. A button pinned to my vest read WILL HACK FOR FOOD. I had a monitor window open in the upper left corner of the vidscreen and I could see the image that Dmitry was looking at. Rolling green hills dotted with grazing sheep spread out behind me. The sky was a deep, cloudless blue.

He cleared his throat. "You know that Cellular has recently purchased shares in the Velikovsky Orbital."

I nodded. Of course I did. I'd hacked a substantial portion of the background documentation on orbital biotech for their Stockholder's Report.

"We're putting together a small community up there to get a facility going – pharmaceuticals, protein construction, genetic mods. Not just biotech, though – we've got plans to start a substrate farm, grow high-T superconductors, micro-gee metallurgy, the works."

I nodded again. No surprises there. Everything he'd mentioned required a zero-gravity environment for profitable manufacturing.

"Let's cut to the chase, Dmitry. I *wrote* that p.r. pitch."

He smiled and nodded, his head bobbing up and down. "Yes, yes, you did, didn't you? Very well." He cleared his throat again. "We need a – well, kind of a sysadmin up there, someone to coordinate all of the info-hacking facilities. Of course, we're hooked into Globalnet via microwave, but we also want to have an autonomous system for the Orbital itself. There'll be all the usual personal support stuff – you can delegate that – and we'll have a cluster of teraflop nodes for process simulation. Lots of bit-hacking there and microwave links just don't have the bandwidth for that." He paused. "I floated your name up the food-chain here and so far the echoes have all been pretty favorable. I'm

sorry I didn't ask you beforehand, but I wanted to test the water first."
He looked at me, his eyebrows raised, a slight smile playing on the
corners of his mouth.

I didn't know what to say. I expected a lucrative project, enough
consulting work to keep me solvent for awhile, but nothing like this. My
knee-jerk reaction was *No way*, but there was a small, still voice
underneath that I couldn't quite smother. *Why not?* it asked.

I was silent for a long time.

"Stacey?" he said, finally.

"Look, Dmitry, I ..." I saw my Proxy up there in a corner of the
screen mouthing my words. It brushed a strand of windswept hair from
its eyes. I reached up to the screen and tapped twice on the image – it
rolled up like a window shade and disappeared. "Can we drop the
Proxies, Dmitry? I need to really see you."

His eyebrows rose, then he nodded slowly. "Sure," he said, finally.

He reached offscreen and did something. His image collapsed and
was replaced immediately with another. A plain, pleasant looking man
of young, middle age looked through the screen at me dressed in a
conservative, corporate-style vest. There was a streak of purple in his
straight, black hair and a pair of gold hoops dangled from his left
earlobe. Behind him was a cluttered, windowless office, unremarkable
except for a shelf of real books. He smiled questioningly at me.

I expected to be surprised by his appearance, but I wasn't – I already
felt like I knew him. I stretched my hand to punch in the escape
metacharacter on my own keypad, and when his eyebrows rose, I knew
he was seeing the 'real me' as well.

"Better?" he asked. The Slavic accent was gone, replaced with a
flat, Midwestern drawl.

I nodded. "Yeah, much." We just sat there looking at each other for
what felt like a very long time, even though it was probably less than a
minute. Finally, I sighed and shook my head. "I don't know what to say,
Dmitry. I'm going to need some time to think."

"Sure," he nodded. "But don't take *too* long. You know how these
things go – sooner or later, the posting winds up on Globalnet and we
get flooded with applicants, most of them cranks. It gets a lot harder to
separate the wheat from the chaff. The Powers That Be would rather see
this nailed down through word of mouth."

"I'll let you know," I said.

"Good." He looked carefully at me. "Take care of yourself, Stacey."

"Bye," I said, but his image had already collapsed into a thin line and disappeared. I sat looking at the flat, blank space on the screen where the vidscreen window had been. I imagined I saw shapes rolling and shifting there, submerged in the depths of the phosphor.

Afternoon sunlight streamed through the Venetian blinds, throwing a pattern of stripes across the hospital bed. Michael sat propped up on a mass of pillows, looking very small surrounded by all that puffy whiteness. He was playing some sort of hand-held simulation game – crude holos a couple of inches high swarmed across the bed. They were barely visible in the bars of intense sunlight, coming alive with color when they scurried into the shadows. The high, tinny sound of their combat filled the room.

I stood at the door watching him. His eyebrows were drawn down in concentration; the pink tip of his tongue protruded from the corner of his mouth. Tubes snaked from a patch on his arm to an array of soft, plastic bags hanging from a rack next to the bed.

"Hey, champ," I said.

He looked up and smiled. Dark circles framed his eyes and the curve of his cheekbone seemed impossibly sharp.

"Hey, Mom. Just a sec..." His fingers danced on the little console for a few seconds longer. He leaned towards the panel. "Save," he said. The armies of tiny simulacra froze, then disappeared.

"I made it up to Level 7," he said, smiling.

"That's great, Mike." I walked over and sat down in the chair next to the bed. I reached out and brushed a strand of hair from his forehead.

"When you get better we'll take you to one of those places where you can play with sim-holos as big as houses..."

He looked at me and frowned. "Come on, Mom. I'm not *gonna* get better. I'm gonna *die*." It was a simple declaration, not a complaint – as if he were explaining the facts of life to a slightly stupid friend.

It felt like he had physically struck me.

"I...why do you say that?" I stammered.

"I'm not *stupid*, Mom." He lifted his arm, showing the tubes trailing from the patch in his arm. He gestured around the room at the menagerie of stuffed animals resting on every available surface. "Med-net says that they'll be able to cure leukemia in ten years with nanocritters, but that we just aren't there yet." He shrugged. He looked and sounded for all the world like a wise old man. How did little kids learn so much?

I sighed. "I know you're not stupid, baby. It's just that ... it's hard ..." I didn't want to cry in front of him, to put him in the position of having to parent me. It wasn't supposed to work like that. But the tightness across my forehead got worse and soon I could feel hot tears on my cheeks.

"I'm so sorry, baby...." I said.

He reached over and put his small hand on my shoulder.

"It's not *your* fault, Mom. *You* didn't do anything."

I *felt* responsible, though. We poisoned the world, killing off millions of our own children – *our own children* – so we could have dishwashers and computers and microwave sat-links, and we were only beginning to step back from the brink. I didn't know if it was too late for us. But it was too late for Michael.

"It just *happened*, Mom." His voice jolted me out of my fog of self-pity. "Stuff just happens."

Alice sat behind her desk, waiting for me to say something. In the window behind her, the New York skyline glittered in the afternoon sun. There was a subtle quality about the colors and the distance resolution that told me it was real.

"I'll say this for you," I said, finally. "You're good. You're very good. It's uncanny how well you ... simulate him. I almost feel like I could forgive myself..."

She smiled gently. "I want to show you something," she said. She punched some buttons on the console at her desk and swiveled the monitor around so it was facing me.

VIRTUAL SESSION LOG
Name: Donovan, Stacey
Status: Solo
On: 13:10
Off: 14:04
Date: 4/22/18

215

Binding Energy

I looked up at her. "Solo?"

"Yeah. If we'd been doing another tandem session, my name would be on the log, too. You were all alone in there."

I felt something give inside me, like a door you've been leaning on with all your strength just beginning to budge. Alice nodded and smiled in the slightly smug and annoying way she has when she thinks she's made some sort of breakthrough with me. I didn't mind much, though. I even smiled back a little.

Keith was sitting in his beanbag chair in the corner, curled up like a loosely-tied bundle of sticks. I walked over to the window and de-polarized it. Sunlight flooded the room. Keith looked impossibly pale in the light. Oozing sores stood out on his skin like bright, red stars. He'd pulled the glucose drip again and a crust of dried blood peeked out from under the ragged bandage on his arm.

I turned off the console and waited. It took a few seconds, then he squeezed his eyes together and brought his arm up to shield them. Whimpering noises came from somewhere deep in his chest.

After a little while, the whimpering stopped and he lowered his arm from his face. He looked at me accusingly. It was like playing a tape loop, those pain-filled eyes burning into me again. It was going to be different this time, though.

"I know you can understand me, Keith," I said. "I can't take care of you any more. I've arranged for you to go to a treatment program out on the Island. It's thirty days, and after that you're on your own. I don't know if I'm going to be here or not when you get out, but you can't come live here again." I paused, not knowing what else to say. "I'm sorry," I said, finally. "It's got to be this way."

I couldn't read his expression. I looked for Michael there in his hurt eyes, in the angry set of his shoulders, but I couldn't see him, not a trace. He opened his mouth again like he wanted to say something, but all that came out was a raspy croak. I stood there in the sunlight, waiting for him to find his voice.

216

More quality fiction from Elastic Press

☐ The Virtual Menagerie	Andrew Hook	SOLD OUT
☐ Open The Box	Andrew Humphrey	SOLD OUT
☐ Second Contact	Gary Couzens	SOLD OUT
☐ Sleepwalkers	Marion Arnott	SOLD OUT
☐ Milo & I	Antony Mann	SOLD OUT
☐ The Alsiso Project	Edited by Andrew Hook	SOLD OUT
☐ Jung's People	Kay Green	SOLD OUT
☐ The Sound of White Ants	Brian Howell	SOLD OUT
☐ Somnambulists	Allen Ashley	SOLD OUT
☐ Angel Road	Steven Savile	SOLD OUT
☐ Visits to the Flea Circus	Nick Jackson	SOLD OUT
☐ The Elastic Book of Numbers	Edited by Allen Ashley	SOLD OUT
☐ The Life To Come	Tim Lees	SOLD OUT
☐ Trailer Park Fairy Tales	Matt Dinniman	SOLD OUT
☐ The English Soil Society	Tim Nickels	£5.99
☐ The Last Days of Johnny North	David Swann	SOLD OUT
☐ The Ephemera	Neil Williamson	SOLD OUT
☐ Unbecoming	Mike O'Driscoll	£6.99
☐ Photocopies of Heaven	Maurice Suckling	SOLD OUT
☐ Extended Play	Edited by Gary Couzens	£6.99
☐ So Far, So Near	Mat Coward	£5.99
☐ Going Back	Tony Richards	£5.99
☐ That's Entertainment	Robert Neilson	£5.99
☐ The Cusp of Something	Jai Clare	£5.99
☐ Other Voices	Andrew Humphrey	£5.99
☐ Another Santana Morning	Mike Dolan	£5.99
☐ Binding Energy	Daniel Marcus	£5.99

All these books are available at your local bookshop or can be ordered direct from the publisher. Indicate the number of copies required and fill in the form below.

Name_____
(Block letters please)

Address_____

Send to Elastic Press, 85 Gertrude Road, Norwich, Norfolk, NR3 4SG.
Please enclose remittance to the value of the cover price plus: £1.50 for the first book plus 50p per copy for each additional book ordered to cover postage and packing. Applicable in the UK only.

While every effort is made to keep prices low, it is sometimes necessary to increase prices at short notice. Elastic Press reserve the right to show on covers and charge new retail prices which may differ from those advertised in the text or elsewhere.

Want to be kept informed? Keep up to date with Elastic Press titles by writing to the above address, or by visiting www.elasticpress.com and adding your email details to our online mailing list.

Elastic Press: Winner of the British Fantasy Society Best Small Press award 2005

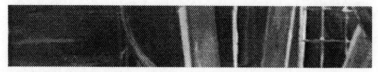

Forthcoming from Elastic Press

The Last Reef by Gareth L Powell

Gareth L Powell's first collection of short stories is stuffed with mind-bending ideas and unforgettable characters. Ranging from the day after tomorrow to the far-flung future, these fifteen stories are perfect for anyone with a craving for intelligent and thought-provoking adventure. From noir-ish cops to disaffected space pilots, blind photographers and low-life hackers, everyone here is struggling to find a little peace amid the tumult of the future.

With an introduction from Interzone co-editor, Jetse De Vries.

Forthcoming from Elastic Press

The Turing Test by Chris Beckett

These fourteen stories, among other things, contain robots, alien planets, genetic manipulation and virtual reality, but their centre focuses on individuals rather than technology, and how they deal with love and loneliness, authenticity, reality and what it really means to be human.

With an introduction from Alistair Reynolds.

For further information visit:
www.elasticpress.com

46.99